About the Author

Nicola Lindsay was born in London in 1944. She went to school in Cambridge before moving to London to train as a nurse. Over the years she has worked as, amongst other things, a model, flautist, garden designer and medical secretary. She started writing seriously when she was in her early fifties. Poetry for adults and children, a children's book, monologues, revues, scripts for radio, articles and five novels have been written during the last ten years. Her work is included in several anthologies in Ireland and England and she has broadcast extensively in both countries.

She has lived in Africa, Italy and France and travelled widely in the USA and Europe, often using the countries she's visited as locations in her books. She has three adult daughters, of whom she is extremely proud, and she now lives in County Kildare with her husband – and gardens whenever she has a spare moment.

Also by Nicola Lindsay

For Sofia
with my love and admiration

Chapter One

I can't believe that, by the end of the week, I shall be out of here. Feeling fragile and not a little nervous but free to finish the task of getting back on my feet in the outside world. As part of my recovery Dr Scheller suggested it might be a good idea to write down my thoughts to give me an idea of where I'm at now. I don't know if it will help but I'm willing to give it a try. I'm not going to think of it like a diary – more as a sort of life-saving device to help me find myself again. I'm going to pretend that I'm talking to someone who doesn't know me and who won't judge me. That will make it easier to be honest.

I really can't remember how long I've been in this place – here in this home for the dysfunctional and unstable. It seems like forever. I do know that I haven't had any major sort of wobbly for some time. No going AWOL and wandering the streets looking like a badly wired zombie or throwing tantrums that invariably ended in floods of tears.

Mind you, at the start, I was only too happy to give in and go along with being dosed up to the eyeballs. I think I must have slept for weeks when I first got here. I feel a bit ashamed now because I think that even then, at the back of my overheated brain, I knew perfectly well that I was chickening out of life. But I realise now that I had no choice if I wanted to come out of the other side of all of this. I couldn't have gone on the way I was any longer. Half the time I was on automatic pilot. Everything was a blur. I can still see the expression on Cassandra's face when I poured tea all over my Special K. It wasn't until she'd pointed out what I'd done that it registered with me. If she hadn't said anything, I probably would have munched my way through it without noticing.

Poor Cassandra – with her moody silences and chewed nails. My daughter doesn't know what to make of me at the moment. Oh, I know she *loves* me but, some of the time, that gets forgotten amidst all her confusion. I was lying on the bed this morning trying to remember what my feelings were for my own mother when *I* was twenty. I think they were pretty ambivalent if I'm honest. But I was polite – most of the time – and I'm pretty sure I went out of my way not to say and do things that would upset her. Was that because I was a reasonably pleasant daughter or was it just that I'd discovered that life was easier if I didn't rock the boat too much? Probably the latter.

Anyway, Cassandra finds me a trial. She's been so taken up with pretending that she's strong and coping that she's stifled feelings that should be talked about. It's been like this ever since . . . ever since Pandora.

Dr Scheller understands. He knows all about loss. You

can see it in his face, in those tired, dark, shadowed eyes of his. I think he's just possibly the kindest, gentlest human being I've ever met. And I do know that I'm incredibly lucky to have him as my doctor here in the clinic.

"Don't push yourself so hard, Mrs Sayer," he said in his lightly accented voice as he sat beside my bed. This was when I was beginning to realise I was through the worst and felt that I was making my way unsteadily out of the tunnel. The process seemed so slow. But he was well aware of how frustrated I felt. "For now, just concentrate on being. Don't worry about all the rest. Everything will fall into place when the time is right."

He never calls me Hebe. It's always been Mrs Sayer and I like that. It's not that he's distant – not at all – or I couldn't have told him all the things I have. No, I think it's more a professional, considered courtesy that helps me hang on to a few shreds of dignity. Not that I'm a dignified sort of person. You have to be tall to be really dignified and I'm only five foot six and I'm too tuned in to the quirky, alternative side of life to keep a straight face for long. People spend so much of their time pretending to be sensible, wise, logical. They want to be taken seriously. I don't at all mind making a fool of myself. I often have and I will no doubt continue to do so!

That's one of the many things that Cassandra finds hard to swallow – the fact that her mother – well, the one I was before all this happened, gives into urges. She doesn't like it when I act spontaneously, when I talk in bus queues to people who I don't know from Adam, when I have chatty love-ins with stray dogs and cats at the side of the street or when I sing at the top of my voice because I suddenly feel sublimely, ridiculously, inexplicably happy.

"Why do you *do* it, Mum? Why can't you be normal?" she asks, cheeks flushed because a startled stranger has turned around to look at me squatting on the pavement stroking a friendly dog and telling it that it's gorgeous.

"Because it's the way I am," I say. "It's just me being me."

There's no point in trying to explain why I do these things but I wish she'd understand that I'm not doing them out of sheer bloody-minded wickedness, just to bug and embarrass her!

It must have been awful for her when I was brought in here, so confused I didn't know what day of the week it was. And yet, in a way, easier too because at least she knew where I was and they kept me so sedated she knew I was unlikely to suddenly break into a few verses of a bawdy drinking song. Things had become so difficult and unreal between us. I can see that it's going to be an uphill battle to get back to how we were before I became ill.

* * *

Dr Scheller spent a long time with me a few mornings ago when we did a sort of look back at my past life. I'm not sure what the technique is called but he's too sensible to go in for long-winded names. He says life is complicated enough without having to put labels on everything and tying oneself in knots trying to pronounce the unpronounceable!

He said he wanted me to talk about my earliest memories. I could imagine myself feeling irritated if any of the other members of the staff had asked me to start delving around in my distant and, for the most part, rather hazy past. But with him, I got the feeling that it wasn't just some clever medical device he was using to unravel my problems but that he was doing it because he genuinely wants to help make me get better. I know, that's typical of me – romanticising the situation whereas I know perfectly well that it's for my benefit and it's stupid of me to read more into his kindness than that he's a good man who has a real vocation for healing troubled minds.

He seems to find the flotsam and jetsam I unearth, from goodness knows where, fascinating. Especially when I mentioned the time when I was five and threw myself into the river, goaded by a smug friend of the same age who said (she was lying) that she could swim.

"Were you not frightened?" he asked, leaning forward, the light catching on his glasses so that, for a moment, my reflection disappeared from their considerably curved surface. "A little girl beside a river that must have seemed immense to someone so young."

"I don't think it was pride," I told him. "Although that possibly came into it. She'd been pissing me off ever since the time our mothers first sat us down side by side on the floor when we were just about able to sit without wobbling over. Even then, Janie was the first to crawl and then the first to stand and walk. She started talking before I did too. I must have found that rather galling, I suppose!"

"Yet you think that it was not rivalry that made you jump into the river?"

"No, I think it was the first stirrings of something that became important in my life – and still is." I remember looking at him closely, wanting him to understand what I meant. "I have always been blessed, or cursed, depending on what way you look at it, with a surfeit of imagination, of believing that anything was possible if you wanted it enough. *Nothing* was too difficult or too off the wall for me; whether it was becoming invisible, flying – or plunging into that extremely cold river. I *knew* I had never learned to swim but I felt that if I was brave and jumped, something, someone would give me the instant ability to surge through the water like an extremely adept mermaid. It came as a bit of a shock to find that I sank like a stone and got all tangled up in riverweed. If it hadn't been for my father diving in and hauling me out by my hair, I probably would have gone to a watery grave. Daft, isn't it?" I laughed, waiting for him to laugh too at my childishness.

But he didn't. Instead, Dr Scheller sat back in the chair, stretching his long legs out in front of him with his hands resting on the file on his lap (he has the most beautiful, slim, long-fingered hands). He looked at me with a serious expression.

"No, my dear Mrs Sayer, quite the reverse! I think it is this particular trait in your character that has seen you through this difficult time in your life and will continue to do so. It is this same, irrepressible instinct of yours to nurture the miraculous, the inexplicable, that will bring you out to the calm water that waits for you beyond." He smiled. "I think it is an excellent quality and I wish for their sakes – and for my own – that more of my patients possessed it."

"It annoys the hell out of Cassandra."

"But it is the task of the parent to annoy the children, don't you think? Especially at Cassandra's age – she is twenty, is she not?" I nodded. "That complicated age when she believes she knows all the answers and that both her parents are ignorant and misinformed on all topics while secretly, deep down inside, she is aware, and resents the fact, that she still needs nurturing and supporting and reassuring – *ad infinitum*."

"Do *you* have children, Dr Scheller?" I asked suddenly. I hadn't meant to say it. It's not the sort of thing you do ask in this delicate doctor-patient situation. I immediately wished I hadn't. Especially when I saw the sudden tremor that crossed his features. It only lasted the briefest of moments, but I knew straight away that, for some reason, it was not a topic for discussion. "I'm sorry," I said hastily. "Sometimes I forget that you are my doctor. I feel that I'm chatting to a friend." I wanted to add, 'to a very special friend' – because that's how I feel about him – but I'd planted my size seven foot firmly in my mouth once already.

His face relaxed into a smile. "But I am your friend – as well as your doctor. But only for as long as you need me. Then you will emerge like a butterfly into the warm sunshine and take up your real life once more. Isn't that right?"

"But when that happens, how do you know that I won't need you again – that I won't get caught up in some nasty sticky spider's web – or be gulped down by a passing bird?"

He patted my arm lightly and then got up, pulling his white coat around him. "Believe me, when you are recovered, you will not need me." He smiled slightly. "And that is good. That is how it should be."

When he'd gone, I thought that what he hadn't said but had gently implied was that, when I finally got my act together and left the clinic, he needed all his strength to deal with the next batch of sadly diminished Hebe Sayers so that he could concentrate on helping them too. I cursed myself for being so greedy. No one had the right to expect continued access to the man's unlimited care and attention.

Not even this forty-six-year-old, loopy woman of diminished responsibility with the character of an occasionally somewhat reckless child who, if the truth be told, sometimes finds it hard pretending to be an adult in an adult world. It's really no wonder that Cassandra finds it difficult to cope with me some of the time.

* * *

Later, same day. I've just been standing in the small bathroom off my room, looking at myself in the mirror over the basin. It's not a very edifying sight, let me tell you! My hair was never my strong point but, after all the days in bed, it's got a permanently flattened look to it and I swear the grey hairs are increasing by the hundred each time I summon up the courage to peer at myself – which isn't very often. I think I look rather like one of those pathetic elderly chimpanzees with the soulful eyes that sit around in their cage, grooming each other in a bored way. The only difference being that I haven't got anyone to groom.

There are so many things whizzing around in my brain. So many worries. And I used to be the sort of woman who never worried. Live for the moment and deal with any problems if and when they crop up. That was fine until last year. If only I'd been a little less laid back, a little more aware, perhaps it would all be different now and I wouldn't be here and Cassandra would be able to look at me without that questioning, slightly wary expression I so often see and my ex-husband wouldn't be quite so embarrassed by his ex-wife's behaviour.

One of the things that's really bothering me is my seventy-four-year-old mother – stuck in that nursing home in Dalkey, not knowing where or even who she is. She has a lovely view of the sea from her window but I don't know how often she looks at it or if it registers as very similar to the view she had from her own bedroom window all her married life. I realise that, now the Alzheimer's has progressed, she's not suffering in the way she did at the beginning.

It was dreadful then because she knew that something was wrong when she was in her early sixties and, each time she couldn't remember where she'd parked the car, and later on, where she lived, it made her so frightened. She tried to pretend that everything was all right – even after the diagnosis had been confirmed. But you could see the fear in her eyes. I used to find her standing in the kitchen, staring out into the trees at the back of the house and I knew she was wondering how long it would take before she had to leave her home and beloved garden. She hated the thought of having to be looked after.

"I don't *want* anyone telling me when I have to have a bath and what clothes to wear," she said one day, her eyes suddenly brimming.

Seeing her like that made me ache inside. My mother never cried.

This was when the periods of lucidity were becoming less and less frequent and we both knew that something would have to be done – and sooner rather than later.

"Oh, Mum! Come and live with me and the girls. I promise I'll never tell you when to have a bath! Not even if you start to get a bit whiffy!" I said, trying to lighten the atmosphere.

She just looked at me. Such a look. She let me put my arms around her and hold her – for a short while. She was never the sort of person who cuddled me when I was a child. I don't remember her ever being demonstrative with my father. When he died I was ten and I clearly remember that my mum stayed dry-eyed and quietly dignified all through those painful days leading up to the funeral. Perhaps she felt she had to make up for the deluge of tears I shed, almost non-stop, which threatened to flood the house.

When I was still lying on my bed, crumpled and damp from crying, several days after my father was buried, she remonstrated with me.

"Hebe, it's time to pull yourself together. All this is very self-indulgent. It doesn't help."

Self-indulgent! I was furious.

"I loved Dad!"

She looked down at me with a slight shake of her head and sighed. Without saying anything more, she turned and left the room, closing the door quietly behind her as though she wanted to shut out the scene as quickly as possible.

But the look on her face as she turned away made me wonder if I was mistaken in thinking that she hadn't loved my father. He, who was always so even-tempered and calm, had seemed perfectly content to be with her. Was it possible, I wondered, that in some strange, grown-up way, they had been happy together? I had never seen them arguing or even more than mildly irritated with each other. To my inexperienced eye, they'd always been what parents should be – constant, solid and unchanging – if a little dull. But they made me feel safe and I realise now how important that was.

Of course, as the weeks passed, I gradually got over his

death. I still missed his bad jokes and the smell of his pipe that he used to smoke in the tiny conservatory that clung to the side of the house, in between the yew hedge and the fishpond. Mum wouldn't allow smoking in the house itself but he was perfectly happy to decamp with the Sunday papers – which seemed to take him all week to get through – and settle down for a read after supper with a cup of coffee, puffing away like mad from time to time when the pipe threatened to go out. I used to be fascinated by the strange spitting, sucking and tapping rituals that appeared to be imperative in mastering the art of successful pipe-smoking. He once let me have a go but, after coughing and spluttering until my eyes watered, I quickly decided that once was enough!

If my mother loved my father in a quiet sort of way, she never talked about their life together after he died. I realised when I was quite small that the thing that she was truly passionate about was her garden, her trees and flowers – in fact, anything that pushed itself above soil level where she lived from the first day of their marriage until she left, confused and frightened, over forty years later, to go into the nursing home.

I never did manage to persuade her to come and stay with us. I begged her to give it a try, insisted that she wouldn't be a burden, that it would be lovely for Pandora and Cassandra to have their gran around. But she wasn't having any of it. Each time I brought up the subject, she'd just shake her head and turn away. Even in her troubled confusion, it seemed to be the one decision that stuck like glue in her mind and that obstinately refused to budge.

Since I've been in here, I know that Cassandra's only visited her a couple of times.

"What's the point?" she observed the other day. "She's away with the fairies. She hasn't a clue who I am."

"But, darling, she might know at *some* level that you're there and that might be comforting to her."

"Oh, Mum! Last time I went, she was doing her best to plant her toothbrush in a pot of begonias. When the nurse took it away from her and made her sit down, Gran asked her if the courgettes were in flower yet and had she remembered to spray the roses?"

"It's not her fault. She can't help the way she is."

"I *know!*" Cassandra looked contrite. "It's just so depressing. I don't feel as though it's Gran any more sitting in the chair. It might as well be a complete stranger – who can't speak or understand the language." She gave me one of her bleak stares. "But if it makes you happy, Mum, I'll go again. I'm not sure when though," she added, just to rub it in that her life was extremely busy.

"Thank you, Cassandra," I said, giving her a grateful smile. "How's Keith?" I asked, changing the subject.

Keith is my daughter's often taken-for-granted and very sweet boyfriend. He's a few years older than Cassandra and deeply into music. From Baroque to Modern Jazz. It flows out of him, over him, through him. He soaks it up and if he's not plugged into his Walkman or at a concert, he's sitting at the piano or hugging a saxophone. If Keith goes missing, it's because he's in Salzburg or London or at the Kilkenny or Cork Festivals or involved in a studio recording or concert. He's even been known, on the spur of the moment, to travel hundreds of miles just to hear a favourite singer. He's a freelance musician and I love him. I love his uncomplicated approach to life, his acceptance of other people's not-so-pleasant characteristics and, most of all, I love the way he copes with Cassandra and her difficult, sometimes unattractive behaviour. Although he's only twenty-three and, apparently, unmarked by life, he's also remarkably mature. When my daughter's playing up and being a downright pain, he just leaves her to stew and when she's finally come to her senses, he never holds a grudge. She's welcomed back as if nothing had happened. I *love* that!

He's been very kind to me. It's as though he understands what each of us has gone through since Pandora. I'll never forget how he acted as a sort of buffer for me after her death, fielding phone calls and doing his best to protect me from Owen and Dervla. A few weeks ago, he even went to see my mother, taking her a mass of flowers from his own mother's beautiful walled garden. He told me that, when he offered them to her, she practically snatched them from him and buried her nose among the sweet peas, honeysuckle and phlox, breathing in their scent in long, deep breaths. When she eventually looked up at him, he said that she gave him the most enormous smile. I can't tell you how good it was to hear that. It was like balm and, for a while, some of the worry faded a little.

* * *

Next day. Only six days to go now and I'm trying to stop myself thinking too much about what it will be like to walk through the door into my home again. I'm worried that all the memories will come flooding back and that I might have a major wobble.

I spent a long time during the night trying to sleep. I've asked them to stop giving me sleeping pills as I think I've started to rely on them too much. As I lay there, watching the moonlight making jigsaw patterns on the floor out of the Venetian blinds and the tangle of wisteria that frames the window, I found myself thinking about Owen.

My ex-husband hasn't exactly been beating a path to my sickbed over the past weeks but that doesn't surprise me. In fact I'm glad. As the days go by and I feel stronger, I realise that there has always been a distance between us, which used to bother me. Now I see that we've both moved on – in very different directions, it has to be said. My path has been rather more bumpy and torturous than his. I'm not saying that he hasn't suffered because of what's happened but what strikes me now is how extraordinary it is that we stayed married for as long as we did. He is ambitious – ruthlessly so when it comes to his business. Never having been ill, he thinks that any manifestation of physical and certainly mental malfunctioning is the sign of a seriously flawed personality. It's just as well that he is so single-mindedly successful because he's footing the bill for this place. I'm grateful for that. Although I like to think of myself as a staunch, standard-bearing member of the Workers' Party, when it comes to the crunch I like my comfort as much as any soft-skinned Liberal. And although I usually get along with people well, I preferred to do my disintegration bit in the privacy of my own room. I didn't want to have to exhibit my chaotic state to the rest of the world and I hadn't got the energy to listen to the rest of the world's worries. Selfish, but there you go!

It's not that I don't earn a reasonably good living from my work but I think that Owen feels that it would look bad if it appeared as though he'd walked away and left me to cope on my own. And he *is* the managing director of his own company with a regular income and stocks and shares and property and what have you. I think he also owns a chunk of racehorse as well. Whereas I rely mostly on royalties from my books and the odd public reading date and magazine article.

I tried my hand at journalism once and quickly discovered that I was hopeless at it. I kept forgetting to ask the right questions, kept getting sidetracked. The interviewee and I would end up, rather merry on several glasses of whatever was to hand and swapping stories about mutual acquaintances and, as so often happens in a small country like Ireland, finding to our delight that we had distant relatives in common. It was fascinating for me but didn't make for good copy.

I write novels, some poetry and children's stuff – but mostly novels. I don't kid myself for one second that what I write is important or of great literary merit but I have the satisfaction of knowing that it's the very best *I* can do and I think I was getting better at it – that is, until I started to unravel. A surprising number of people seem to get pleasure from reading my books and, as far as I'm concerned, that's what matters. I love the idea of making a complete stranger laugh and become involved enough in the story I'm telling to care about what happens to the characters I've dreamed up or rather cobbled together from different bits of various people I've come across.

Mind you, until I started scribbling down these notes, I hadn't been able to write a complete sentence for nearly a year now. If I'm not careful, my income will eventually dry up and I can't let that happen. I like the feeling of being capable of standing on my own two feet without any handouts from either Owen or the government – and I like writing. I like the tension that builds up inside me when I sit down in front of the computer; that moment when I decide on the first word of the first chapter of the next book. It's a weird and marvellous feeling. Alarming and yet exciting.

I think one of the reasons I derive so much pleasure from it is because I was such a dunce at school. I got, if not used to, indifferent to people dismissing me as a non-performer. For me, school was a disaster of enormous proportions – a disaster that lasted twelve bloody long years. I loathed the stuffy classrooms, the smell of chalk and sweaty gym shoes, the strict teachers, the uniform with its slippery tie that refused to stay in place, the lumpy food, the punishments and, above all, what I saw as, all those ridiculous rules. Imagine making twelve-year-old girls go on cross-country runs in a blizzard, wearing only their sports shirts and shorts, tennis shoes and short socks because that's what you wore for cross-country runs!

"You're far too soft, the lot of you. Do you the world of good!" the games mistress used to bellow at us as she watched us jog out into the freezing whiteness.

I used to suspect that she'd been badly treated as a child and this was just one way to get her own back on society. She had a particular dislike of me. I was no good at games and she seemed to take great pleasure in tracking me down to wherever I'd hidden and hauling me off to 'be a sport and join in like a sensible creature'. It didn't matter how imaginative I was in the choice of hiding places. She always sniffed me out like some great bloodhound. I seem to remember that she had bloodshot eyes and heavy jowls. I can't recall if her nose was cool and moist. Probably.

I wasn't much good at academic work either. I spent too much of my time reading books that weren't on the curriculum and imagining what I would do with my life if I could only escape. You could have added a wing to the school library with the number of books I had confiscated from me.

It came as no surprise when I didn't do well in my final exams. In those days, you didn't have to be so bright to get into nursing. As I had just been ill in hospital, where I had been nursed by a particularly sweet girl who'd impressed me with her gentle efficiency, I bit the bullet and decided I too wanted to do my bit for the unsuspecting human race. I applied to train as a nurse at a London teaching hospital. I was interviewed and, to everyone's amazement, including my own, I was accepted.

I never finished the training. I can't really remember why. Well, I do, sort of. It got to the point where I couldn't cope with the officious Sisters and patronising, rude medical staff and the long hours and seeing nice human beings dying often quite horrible deaths. But it was the children dying that really got to me. The three months I spent on the children's cancer ward were the bleakest in my life. I can still remember some of their names and the pale, trusting faces of one or two have stayed vividly in my memory. I know it sounds weak but it upset me so badly that I started to become ill and every time I went back on duty, I came down with another ear or urinary tract infection or back trouble. In the end, I gave up. I felt ashamed that I wasn't apparently cut out to care for suffering humanity. In fact, I realised after I'd left that suffering humanity was probably a lot better off without my inept interventions.

Then I came home and worked in a market garden in County Wicklow – as a sort of placatory gesture to my mother more than anything else. I rather liked the six months I spent there. It was a welcome antidote to the previous two years. It was a chaotic place, run by one of the brotherhood of the kind of local Irish Mafia that you find dotted around this country. You know the type. They have unlimited funds, extensive connections to people in power, drive a Lexus and go on expensive holidays at least three times a year and yet they seem to run only rather small and insignificant businesses.

He was a lovely man, whom everyone addressed as Ant. I suppose his real name was Anthony but I never heard anyone call him that. He didn't know much about plants but would disappear off to Amsterdam at regular intervals 'on business'. I quickly cottoned on that his business didn't have anything to do with purchasing tulip bulbs. I remember he had a habit of handing me a bunch of assorted, badly written labels, pointing me in the direction of a positive jungle of rose bushes and telling me to label them. When I pointed out that I didn't know what label should be attached to which rose, he just smiled disarmingly and said I shouldn't worry, neither would the punters until the plants came into flower and, with any luck, the labels would have blown off by then and they'd be none the wiser.

After that I taught the recorder in a nursery school. I didn't enjoy that experience nearly as much as I thought I was going to. I'm afraid that the problem was me – and only me. I found that some of the kids were gut-wrenchingly adorable and others were just simply death-defying little fiends from hell. I could easily imagine how the hellish ones would turn out as adults. I found it impossible to treat the fiends the same way as the adorable ones and spent my whole time there out of breath and feeling guilty. My self-confidence deserted me for a while and I came to the conclusion that I wasn't a very nice person.

And then, in a sort of blind desperation, I married Owen. I stupidly fell into the trap of feeling that time was marching on and this was the next logical step to take. Every single one of my school-friends was married by that stage. Some of them already proudly sporting two or three children. By the time I realised that I'd made a mistake, it was too late. I had made a commitment to love and honour (I'd refused to say the obey bit) my man and, by God, that's what I was going to do, even if it killed me.

It very nearly did too. It wasn't that Owen was so terribly unkind or unreasonable. We were just completely unsuited to each other. He wanted to be seen in the right places, mixing with the right people and I couldn't care a fig about going to the latest trendy restaurant and the right people were usually fairly painful characters with, as I saw it, their priorities upside down. I wanted fun and laughter and as little routine as I could get away with. Owen was punctual to a fault and neat and tidy and hated mess. Why he asked me to marry him, I'll never know. Well, that's not strictly true. I know perfectly well. It was a case of sheer unbridled lust on both our parts. He was quite *marvellous* in bed! I thought the fun we had in the bedroom would last and spill out into the rest of our marriage. But, sadly, I was wrong.

It wasn't until I was trundling absent-mindedly towards the forty mark and just divorced that I actually got round to discovering what I *should* have been doing all those years. I think I'm a slow learner. It took me all that time to find out that standing by your man is not a good idea if it's slowly killing all your ability to feel like a whole, useful person who exists, not just as an addendum to a successful husband but as an interesting, viable being in her own right.

Still, I suppose all those difficult years of wedlock and all the different activities I indulged in before and with Owen are fodder for books, written and as yet unwritten. I try to cheer myself up with the thought that perhaps I write better now than I would have done in my inexperienced twenties.

"Well," as Maggie Hapgood, my lovely literary agent said when she signed me on, "who wants more chick-lit books? They're crying out for something more substantial to get their teeth into and I have a feeling that you've come along at just the right time!" I could have hugged her! She was the first person to take my work seriously – and it was magic! I must have looked a little shell-shocked. I'd become so used to rejection slips or polite letters thanking me for sending a manuscript but I'd be better off trying elsewhere as that particular outfit didn't go in for my sort of writing. The implication being that what I had sent them was tremendously inferior and I'd be damn lucky if I found anyone the slightest bit interested in tangling with my work.

"You look as if you don't believe me," she said, with an amused expression.

I remember stammering, "Oh, I do, I do. It's just you're the first person to react in this way – and it's hard to take in."

Suddenly, all the hours spent trying to be a good mother to my daughters, getting up at the crack of dawn before the breakfast and school-runs routine so I could write, all Owen's indifference to the very idea of my becoming a proper, published writer – it was all gloriously worth it.

I remember bounding to my feet, rounding her desk at high speed and giving her a hug. I know! A bit much but I couldn't stop myself, I felt so happy and so *relieved*. And she didn't seem to mind one bit.

She's a tremendous person is Maggie. Short, slim, with the brightest blue eyes and a wild halo of fuzzy fair hair and she's always simply bursting with energy. She makes me think of those ads on the telly with the battery-powered rabbits that give up the ghost one by one until there's only one left, who steams off over the horizon, still going like the clappers. She's only thirty-five and as sharp as a scalpel – when it's appropriate. She doesn't stand any nonsense from anyone and yet, she has been so sweet and supportive during this last awful year. Right from the start she was an absolute rock for me when I nervously sent her my first efforts at novel writing. In fact, I wonder how long it would have taken me to get a publisher interested without her help and know-how. I suppose my continued belief in achieving the impossible would have won out in the end but I'm convinced it was a lot easier – and infinitely more pleasant – with her guidance and advice.

Now, I count her as a good friend. She rang several times each week to find out how I was when I was too out of it to talk and, since I've been feeling better, we've spoken regularly on the phone. She wants me to go over and see her in London as soon as I'm up to it. A few weeks ago that seemed an impossibility but now, I almost dare to think that the idea is not so mad after all.

Chapter Two

A day later – after recovering from a stiff neck and sore right hand from all that writing.

I had another session with Dr Scheller this morning. He asked me if I could go further back in my memory than when I was just five. I know some people say they can remember being in the womb. I wonder? I would have thought that would have been a sort of limbo period in one's existence. You'd be pretty anaesthetised by all the swishing and gurgling and heart-thumping noises bombarding you. Just think, if you opened your eyes or mouth, you'd be inundated with amniotic fluid. Perhaps I just sensibly stayed in shut-down mode, sucking my thumb and saving all my energies for the great push out into the big, wide world.

Instead, I started to talk about an uncle. He wasn't a real uncle – more an adopted one. My parents decided to let out a room and he came to live with us in our house in Blackrock when I was five. He was a retired doctor. He appeared to have no relatives and was a quiet, undemanding sort of man. I think my parents felt sorry for him. So, instead of treating him like an ordinary paying guest, he quickly became one of the family.

Dr John, as he came to be called, used to take me out for long walks along the sandy beaches of County Dublin. He always seemed to know when I was getting on my mother's nerves and he would whisk me off and buy me an ice cream. We would sit on a bench or rock while I licked round and round the melting ice until I was left with the small bottom section of cone and then we would go in search of a friendly dog, who'd be delighted to polish off the remainder.

I probably learned more from that man than I ever did at school. Certainly I learned some of the more interesting details about the world around me from him. He was interested, not just in medicine and scientific research, but in geology, botany and astronomy. He had a small telescope in his bedroom and would let me use it, helping me up onto a stool so that I could look through it. I remember being stunned into delighted silence by the sheer numbers of stars and the way they looked like vast clusters of diamonds caught in a gauzy net that trailed haphazardly across the heavens.

My mother told me many years later that he'd described my reaction to my first close encounter with the night sky with quiet amusement.

"That's where the angels live," I'd apparently informed him solemnly when I finally found my voice again.

He never talked down to me but imparted titbits from his enormous store of knowledge in an easy, conversational way that I found irresistible – even though I often didn't understand all the words he used. He encouraged me to ask questions. In fact, the more questions I asked, the more pleased he was. When we walked on the stonier beaches, he would pick up pieces of rock and tell me where they came from and how they were formed. We once found a small lump of amethyst. I still have it on a shelf in my bedroom. Even though he was well into his seventies when I knew him, his eyesight was perfect and I don't ever recall him wearing glasses. Eventually, we would stroll back to the house with our pockets full of interestingly shaped shells and pieces of seaweed and small bunches of the wild flowers that clung precariously in the wind-blown sandy grass at the side of the cliffs. I remember how my mother used to get fed up with me sprinkling sand all over the floor, as I unearthed the precious treasures in my pockets and spread them out in front of her.

He had never married and I think I became a surrogate daughter to him. And, in a way, he was like a second father to me. I certainly loved him. Perhaps not as much as my own father but with more awareness. Even though I was very young, I think I knew that he was a special sort of person and I didn't take him for granted. I was heartbroken when he died suddenly of a stroke just after my eighth birthday. He left a large gap in my life that I thought no one else would be capable of filling. I think, in a way, part of me was still grieving for him when Dad died eighteen months later.

As I described all this to Dr Scheller, I suddenly had a mental picture of the tall, gangling figure of Dr John, striding along a beach, suddenly stooping to pick up some object that had caught his eye – like a long-legged heron swooping on a fish. Running up to see what he'd found was this small girl with sturdy legs and untidy hair. I knew that child was me but suddenly she became Pandora at the same age.

I stopped talking and took a deep breath.

He waited patiently. After a while, he leaned forward, searching my face.

"Are you feeling all right, Mrs Sayer?" I nodded without speaking. "You were remembering your daughter just then, I think? Your Pandora."

Again I gave a slight nod, stunned by the sharpness of the image I'd just experienced. Then he too fell silent. It was comforting – having him sitting there beside the bed. He has that amazing quality of stillness that very few people possess. I just knew that I didn't have to say anything and that he understood.

I must have fallen asleep because, when I opened my eyes, there was no sign of Dr Scheller and two hours had gone by.

When I woke, I was still feeling a little shaken from the morning session but I was calm again.

As I waited for lunch to arrive, I splashed my face with cold water and combed my hair. Then I sat down in the comfortable chair by the window. I felt I needed to try and unravel my thoughts, to attempt to sort out what had happened two hours earlier. I know all this examination of self is a delicate operation. Even after all the sessions we've had it is still rather like tiptoeing around a minefield. Powerful emotions seemed to lie in wait, threatening to grab me by the throat and give me a mental mugging.

I was sitting beside the open window, trying to think positive thoughts when the door opened. It was Cassandra. For a moment I felt resentful. I needed to have my space un-invaded and my uncertain tranquillity undisturbed for just a little longer.

Summoning up a smile I greeted her.

She collapsed onto the end of the bed with a sigh. "How are you, Mum? Are you feeling any better?"

"Yes, I'm definitely on the mend. Dr Scheller seems to think I'm doing well."

Poor Cassandra! She must be feeling that this has all gone on quite long enough.

"So, do you think they'll be letting you out soon?"

It sounded as though she was wondering if the keepers might be considering the release of a caged animal.

"The good news is that I can come home at the end of the week."

"That's great," my daughter said.

I couldn't help noticing the anxiety in her eyes.

"Don't worry. They wouldn't let me go home if they didn't think I was up to it."

She scanned my face worriedly as if searching for confirmation that I was no longer the frantic, troubled woman of three months ago. There was a silence – the sort of silence that I knew was filled with a mass of things she wanted to say but couldn't or wouldn't.

I watched her as she fiddled with the strap of her bag. She was wearing black jeans and a black T-shirt that looked rather hot and un-summery. But her long blonde hair looked lovely, spread silkily over her shoulders. Because she's so tall – almost five feet ten – and has legs that go on forever, she always looks good and can more or less get away with wearing anything. Pandora was like that too, I found myself thinking.

"What's wrong, Mum?"

I hadn't realised that, for a moment, I'd closed my eyes

and my hands were clenched into fists. My daughter had come over to where I was sitting. She was crouched in front of me, looking concerned.

"I was thinking of your sister."

"Oh!" She moved away from me slightly.

I don't think she knew she'd done it. It was a kind of involuntary withdrawal. Judging by the stony expression on her face, she wasn't ready to talk about it either.

"Would it help if you talked to Dr Scheller?" I asked on a sudden impulse.

"God, no!" she said quickly, moving back to the bed. "I don't need a shrink."

Then, seeing the look on my face, she said hastily, "I'm sorry, Mum. I didn't mean . . ."

"It's all right, darling. I know you didn't. I just thought it might do you good to talk to someone wise, someone who can look at all of this from the outside and who won't put you under any pressure. I know he wouldn't make the mistakes I make when I talk to you. I know you feel that I've been pretty useless for some time."

Suddenly, she gave one of her rare smiles. It lit her face, making her look beautiful.

"You're *not* useless, Mum," she said in a surprisingly gentle voice. "It's just that you've been a bit . . ." She groped for the appropriate word. "All over the place. You know, sort of unglued. I didn't know what to say to you. But I do know that I wouldn't swop you for anyone else's mum."

* * *

Next day – with only five days to go.

I think I slept very well last night. I don't remember having had such a nightmare-free eight hours in a long time.

I suspect that a large part of that was due to Cassandra's visit yesterday. We didn't talk very much but she was gentler and sweeter than I've seen her in ages – as though it had suddenly struck her that she isn't perhaps the only one who's finding the going rough. It was good to be together and not at odds. Oh, I know I shouldn't think that everything's all right between us. It will take a long time to really get back to the way we used to be and I know there's a reticence there that didn't exist before. She's hurting and miserable and she's still angry. Understandably. They were so close, closer than a lot of sisters. Well, they would be, being twins.

Pandora was always the more biddable of the two of them. She didn't like confrontation and would go out of her way to smooth things when Cassandra was being awkward and trying to pick a fight. Although they looked so alike, with their long fair hair and amazing legs and their blue eyes, Pandora's expression was somehow more open. She had an aura of calm, even as a little girl, that was delightful. She was every bit as enthusiastic about things as her sister but she never went over the top like Cassandra. There always seemed to be a kernel of self-knowledge somewhere deep inside her that she relied on and that helped her to make the right choices. Until that last night.

When the sheer waste of it all hit me it was like a sledgehammer. Then the anger kicked in. I remember coming back from visiting her grave, several weeks after the funeral, and stopping on the path and suddenly not knowing what to do with myself. I felt breathless with anger. I wanted to lash out and destroy and hurt and do damage on a cosmic scale. Stupid, I know! The recriminations had begun by that time and Cassandra and Owen were both doing their own bit of lashing out. We were all caught in the crossfire. The atmosphere at home was sour and dangerous and filled with pain.

It seemed to me as if the name I'd given Pandora was a curse. In the legend, she was the first woman to be made from earth as a punishment for man stealing fire from Prometheus. Then she herself defied the gods and opened the forbidden casket, letting free unimaginable torments and woes to stream out into the world. I found myself wondering if everything might have turned out differently if I'd given her another name.

I had chosen Pandora and Cassandra as names because I liked their differentness and I'd loved reading all the books I could get my hands on about Greek and Roman mythology when I was pregnant. Owen thought I was mad, of course. He would have preferred nice, normal Irish names. He even suggested Dervla – which wasn't too smart of him. Dervla is his mother's name and she and I disliked, and continue to dislike, each other – intensely and overtly. Every now and then I come across the phrase that someone cordially dislikes some one else. There is *nothing* whatsoever cordial about her relationship with me. Interfering, pot-stirring snob (with absolutely nothing to be snobbish about). Anyway, in the end, he gave in and humoured me. I didn't stop to think that the girls might not like the names they'd been landed with. As she grew older, Pandora would just give a wry smile when anyone queried her name but Cassandra resented hers bitterly.

"Why did you call me that? *Why?*" she demanded to know, after being teased at school by one of the older girls.

After that incident, she insisted on being called Cassie

all through school. Funnily though, now she seems to rather like having a name that's unusual.

Thinking back over those terrible, anger-suffused days, I realise how destructive it all was. But, true to form, I didn't learn quickly. Even when I first came here, after the initial phase when I did nothing but sleep, it flared up again. I'm ashamed to say that I vaguely remember hurling my tray at the rather po-faced sister when she insisted that I had to do something that I thought unnecessary. I can't even remember what it was now. She was the worst one for persuading the house doctor to sedate me if I so much as blinked out of turn. She didn't try it on when Dr Scheller was around, of course. And when I was more with-it and told him what went on, I know he must have spoken to her because she's a lot more careful around me these days. Plus the fact that, perhaps having a breakfast tray whizzing past her head concentrated her mind somewhat!

But I do now realise that she had grounds to consider me unstable and unpredictable. Perhaps it was the cocktail of drugs I had rattling around inside me, but I dimly remember escaping into the garden in my dressing-gown and slippers at some point early on in my stay here. They caught me trying to shin up one of the old lime trees. I'd picked the one that was closest to the high wall, being just about *compos mentis* enough to realise that the porter would hardly let me saunter out through the gates in my nightwear. Dr Scheller told me later that, when the sister caught up with me, I hit her with my flipflop – several quite hard whacks – before they managed to disarm me. He didn't tell me in an accusatory way but just as a fact, perhaps to demonstrate that I was on the mend and hardly likely to do a repeat performance. Oh, dear! No wonder she isn't too keen on me. I see her glancing at me uncertainly sometimes as though she's not quite sure that I'm sane again. Perhaps she thinks it's all a clever ruse and that my docility is faked and, at the first chance, I'll give chase and stab her with my supper fork! Not that I haven't been tempted. She's one of those people you meet from time to time as you stagger through life that just ask to be chased and superficially stabbed. No arteries involved, of course. I'm not that vindictive!

That happy memory made me smile – and I haven't done much of that for some time. I think that, possibly, writing down all this stuff *is* a good idea.

* * *

Some time later after a rather revolting evening meal of shepherd's pie. I hate to think what the poor man died of because he tasted awful.

Dr Scheller says that it's good to write down my moans too.

"We all moan sometimes. Why not write them down? Then you can come back to them, look at them and either dismiss them as irrelevant and trivial or perhaps make the decision that they are justified. If they are, you move on to the next step of deciding what you will do about these justifiable moans of yours. It can be quite educative," he said, giving me one of his slightly lopsided smiles.

"Isn't that rather self-indulgent?"

"Why? Do you think that a cold shower and a brisk, motivating pep talk is the answer? I don't think it is self-indulgent to want to understand yourself better and, in a small way, this is a method of doing just that." He took off

31

his glasses and pinched the sides of his nose, screwing up his eyes as he did so. I saw that, without them, he seemed even more tired than he usually did – and his sallow face looked strangely naked. When he'd replaced them, he continued, "From several things you've said over the past weeks, Mrs Sayer, I get the strong impression that, although you are kind to others, you are hard on yourself. Where did you get this idea that you shouldn't allow yourself a little leeway, a little spoiling from time to time?"

I considered the question for a moment but it wasn't all that hard to answer. "I suppose from my mother. She was constantly telling me that I was too easy on myself; that I was always ready to sit back and let others do the work. And she was right – I was very lazy." I laughed. "If you want to know the truth, I still am but I have unfortunately developed a conscience that stops me from giving in too often – and it's a damned nuisance! There are many occasions when I'm severely tempted to opt for the glass of gin and tonic and a good book rather than do what I'm supposed to be doing."

Then he laughed too. "Oh, yes, to have a conscience can sometimes be a drawback, I agree. But," he paused and gave me a penetrating look, "it is unwise not to occasionally give in to your instincts and take the path that is less hard. It is no sin at all to nurture the child that lurks within the most successful, the most pompous and the most self-righteous among us." He sat back in his chair, regarding me with raised eyebrows. "Where do you think I would be if I didn't once a week go to the cinema and indulge my love of, what you in Ireland endearingly refer to as, foreign films?"

"But that's a very sophisticated, adult pastime," I remonstrated.

"With the biggest tub of popcorn I can lay my hands on and the largest paper cup of Coca-Cola?"

The idea of him sitting in a cinema seat, clutching a Coke in one hand and popcorn in the other made me laugh out loud – a proper laugh – that came from somewhere deep down inside me, taking me by surprise.

"There, you see! The very thought of my particular indulgence has a good effect on you! Imagine how beneficial it will be for you to treat yourself with your own variety of indulgences. Will you remember that?"

I smiled at him. "I will, I promise."

And, what's more, I meant it.

* * *

Next day and the sun is streaming in through the open window. I can hear a blackbird singing in the chestnut tree outside.

I woke up this morning and found myself looking around my room and, for the first time, really taking in what it was like. I realised that, up until now, I've sort of existed in this space, because this was where I happened to be, without really noticing any of the details. The walls are a restful, pale primrose yellow. On the wall above my bed is the ubiquitous Monet print of his wretched pond at Giverny. I'm sorry, I like good, Impressionist paintings but I've seen enough of his damn water lilies to give me webbed feet. And this one's faded so that it has a slightly mauvish tinge that makes it appear as though the pond – and the lilies – could do with a good scrub with Harpic.

There's the comfortable chair by the window in soft, cream-coloured leather and there's a bedside locker that is pretty much a bog-standard bedside locker. There's a long shelf with an assortment of flowers, including a really beautiful bunch of freesias and gardenias from dear Maggie. Opposite the window is a wardrobe that, I expect, houses the clothes I was wearing when Owen brought me here. I can't for the life of me remember what I *was* wearing that day. That's part of the erased bit I suppose.

I do remember that Cassandra told me after I'd been here for a few weeks that I'd really lost the plot during those last days at home. So much so that she been frightened into ringing her father. Usually she does her best not to be caught up in anything that involves both her parents. When Owen and I broke up, she insisted that she would not be drawn into a discussion of either parent by the other one. I think that was probably wise of her. That way, nothing was repeated that might up the ante. Life was difficult enough without any passed-on spitefulness.

I've just been trying to remember exactly what *did* happen on the day I came here. I know I didn't realise that my behaviour was becoming more and more alarming by the day and that Cassandra had got to the point where she was regularly ringing up her father to ask him what she should do. All I know is that the silly, forgetful sort of things I was doing gradually escalated into more potentially dangerous situations.

Like the time I felt that, if I didn't get out of the house and away, I would go mad. So I took off in the car, leaving all the lights on and the front door wide open. I drove around for hours, deep into the Wicklow Mountains, finishing up at Djouce woods. I must have been away for a long time. It was late at night and freezingly cold when I finally got home to find Owen and Cassandra pacing the floor, angry and worried.

Poor Cassandra had arrived home to find the front door

open and my car gone. She immediately jumped to the conclusion that the house was in the process of being burgled and, it was only after a lot of tiptoeing around, listening for the slightest sound, that she realised there was nobody in the place – only Busby bawling for his food.

Since I came in here, I haven't thought about poor old Busby but in the last few days, I realise that I've started to miss that silly cat! Busby's fat and his coat is black and shiny. He would make an excellent stand-in for a Buckingham Palace guardsman's headgear if needed. I'm sure the old Queen would never notice the difference! The remarkable thing about Busby is his ability to really cuddle you. His technique is unique. I've never seen any other cat behave in the same way. He mountaineers up your front and then, back legs resting on your stomach and with his head snuggled into your cheek, he wraps a paw around each side of your neck and purrs at full volume. He gets extremely put out if you try to remove him before he feels he's had a proper love-in and stalks off into the garden with his ears flattened and his tail in the air – as though to say, 'Right, mate. Stuff you! That's your lot for the rest of the day'.

I know that, as the weeks went by, my wanderings became more frequent and prolonged. I scared myself and I know I scared Cassandra. That made it even more difficult for me to help her deal with her distress and feelings of guilt. From things she'd said, it sounded, right from the start, as though she'd decided that what happened to Pandora was mostly my fault but I know that, deep down, she's smothered in guilt.

Owen blamed me for not being more on the ball, for not anticipating what could happen. He hasn't actually said as much but I know him and I'm sure that's what he thinks. It's all very well. It's easy to be the perfect parent when you're not the one doing 90% of the parenting. The times the girls were with him were during the holidays, the fun times and the special occasions when he'd take them to London for the weekend and treat them to a show, a delicious meal and some expensive shopping. No wonder he never had any problems with Cassandra when all that was going on. She was being spoiled rotten and so, of course, she behaved like an angel.

And, of course, bloody Dervla has given her cauldron a good stir. *She's* made sure to put in her tuppence-worth of criticism and innuendo ever since it happened. I'm sure she must be sad about losing one of her granddaughters but she's hidden it very well. Having overheard a couple of conversations that I wasn't supposed to hear, it seemed to me she was much more interested in fanning the flames of doubt as to whether I should even be allowed back into my own house than trying to be constructive or supportive. That woman is such a witch! An extremely elegant and excessively thin one but a witch all the same. She's part of a coven of wealthy, elderly women who spend their time suiting themselves but giving lip-service to a host of good causes. They're always swanning around from one strategy-planning lunch to the next. If they donated all the money they spend on wine, *cordon bleu* lunches and Gucci suits, they'd sort out third-world debt in record time – no problem.

I *must* be getting better; I'm starting to sound like a real cow! But when I compare her to my own mother, it's hard to believe that they're the same age. Whereas my poor mother's mind is full of cotton wool, Dervla has all her wits and they are razor-sharp. I can just see her whispering into Owen's ear that perhaps, in everyone's best interest, I should have been sectioned. Luckily, her son's not that stupid and he's done nothing of the kind. He probably also realises that if he attempted such a thing, he would live to regret it. He wouldn't be too keen on getting on with his life minus a few essential body parts. I have an awful temper when really roused.

* * *

One of the nurses has just reminded me that it's nearly the end of August. I have been here for over *two and a half months!* I can hardly believe it. The days have slid imperceptibly into each other and I almost feel that I've spent half my life in this place with its plush carpets and hotel-standard food. It's only when you inadvertently glimpse through an open door some poor creature with restraining bandages attached around their wrists to the cot bars on their bed that you remember that where I am is where some of the mentally fragile of this world are held.

Every now and then I hear a woman's voice wailing – a high-pitched unearthly sound that increases in volume as a door is opened and then stops as suddenly as it began. When I hear that chilling sound, my heart misses a beat and a rash of fear creeps over my skin like some horrible freezing acne.

I know I got up very early on that last morning before I came in here. It was just beginning to get light and I remember it was raining. Not hard but that constant, wetting, silent drizzle that soaks you within minutes. For some reason, I went outside into the garden. I think I must have been in my nightdress still. Yes, because I remember

37

that my slippers got muddy very quickly and I took them off . . . I don't know how I ended up in the street but I *do* remember cars and an early-morning dustbin lorry.

I think I had a sudden desperate urge to see my friend Suzanne. We've known each other since the children were small and her son is six months younger than my girls. I think that I desperately needed to speak to her, for her to put her arms around me and just hold me. I don't know why. Oh, Hebe, don't be a fool! Of course, I know why. My own mother wasn't capable of holding me, neither were Owen or Cassandra and I must have been frantic for some form of affectionate physical contact. I knew she'd gone to live in Australia for a year but, for some reason, I thought that if I went to her house she'd be there. Suzanne lives a good five miles from where I do – so that was going to require a lot of walking – and in bare feet. I must have been off my trolley!

And I definitely remember the poor woman with the fair hair, who stopped her car and wound down the window and asked me something. I haven't the slightest idea what we said to each other but I expect she wanted to know if I was all right. It must have looked very peculiar, me all bedraggled and in my nightclothes wandering along the side of the street. I probably made very little sense because she must have rung the police on her mobile. I vaguely remember refusing to get into a squad car a little while later. In fact, I think I became quite abusive. On the whole, I only resort to swearing when I'm really pushed. It has much more of an effect that way. But I've a horrible feeling that I told those poor lads to bugger off and arrest some real criminals.

I wonder how many people am I going to have to apologise to when I get back home?

Chapter Three

29th August. The first anniversary of Pandora's death.
Early this morning, I lay on the bed and shut my eyes and remembered. I wanted to remember all the times that were connected to Pandora and to laughter and affection and joy.

I remembered holding my two newborn daughters in my arms, enchanted by their miraculous completeness, happier than I think I'd ever been and yet, at the same time, bewildered. As I looked down at them, it struck me for the first time that I was responsible for their welfare and I nearly dropped them I felt so overcome by the thought.

I remembered when they were small and the family holidays we spent in France with the two girls playing on the beach, naked and brown and happy. I relived the look of surprised delight on Pandora's face when she won a singing competition at school. I remembered how she would sneak Ziggi, the springer spaniel puppy, into her bed at night and how content she looked, fast asleep with her cheek nestling against the animal's soft fur. I remembered seeing both girls leaving for their first dance on their so very young-looking escorts' arms, Cassandra in a dress of pale gold and Pandora in the deepest green. I remembered how excited they both looked and how beautiful – and I remembered thinking how they had their whole lives in front of them and wondering what each of them would do with that life. After they'd left, I stood at the open door and I wished that I could ensure their happiness and that they would live useful, interesting lives that would make them content and well-rounded human beings. I wished for them all the things that every parent wishes for their children. Even then, I didn't see how vulnerable they still were, in spite of the make-up and elegant dresses and the pretended sophistication. I didn't realise that I'd already relaxed my guard. I had started to forget to watch out for them as carefully as before.

I remembered until I couldn't remember any more and then I cried a little. But not that dreadful, gut-wrenching crying that leaves you feeling like a wrung-out dishcloth.

I felt strangely light-headed this morning. Not quite real. When Dr Scheller came in he gave me one of his gentle smiles. I'd told him yesterday that today was the anniversary of Pandora's death.

"I can't tell you how happy I am that you have got so far, Mrs Sayer. How are you feeling? You look a little tired."

"I feel very tired but I've spent a lot of time this morning thinking about my daughter in a good way. I want to try and stop today from becoming the first of many anniversaries that concentrate on the loss of her and the hopeless waste. It will help Cassandra too if we try and think about the joy Pandora brought into our lives – about all the good times – and there were lots of those."

"Now that you can put Pandora's death into words and say the sort of things you have said to me just now, I believe that your climb back to the sunlight will be faster than you think." He held up a hand in a warning gesture. "But don't expect too much too soon. There will be setbacks. Life rarely allows us to travel smoothly in the direction we would like. Don't be disheartened if, tomorrow or next week, you feel that the light at the end of the tunnel has not become as strong as you want or if it seems as far away as ever. Be patient. You are well on your way to feeling that there are good things waiting for you. Like love, don't go looking for them and then they will creep up on you and take you by surprise!"

I found myself suddenly wanting to fling my arms around his neck and hug him in gratitude for all his attention, his patience but, above all, for his compassion. The man seems to have a bottomless well of that commodity. But I didn't. I gather it's a common enough occurrence, grateful patients falling for their doctors. I seem to remember that Freud suffered from it all the time but he made the mistake of loving at least one of his female patients back. And I know that Dr Scheller would never allow himself to give in to such weakness. Not that I think for one minute that he has the slightest urge to take me in his arms and embrace me. So I can also add common sense to his list of good points!

* * *

Later, same day. Sun has disappeared but I feel surprisingly together.

I had visits from both Cassandra and Owen today.

Luckily his mother hasn't been near me since I came in here. Owen probably told her that it would not be a good idea but, on second thoughts, she more than likely never had the slightest intention of dropping in. Having a basket-case for a daughter-in-law doesn't go down well in the bridge-playing, fund-raising, ladies who lunch – and lunch – set. I wonder how she explains my absence from the scene. After all, Dalkey is a small enough place and my sudden disappearance and the cancellation of various readings I was supposed to be giving must have been fairly obvious. No doubt hair-raising and highly embellished versions of my lunatic wanderings before I was incarcerated have caused her considerable discomfort. *Good!* I hope she has repeated nightmares in 3D of me doing all sorts of totally off-the-wall things – that I don't think I actually got around to doing – to disturb her slumbers. But I somehow can't imagine that one waking up with a scream of terror. Terror just isn't in her vocabulary. It wouldn't go with the image! She just likes to terrorise others. Oh, she does it fairly subtly with a gleam in her eye and a curl of her lip but when she really lets rip it's devastating for the recipient. I should know!

Like the time she came to lunch shortly after Owen and I were married. He had invited several colleagues from work and I had pulled out all the stops to prepare a suitably impressive meal. She knew I was nervous and played on it, taking over the role of hostess, ignoring me and treating me more like a paid help who had somehow wangled a seat at the dinner table than her son's new bride. But I have to admit that she's consistent. You have to give her that. She is every bit as ghastly now as she was then!

Cassandra arrived first, looking as though she too hadn't

slept much. It makes me sad to see the blue smudges under her eyes and the way her mouth turns down at the corners. When I saw her standing in the doorway, it struck me that she seemed older than her twenty years. She looked as though she was determined to put a brave face on things but was finding the effort extremely difficult. I wanted to put my arms around her and hug her tight. But that didn't happen, I'm afraid. I knew that today of all days was going to be hard on both of us. But I took a mental deep breath and greeted her with a smile.

"Hello, darling!"

She stood by the door for a moment before moving into the room, letting it bang behind her. "I don't know how you can smile. I suppose you realise what day it is?"

"Of course, I do but that doesn't stop me from being pleased to see you." I gestured for her to come over to where I was sitting by the window. "Come and sit down. You look tired."

She gave me a baleful look. "Of course, I'm tired. I didn't get much sleep last night." She came to a sudden stop in the middle of the room. Then she surprised me by breaking her strictly observed rule of not discussing Owen with me. "Do you know, I rang Dad last night."

"Good. Was he pleased you'd rung?"

She gave a mirthless laugh. "It turned out that it wasn't such a good idea after all. He wasn't there. In fact, dear Daddy was out on the town."

"What do mean 'out on the town'?"

"Out!" she snapped. "Enjoying himself with some bimbo or other."

"How do you know he was out with a woman? He might

have been at one of his business dinner things. You know how many of those he has to go to."

"Joan told me. I asked her. So you can stop making excuses for him, Mum."

Joan is Owen's housekeeper – it was I who discovered her before the divorce and we've been friends ever since. I like her. She's solid, physically and emotionally, dependable and loyal and completely unflappable. The thing I like most about her is that she deals with all Dervla's nonsenses without batting an eye.

I held out my hand to Cassandra. "Please come and sit down beside me."

Slowly she came over and sat on the end of the bed rather than on the other chair, which was nearer. I could see the tension in her face and shoulders and hands. It was rather like being close to a land-mine. If I didn't tread very carefully, she would explode, harming us both.

"Surely you realise by now, Cassandra, that people deal with grief in different ways?" I asked her cautiously. "Would you have preferred it if he had been at home, feeling miserable? How would that help anyone?"

"It would have helped me to know that Pandora's death meant something to him," she replied stubbornly, fixing her gaze on the distant sea. "I *needed* to talk to him. After all, he's been the only semi-functioning parent I've had for some time."

That really hurt. I know I haven't been there for her for ages but I am doing my best to start functioning again.

She looked over at me, perhaps feeling that she'd gone a bit far. When she next spoke there was a slight tremor in her voice. "Mum, it's only been one year. Surely on the night before her first anniversary you'd think he wouldn't want to go out and enjoy himself. It's so – selfish! Especially after what he . . ."

"Especially after he what?"

She shook her head and added sourly, "Especially as she was always his golden girl."

I knew that she'd been going to say something else and had changed her mind at the last minute.

"He loved Pandora. You can't pretend he didn't. Perhaps he went out because he wanted to forget. Perhaps he went out because he couldn't bear the thought of staying in. Men behave differently from us when they're upset. They deal with emotional stuff in ways that wouldn't work for us. Dad doesn't have close men friends to confide in. *You* have a circle of really good friends but most men don't have that comfort."

"He wouldn't have gone out if he was a normal, decent person!" she said, angrily. "But he thinks that because I miss her and think about her all the time that I'm a freak. Anyway, what I think and who I am don't count as far as he's concerned."

"Of course, you count, Cassandra!"

"I wonder!" Her voice became ominously quiet. "He was always telling Pandora things. It never seemed to be a problem for him, sharing what he felt with her. You'd have to be blind not to see that he thought she was special."

Why hadn't I seen it before? Cassandra is jealous of her dead sister's place in her father's heart. She thinks that Owen preferred Pandora.

"Your father adores you, you silly girl. I know he loves you every bit as much as he loved Pandora."

45

She gave me a strange look that I found disquieting. Then, as though she didn't want to continue the conversation, she said quietly, "Well, he's got a funny way of showing it, that's all I can say."

A troubled silence stood between us like a wall. I didn't know what to say or how to comfort and reassure her. But I didn't want that wall to grow until she was hidden from me and unreachable.

"Cassandra, darling, I . . ."

It was just then that Owen arrived.

As soon as she saw him, my daughter got to her feet. "I have to go. I'm meeting Keith. We're going to take some flowers down to the cemetery." She gave her father a meaningful look. Then, brushing the side of my cheek with her lips, she added, "I'll see you, Mum."

And she was gone, leaving Owen standing by the bed looking annoyed.

"What was all *that* about?" he asked, dumping a bag of fruit on the bedside table.

"She's upset." I looked at him curiously. Surely he hadn't forgotten what day it was, had he? "She rang you last night, hoping to talk to you."

"I was out," he said dismissively.

"I know. She told me."

I watched him as he moved over to the other chair. He was impeccably dressed – as always – in a beautifully made lightweight summer suit of pale grey that showed up his tan. He must have been sailing recently. His brown skin made his eyes look even more blue than usual and the sun had bleached his fair hair so that you couldn't see the grey. All in all, he's a very attractive-looking man – perhaps even more so than when he was younger. He undoubtedly has presence. No wonder he's never short of a companion when he needs one.

"She was upset because of today being –"

"I know perfectly well what today is," he said, quickly. "And, what's more, I don't need Cassandra dropping heavy-handed hints about going down to the cemetery with flowers."

"I know, I know!" I said in a placatory way. "But it's been difficult for her. You know, with me in here and she can't talk to her gran."

"It's been difficult for *everyone*." He sounded stiff and formal. "But that's no excuse for rudeness. And she could always talk to Mother," he added reprovingly.

I didn't even bother to argue. He knows perfectly well that his mother is not the sort of person to give solace to a grieving granddaughter. He just doesn't like the fact that the girls were always much closer to Mum than to Dervla.

Owen was looking belligerent. He gets that look when someone had got to him or when he's feeling guilty about something and is made to feel uncomfortable in spite of himself. It's easy for him to sort out more or less any drama to do with work but, when it comes to his personal life, he gets decidedly awkward when things don't go smoothly.

"*Will* you be going to the grave today?" I asked.

"No, I won't. It's ridiculous – being expected to perform in a certain way just because of a date. Pandora's dead. It doesn't make any difference what day it is, nothing is going to change that fact."

I just managed to stop myself from putting my hands over my ears. I wanted to shout I know, I know! I wanted to drown out what he was saying. Why does he have to be so brutal about it?

After what seemed like an age, he got up slowly. "I'll give you a lift home at the end of the week."

"I was going to get a taxi. Are you sure?" I asked, surprised.

"Yes, of course, I'm sure."

I could see from his face that he'd had enough. I know he doesn't enjoy coming to visit me and the little *contretemps* with Cassandra had obviously got to him.

I must have sat for a long time after he'd gone – trying to work out how I was going to cope with all the turmoil and anger that apparently still seethes unabated in Owen's and Cassandra's lives.

* * *

Next evening and the sun was shining again – all day. I know it's the end of August and it should be shining but it feels like a good omen.

"You do look quite a bit better, Mum," Cassandra commented this afternoon when she came to see me. It was obvious she was trying to make up for yesterday. She peered at me critically. "The circles under your eyes are just blue now. They used to be almost black."

I know she was trying to sound cheerful but I wish I didn't have *any* circles under my eyes. Above all, I wish, wish, *wish* that the reason for those circles didn't exist. I would give anything in the world to just have Pandora back, safe and happy.

"Mum? *Mum?*" Cassandra was looking annoyed.

"Sorry! What did you say?"

"You were miles away." She gave me a sideways glance. "I suppose you were thinking of Pandora."

"Yes," I said, feeling guilty. "I was."

"You do that all the time. I say something and you don't hear. I do try, you know. I can't think why I bother sometimes. It's as if I'm invisible."

"I'm sorry, darling!" I said, smiling at her, willing her not to make a big thing about it. "I'm sure there are lots of times each day when you think of her too."

"Not to the exclusion of everything else." Her voice sounded flat with bitterness.

I immediately made a silent promise that, from now on, I would try not to let myself wander off like that but would give my surviving daughter the attention she deserves – and plainly needs.

But, as so often happens when Cassandra makes up her mind that she's not getting a fair deal, it's almost impossible to undo the damage. She simply pulls down the shutters and scowls for a few hours, sometimes for a few days. The sad thing is, when she's like that, she's so unapproachable that it's impossible to get through to her. It's always been the same. Any perceived slight festers and it takes her a while to recover. Only nowadays, her moods are darker and they last longer.

Then she startled me by suddenly saying, "I suppose you know about that Lucy creature!"

My mind was a blank. I don't know anyone called Lucy. "*Lucy?*"

"Yes! You *know!* Dad's secretary."

"Cassandra, Dad and I are divorced. I didn't know that he had a secretary called Lucy and you know perfectly well that Dad and I don't discuss his personal life – any more than

I talk about mine with him – until I came into this place – and then it was open season for a while." I probably sounded ratty. I didn't mean to but, if Owen has got something going with his secretary, it's nothing to do with me and I'd rather not know any details. "Why are you telling me?"

She shrugged. "Because you should know."

"That's not the only reason, is it?"

"All right! Because it's sad – and it's embarrassing. Dad's forty-eight and that Lucy person is my age. Can you imagine how that makes me feel?"

I looked at her, at a loss as to what I should say. I wasn't interested in Owen's girlfriends and I found myself wishing that he'd been a little more discreet and kept it to himself – at least until Cassandra was on a more even keel.

A sudden thought struck me. "Does Dervla know about this Lucy?"

"Are you joking?" said Cassandra, giving me a withering look. "Of course, she knows! She's got a radar system the Americans would kill for. Dervla should be part of their Star Wars programme."

It's funny how Cassandra dislikes Owen's mother almost as much as I do. Not quite though because she knows if she manages to keep her mouth shut and keep her relatively sweet, the woman's good for an expensive present at Christmas and on her birthday. She's never been allowed to call her grandmother Granny or Gran, like my mum. When they were very small, Dervla said she preferred it if the girls called her by her first name. She said she wasn't granny material. She was right there! I can't ever remember her allowing them to climb all over her or put sticky fingers on her silk wallpaper or brocade chair covers. She usually visited them in our house and it was on her terms and in a way that made it possible for her to escape at the first sign of rowdiness or insurrection! And the idea of asking her to look after them if they weren't well was laughable. The very thought of even the slight possibility of having to face runny poo or vomit that didn't quite make the loo would result in her disappearing into the distance at the speed of light until the threat was over and they had recovered.

Although my mother could be tricky and was impossibly house-proud, she loved being a granny to them. She was always baking them gingerbread biscuits in the shape of stars and moons and dreamily moist marble cake and soft, floury scones that she spread with clotted cream and home-made raspberry jam. When they were small, she'd regularly have them to stay with her and they would return home happy and sunny, clutching the latest book of fairy stories or a packet of sweets each. Granny Molly, as she came to be called, knitted all their jerseys from the time when they first started wearing them until she became too confused to knit. They were lovely, her jerseys, often striped and always in the softest wool and in the most gorgeous colours.

I remember going to my mother's house one day to collect the girls. They were playing in the garden, surrounded by flower-beds bursting with colour. They were wearing their latest Granny Molly hand-knitted tops. Pandora's was shocking pink and Cassandra's was a lovely rich peacock green. As they ran through the curved pergola, smothered in climbing roses and sweet peas, I remember thinking that they were like two brightly coloured butterflies flitting in and out of a scented rainbow of flowers. I can still see how happy they looked.

My mother came to stand beside me at the door. I remember she watched them silently for a moment and then, as she turned to go back inside, she gave a sigh and said, in that rather unemotional, dry way that she had, "I hope you realise how blessed you are. They are lovely children, Hebe."

I was surprised because it wasn't the sort of thing that she would normally say. A word like 'blessed' wasn't in her vocabulary. It was the sort of word she associated with church and my mother had no time for the Church. It was unusual too because she always kept her thoughts to herself and I'd learned the hard way not to expect to share confidences or intimacies with her. I think that the times when she had my two small daughters to stay were possibly some of the happiest in her life. I'd seen how she was with them – when she didn't know I was watching. It was as though their unconditional love made it possible for her to open up and be a softer, gentler, warmer sort of person. They certainly gave her something that I was never capable of giving.

I don't ever remember her being that way with me when I was a child. Perhaps I was too awkward and unattractive. Perhaps she didn't have the time for me when my father was alive and then my extreme reaction to his premature death alienated her. It was only when I was older that I realised how she'd always hated any overt show of emotion. As far as she was concerned, it was a sign of weakness and a lack of any real backbone.

Looking at Cassandra as she stood glumly beside the window, staring out at nothing while she chewed one of her already badly bitten nails, I was suddenly filled with a fear that we had drifted dangerously far apart and, at the moment anyway, I didn't know how to stop that drifting or how to coax her back to talking in a relaxed, open way with me – like she used to when she was younger. I don't want to make the mistake of alienating her permanently. I want her to know that I love her and am proud of her achievements but I don't know where to start.

Realising that I was in danger of losing myself in memories yet again I went over to the window to stand beside her.

"So I take it that Dervla has met this Lucy," I said, already feeling sorry for the unknown girl.

"Joan said that she had." She pulled a face. "But you know what Joan's like. She wouldn't say anything more – just got that 'I'm busy and you're in my way' look about her when she thinks she's protecting Dad."

"Well, it's not her place to gossip about what Dad does and she knows it. You'd be silly to try and pump her. You won't get anything out of that one when she clams up. No wonder he trusts her. She's marvellously loyal."

"Well, it's bloody infuriating! Still, it probably won't last very long once Granny Cruella gets in on the act. She'll make mincemeat out of her!"

"Don't you want your dad to be happy?"

"I suppose so."

I ignored her lack of enthusiasm, "So you want him to be happy – but on your terms," I said, feeling more irritated with them both by the minute. Her for being so intolerant of the situation and him for going out with a young one the same age as his daughter. Of course, Cassandra's put out!

I got another basilisk stare. "If you can't see how pathetic it is, then perhaps you're not as back to normal as you're pretending to be."

"I'm not pretending anything," I snapped. "I'm struggling here, Cassandra, and it all feels very one-way. How about being just a little less aggressive?"

Suddenly, she scooped up her bag from the chair and made for the door. "It's no good. You don't know how I feel. And you don't know what he's capable of. He's totally selfish and yet you always stick up for him. I've got to go. See you, Mum!"

The door closed behind her, leaving me angry and then disappointed. I was doing really well at the non-alienation bit, wasn't I?

Oh, God! I thought that I could sort it all out, bit by bit, given time and a good dollop of patience. But she makes it so hard. And Owen's not helping. Cassandra's right – he is selfish. I know that. He's not exactly a font of wisdom and reassurance at the moment. Well, he never was really, although, for the first few years of marriage, he could be fairly supportive when he wanted to be – until he got bored with me and stopped listening. To be honest, I suppose that I stopped listening to *him* too. And I know only too well from the past that when he's having one of his flings – if that's what he's doing – then family doesn't really come into the equation. I suppose that's another reason why Cassandra's so angry with him. Although, every now and then I get a feeling that it's not just jealousy on her part – that there's more to it. *What* I don't know.

I wish they would give you intravenous gin in this place. A constant infusion of the stuff, plus the odd Valium, might just see me through.

* * *

Day before my release. Remembered to collar the dodgy sister this morning and ask her what time I could tell Owen to collect me tomorrow. She gave me a wary look – like she thought there was something sinister about my question. Either that or she was trying to remember if there was a full moon tonight!

Dr Scheller and I sat on a bench in the clinic garden this afternoon. It was hot and still and it was pleasant to be in the shade of the giant copper beech tree that spread its purple leaves over us like an enormous parasol. The faint quacking of ducks floated up to where we sat. It was lovely there and I felt rested after a good night's sleep – and relieved that he hadn't insisted I should spend any more time in the clinic.

"So, Mrs Sayer, you are determined to leave us behind and take up your life again?" he asked with a smile.

"I know that I have to get on with things. There are so many bridges that need mending and I can't afford to put it off any longer or I'm afraid that some of them might prove to be unmendable."

"I would still like you to come and see me every two weeks for the time being," he said, his eyes scanning my face as if he were reassuring himself that, even though I looked so much better physically, what was going on inside my head wasn't too strange.

"Don't worry," I told him. "I've been remarkably well behaved for a long time now. I even apologised to Sister Costello for trying to decapitate her with my breakfast tray."

His eyes creased slightly at the corners. "Did she accept your apology graciously?"

"I got the distinct impression that she didn't believe me when I said how sorry I was."

"Perhaps that is because, deep down inside, Mrs Sayer, for you, at least, the experience was rather satisfying at a certain level – and Sister Costello knows it?" We both laughed. Then he asked, "On the subject of going home, do you have a friend whom you could ask to come and stay with you until you have settled into more of a routine?"

"My closest friend is unfortunately away in Australia and she won't be back until Christmas. There's no one else I'd want to ask – except perhaps Joan. She's my ex-husband's housekeeper. I've never gone in for many close friends and of the two other women I can think of, one died last year of cancer and the other had to move to the States because of her husband's job. But I'm sure Joan would pop in and give a hand if I really needed it. Although, I don't think I will," I added, full of renewed – and no doubt misplaced – optimism. "I'll manage fine. It's probably better that there won't be anyone else around. It will give me a chance to spend time with Cassandra – just the two of us on our own. Maybe that will help our relationship."

"But remember, please, Mrs Sayer, not to take all this bridge-mending on yourself alone. Others too have to do their fair share. And remember also not to fall back into the trap of blaming yourself for what happened. I can't stress enough how very important that is." He got up from the bench and laid a hand lightly on my shoulder. "I hope you will be able to contain your desire to escape this institution and at least stay with us until tomorrow?"

"Of course," I said looking up at him with a smile.

"And remember too what I said about just enjoying the sensation of being alive and well and of getting stronger every day – because you *are*. Also remember that you are in the process of learning to be happy again. We all of us have that right."

"I can't tell you how grateful I am for all your help," I told him. "The night Pandora died, I felt as though a large part of me shrivelled and died too. I felt I would live the rest of my life as half a being – if I managed to go on living. But now, with your help, I feel that, one day I might possibly become a whole, functioning person again."

As I sit in my room now, I know that's what I want with all my heart. Whether I achieve it or not remains to be seen. I'm certainly going to give it a bloody good try.

Chapter Four

8th September and finally home!

Busby all but sprang into my arms when I walked into the hall this morning. The lunatic cat hasn't stopped shadowing me ever since I came home. Poor animal probably thinks I'm about to do a disappearing act again and he's making absolutely sure that, next time, he's coming along too.

As soon as I came through the door, I realised that I was seeing my home in a different light. It was as if all my senses had become more acute. Before, I hardly looked at my surroundings. I took it all so much for granted – all the trappings of living were there to be used but not necessarily appreciated very much. But, this afternoon, standing in the carpeted hall, looking through the archway towards the glass door that opens into the kitchen with its walls of copper rose, I thought how welcoming and cosy it was. I smelled furniture polish – which was unexpected because I very much doubted Cassandra even knew where it was kept. It mingled with a slight perfume hanging in the air that came from a large vase of flowers on the hall table. Feeling almost as if I were trespassing in some other woman's house, I went down the three steps into the kitchen, Busby nearly making me fall flat on my face as he wound his way through my legs as I walked.

Of course, the first thing I did was make a cup of tea. It's funny how one reaches for the kettle at the most insignificant as well as at the most traumatic times of one's life. The first thing I wanted after the birth of my children was a cup of tea. For some reason, all through the pregnancy, I hadn't been able to look a tea bag in the face. But the moment it was all over, I couldn't wait for a cup. However splendid and luxurious the holidays abroad had been, the thing I longed for, as soon as I put a foot in the door, was a good old Lyons tea bag in a mug!

In the hospital, when your daughter had just died, that's the only thing they can offer you in a kind attempt to bring some tiny grain of comfort while you are still reeling from what they've just told you – and before the unstoppable tears start.

Owen collected me from the clinic after lunch and acted as taxi. He was very quiet during the ten-minute drive and wouldn't come in when we got here. I suggested that, perhaps, he could stay for a little while and have a cup of tea with me.

"Sorry, I haven't got time. I've got a stack of things waiting for me back at the office," he said.

I couldn't stop myself from thinking that one of them was, more than likely, the twenty-year old Lucy.

"Anyway, it'll be nice for you and Cassandra to have some time together on your own," he added, dumping my case just inside the hall door.

I didn't make an issue out of it. In fact, I really don't want him in my home. He doesn't belong here and perhaps his eagerness to get away is an acknowledgement that we are worlds apart now and there's no point in pretending otherwise.

But still, I can't make him out. In one way, he seems to have accepted our daughter's death as fact – but men like him don't waste their energy grieving so now he's getting on with the rest of his life. In another way, I've had the strangest feeling, several times in the past – and again today – that he's actually frightened to come into the house. Is he afraid of what he will see or remember? What are the memories that haunt him most, I wonder? He puts on this undaunted, macho façade but really I think there are things going on inside him that he can't or won't let me know about. I wonder how much he actually tells Lucy – whether he tells her anything. Probably not – unless he's changed since we lived together.

Cassandra was supposed to be here to greet me. She arrived ten minutes after I did, with some excuse about getting held up at a friend's. It sounds unkind, putting it like that, but over the past year there have been so many occasions when she said she would be somewhere at a certain time and then, she would either not turn up at all or would be incredibly late. At first, and until I got too ill to care, I put it down to the fact that she was punishing me for her sister's death. Now, I'm beginning to think it's just become an annoying habit.

She came into the kitchen where I was sitting on a stool, sipping my cup of tea.

"Oh, you're here!" she proclaimed. I knew by the tone

of her voice that she felt guilty but wasn't going to apologise. "When did you get back?"

"About ten minutes ago." I put down the cup and held out my arms to her. "Come and give me a hug."

There was a slight hesitation before she came over, almost as though she was nervous, that seeing me sitting there brought back unwanted memories of the vacant-eyed, distraught woman I had been only a couple of months earlier. I kissed her on the top of her head and held her. She smelled of shampoo and chocolate and a faint perfume I thought I recognised as *Ysatis*. I hadn't bothered to use any in the clinic but I vaguely remembered that I'd left a bottle on my dressing-table all those months ago. I closed my eyes. It was lovely to be back in my own home again and holding her close. I felt I never wanted to let go, that, whatever else happened, I would never let her come to any harm.

"Mum!"

"What?" I asked, releasing my hold.

"You're squeezing me to death, that's all."

I managed some sort of a laugh. "I'm sorry. I'm just thankful to be home and happy to be with you."

As I released her, I felt a pang of sadness. How could I promise that she wouldn't come to harm? She is twenty. Of course, I know that she's got to make her own mistakes – and some of them will probably be big ones. All I can do is hope that she doesn't end up any more hurt and confused than she is at the moment.

Cassandra seemed about to say something but changed her mind at the last minute. Going over to the sink, she picked up a dishcloth and absent-mindedly draped it over a tap.

Then she turned towards me. "I hope you've noticed how tidy the place is. Joan was in yesterday and nearly drove me mad, spring-cleaning the joint from top to bottom. She left a card for you on the hall table by the way. Do you want me to get it for you?"

"Please," I said, feeling suddenly deflated.

I had thought that, in spite of our differences, she might have shown a little more pleasure at having me home again. Then I reminded myself that I mustn't expect too much, that these things take time to resolve.

The card was a large, flowery affair with gold lettering, wishing me *Good Luck*. I feel as though I'm going to need a bit of that somehow! Inside, in Joan's generous, rounded script was a short message, saying that she would be happy to come over any time I needed some help and that Owen had said he wouldn't mind if she gave me a regular Wednesday afternoon slot. *For as long as you want*, the note ended. That's typical of Joan. She's kind and thoughtful. Although we haven't seen too much of each other, I would count her as a friend. Someone who is good to be around and who is there when you need them and who *doesn't* require any long explanations as to why you might need that help. Although she works for Owen now – she's pragmatic about it, she needs the money and I couldn't afford to have her every day the way he can – she somehow manages to remain loyal to him, while still being a dear friend to me. All the times we spent together chatting over morning cups of coffee when she first came to work for Owen and me were good times and the fact that we could talk frankly to each other right from the start cemented our friendship. And, of course, we shared the task of attempting to keep Deadly Dervla at arm's length. In the early days of my marriage, the woman had a front-door key. She would slide into the house unannounced, like some lethally elegant reptile, and surprise Joan and me roaring with laughter over something silly. It took me a while before I managed to get Owen to see that it was not on. He must have taken quite an ear-bashing from her but he did retrieve the key. Dervla was exceptionally glacial the next time our paths crossed!

"I've asked Keith over this evening. I hope you don't mind," Cassandra said, jolting me out of my thoughts.

"No, that's fine," I replied. But I knew why she'd done that. My daughter didn't want to be on her own with me. Or was I just paranoid? "What about food?" I asked, doing my best to sound cheerfully efficient.

I had forgotten about eating until then. It's been so long since I planned any meals or did any shopping, I feel alarmed at the thought of having to wield a saucepan again.

"We could get a take-away, I suppose," she said, rather vaguely, as she wandered over to the fridge and opened it.

I could see from where I stood that it was bulging with goodies. Joan again!

Seeing a cooked chicken on one of the shelves, I said, "How about cold chicken and salad?" There was a minimal nod. "Right!" I said, more briskly than I felt. "You wash the lettuce and tomatoes and I'll get some potatoes on for a potato salad."

As it turned out, my first meal back home was enjoyable. Keith arrived early, bearing an enormous bunch of white daisies and deep blue lupins and a bottle of fizzy white wine.

He thrust both wine and flowers at Cassandra and came over, smiling broadly and gave me an enormous, warm hug.

"Welcome home, Hebe."

"Goodness, Keith!" I said, hugging him back. "Does your poor mother have any flowers left in her garden?"

Cassandra gave us one of her disconcerting sideways glances.

"Don't I get a look in?" She held the flowers in front of her. "I don't suppose these are for me."

Keith went over and kissed her cheek. "Of course not, you idiot! You can't always be the centre of my universe, you know."

His being there lightened the whole evening. He made me laugh and Cassandra relax and come to life. By the time he left, I was feeling exhausted but the atmosphere in the house was a lot happier and brighter than it had been earlier.

* * *

The first day of my new, improved life.

When I woke this morning, the sun was streaming in the open bedroom windows. Because my bedroom is at the back of the house, I can hardly hear the traffic from the small road at the front. I lay in bed, listening to the faint tinkling of the wind chimes hanging from the curtain rail. I never bother to close the curtains. I like seeing the sky and trees outside; the mysterious way in which the clouds race and build and subside has always seemed to me to be a sort of magic. As a child, I would spend hours lying on my back in the grass, imagining that the shifting shapes above me were dragons and one-eyed, multi-horned monsters, their habitat full of castles, towering beside lakes of the clearest blue. To be truthful, I still do that when I get the chance!

The house at the end of the garden has a blank wall facing the back of ours so there's no danger of being on view.

For a long time, I just lay there, feeling delightfully dozy, stretched out diagonally in the double bed, revelling in being back in my own bed in my own room. Somehow, I didn't allow my brain to get into gear. I was so comfortable. I felt as though I were in a silky cocoon, wrapped up safely away from the rest of the world. What was it Dr Scheller said about me emerging like a butterfly? There are times when I think that I'm not completely sure that I want to emerge. The world's not a very nice place for people who are as bruised and battered as I've been feeling.

Of course, it didn't last long, that feeling of comfortable security. Thoughts of my mother made me throw back the duvet and scramble into my dressing-gown. I hadn't been able to visit her for weeks and weeks and although the others had told me she was all right, I wanted to see for myself. 'All right' could mean any number of things. It seemed to me too vague for comfort. And anyway, I wanted to do something about trying to break through the fog that surrounds her, to let her know that I love her – or at least to get her to see that I'm there for her – to make up to her for my (to her) inexplicable absence. Then I started to wonder if she'd even been aware of my absence. *Had* she ever asked for me while I was half comatose in the clinic? And if she had, had there been anyone around to hear her asking?

I got dressed as quickly as I could and went across the landing to Cassandra's room. I paused for a moment before knocking. The door at the far end of the landing was still closed. I hadn't gone into Pandora's room since I came home. That was another hurdle that had to be jumped. But not this morning. One thing at a time, I thought, as I rapped gently on Cassandra's door.

Eventually, there was a muffled, "Yeah?" from inside.

I went in, nearly tripping over some runners, lying between the door and the bed. In the gloom, my daughter was almost completely invisible under the bedclothes. Her blonde hair, lying in tangled strands across her pillow and one limp brown hand, was the only sign that the bump under the duvet was her.

A portfolio of black and white photos from her Media Study course lay open on the floor, its contents leaking out from between the bulging covers.

"Are you awake?" I asked.

"No!" She sounded unbelievably grumpy.

"I'm going to have some breakfast. It's a beautiful morning." There was no response. "Then I'm going to see Granny Molly after I've had something to eat."

"I'll see you when you get back, then."

I stood there for a moment before retreating out onto the landing again. There was no point in insisting she wake up. You never got very far with Cassandra by insisting on anything. I hadn't asked her to come with me to see my mother. I needed to do that on my own.

* * *

I'd thought it might look different somehow. My last visit

there seemed to have been so long ago. But as I turned the car into the entrance of the home, I noticed how nothing had changed. It was the same elderly man in the kiosk, who raised the striped barrier for me to drive through. The grounds were still immaculately kept and the grass freshly cut, with not a weed daring to raise its head in any of the flowerbeds. Even the chapel bell rang out as it had on so many previous visits. It was as though there were some kind of time warp and the only thing that was different was me.

I couldn't say the same about my mother. When the smiling nun took me over to where she was sitting in a wheelchair beside a window in the large, bright lounge, I nearly told her she had made a mistake and that the shrunken figure, head averted, staring out at nothing, was no relative of mine.

"Mrs Forde!" said the nun in a cheerful voice. "Your daughter's come to see you." She leaned over and patted the woman lightly on the hand. "Isn't that a nice surprise?" Then she turned to me. "I'm so glad you're feeling better, Mrs Sayer. You'll probably see a bit of a change in her since you were last here but that's only to be expected, I'm afraid." She went and fetched a chair. "I'll leave you in peace and quiet for a while. Just call me if you need anything."

With a feeling of unreality, I sat down beside the wheelchair. She'd called the woman Mrs Forde. That was my mother's name. She'd addressed *me* as Mrs Sayer.

I instinctively looked down at the left hand, lying motionless on the flowered skirt that covered the bony knees. There was the thin gold wedding ring and the gold bracelet watch my father had given her as a present the year before he died. I looked at the blotched face with its vacant red-rimmed eyes and my heart somersaulted painfully in my chest. How was this deterioration possible in just a few months?

I leaned forward and took my mother's hand in mine. Even though the day was so warm, it was cool and dry. Her skin felt like rice paper. I tentatively slipped my fingers through hers and gave a gentle squeeze. There was no answering pressure.

"Mum?" I said in a low voice. "Mum, can you hear me? It's Hebe."

There was a slight movement of her head and, for a second, her eyes flickered over me and away again. There had been no spark of recognition in that briefest of glances. I tried several times more, searching her face for the tiniest sign of a reaction or glimmer of acknowledgement of my presence. But there was none.

I was still sitting, holding her hand, when the nun returned.

"No luck?" she asked in her soft voice, her expression sympathetic.

I shook my head, fighting to hold back the tears that scalded my eyelids. "Nothing."

At that moment, a sudden gust of wind stirred the curtains beside my mother and the door slammed, making us jump slightly. The nun hurried over to an elderly man, who called out loudly, sounding distressed. Suddenly, the flaccid hand in mine stiffened and the fingers tightened on my own. When I looked at her, my mother was staring straight at me.

"Mum?" I said, excitedly.

Her mouth opened and shut and then opened again. She made a sort of grunting sound, her lips moving as though she were trying to push out words. But it was the expression in her eyes that made me catch my breath. They were wide open and so full of blank confusion, almost of fear, that I felt like weeping. I wished she'd return to her static state again. At least, like that, she seemed calm. To my great relief, that happened almost immediately.

No wonder Cassandra didn't want to visit her any more. I wished now that I hadn't insisted she come while I was in the clinic. Far better for her to remember her grandmother as the busy, sprightly woman who had spoiled her granddaughters and in whose garden they had played for hours, enjoying picnics under the old apple-tree and fishing the green blanket-weed out of the small fishpond with their bare toes, squealing as they threw the slimy strands at each other as they ran, helter-skelter, ducking and diving around the trees.

Suddenly, I couldn't take any more. Muttering to the sweet-faced nun, who was bending over the old man, peering down at her watch as she took his pulse, that I would be back in a few days, I literally ran out of the building, down the stone steps and across the gravel to where my car was parked in the shade of a large weeping cedar. When I reached the safety of the car, I scrambled inside, buried my face in my hands and wept.

I cried at what I had just witnessed – at what my once smart, independent mother had become. I cried because I realised that I'd left it too late. It was no good telling her now that I loved her, that I was sorry for being such a clumsy, often indifferent daughter. My mistiming was monumentally obvious. I think I cried most at the awfulness of the illness that had taken her, twisting her into something she herself would have found repulsive and unrecognisable.

The ridiculous thing is that I think it wasn't until today that I *really* took on board the fact that my mother is going to die – that she's not indestructible. Perhaps, if we'd been closer, I would have noticed all the small things that go towards the realisation that she was past her prime. I sat in the car and tried to remember the first signs of her becoming old.

I knew that I hadn't been very patient about the subject. Growing old was something that happened and you couldn't do much about it. But, looking back, I hadn't really thought about it or how it would affect my own mother. Perhaps I thought it happened only to other people. There was the day when she'd looked down ruefully at her swollen ankles and said in a voice of injured surprise, "These don't belong to me. I've *never* had swollen ankles."

I remember teasing her about spending a relatively large amount of money on buying expensive glasses. She, who was never extravagant, had splashed out on specs that looked both pricey and smart.

She'd rounded on me, saying angrily, "Just because you make do with any old thing doesn't mean I have to. And just because I'm getting on a bit doesn't mean that I have to stop trying."

That was just it! I hadn't realised until now how admirable that was – and how much effort it took as she became older and more unwell – that refusal to give in and stop doing things to the very best of her ability, whether it was cooking an apple-pie or making herself 'look presentable' as she called it. It wasn't that she was vain. It was a matter of keeping up standards.

It wasn't until I started writing seriously that I realised I hadn't known what it meant to strive to do something to the very best of your ability, to go on learning and developing. But then, I always was a very slow learner. No wonder I drove her mad with my *laissez-faire* attitude to everything.

I don't know how I drove home. I have no recollection of the journey. When I got back to the house, I heard voices in the garden. Looking out of the kitchen window, I saw Cassandra and Keith, sitting at the stone garden table with, what looked like, glasses of cold beer. I was going to slip upstairs without letting them know I was back. I wanted to wash my face with cold water apart from anything else. But as I drew back from the window, Keith suddenly looked up and saw me and gave a cheerful wave.

"Hi, Hebe!"

Reluctantly, I went to the open door. "Hello, Keith."

"Come and sit down," he said, getting up from the table and dragging a third chair nearer. "How's your mother doing?" he asked, still standing, one hand resting on the back of the chair. Then he peered at me more closely through his round glasses. He came towards me, looking concerned. "Is there something wrong?"

Cassandra, who'd barely glanced at me, said in an ominous voice, "You're not miffed that I didn't offer to come with you to see Granny Molly, are you, Mum?"

When I didn't answer, Keith took my hand and led me over to the chair. "Sit down and I'll get you something cold to drink."

I smiled briefly. "Thank you. There's orange juice in the fridge."

He hurried into the kitchen. I could hear ice tumbling into a glass and the sound of the fridge door being banged shut. If you don't bang it, it swings open and everything defrosts at record speed. I'd been meaning to get round to fixing it but, somehow, it was never near enough the top of my list of priorities to get it done.

"What's wrong, Mum?" Cassandra's voice sliced its way into my numb brain like a knife.

I realised that I'd closed my eyes, which were hurting, in an effort to keep out the bright sunlight.

"It's Granny Molly," I said slowly, aware of Keith's approaching footsteps on the granite slabs and the sound of ice tinkling in a glass. I opened my eyes and looked at her. "I didn't know she was so ill."

"Well, I told you what she was like last time I went and . . ." I saw Keith give her a warning look and she stopped abruptly, turning in her seat to look at me properly. When she next spoke, her voice was gentle. "Was she very bad?"

"Far worse than I'd been expecting. She never knew I was there."

Slowly, Cassandra put her own drink down on the table. "I'm so sorry, Mum. It must have been a shock."

"It was," I said, bleakly.

Keith handed me the orange juice, which I gulped down gratefully, the liquid soothing my barbed-wire throat. I rested my forehead on the side of the glass, the beads of condensation feeling cool against my hot skin.

"You look done in," he said, in a kind voice. "I don't think you need any extra people hanging around at the moment. I was just going anyway." He looked over at Cassandra. "I'll see you soon, Cass."

"But I thought we were going to . . ."

There was that look of warning again. And then he slipped away, leaving my daughter staring moodily into her beer and me grateful for his sensitivity.

For a while neither of us spoke.

Then, she asked, "How bad was Granny Molly?" Her voice was husky.

I shook my head slightly, feeling too wrecked to say anything more or go into any details. There was another silence and then she got up quietly. I watched her as she moved towards me. She looked troubled, the skin on her forehead puckered.

"Would you like me to stay or would you rather I left you on your own for a while?"

Instinctively, I knew that she'd rather not be asked to stay because she didn't know what to say, and anyway I didn't want to talk just then.

"No, you go. I'll be fine. I'll just sit here for a while and get my breath back. You know how I loathe hospitals and I've had more than my fair share of them in the past few months."

"OK!" she said, looking relieved. "I've some stuff to do for the start of next term. I've got to try and make sense out of my portraits for the photography portfolio or I'll have my tutor on my case. I'll be upstairs if you need me."

She gave me an uncertain smile before padding away on her bare feet towards the house, carefully avoiding the buzzing, bee-strewn patches of thyme growing along the cracks of the uneven paving stones.

I leaned back in my chair and closed my eyes again. Had my illness so alienated her that she still didn't feel safe around me? I couldn't keep putting off making a start on getting her to see that I wasn't going to behave like a lunatic again. I knew that I mustn't use my mother's condition as an excuse for delaying some bridge-building with my daughter. At that moment, I didn't feel I had enough energy to make a start. But, after a little while, sitting in the sun, soothed by the buzzing bees, my once constant sense of optimism made a shaky return. It looked as though I was too late where my own mother was concerned but not Cassandra. Tomorrow, I promised myself. We'll do something nice together tomorrow and that will give me the chance to take a first real step. Nothing too dramatic, just a small move towards reconciliation and normality.

And then, the day after, I'd go and see my mother again. Now I knew the situation, it wouldn't be such a shock. I promised myself that I'd manage it better next time.

Chapter Five

Next day – which makes it 10th September, I think.
I'm sitting in the garden drinking a large – and very strong –
gin and tonic and oh, boy, do I need it! I wouldn't say that
today has been a blazing success – however elastic I'm
prepared to be with the truth.

It really comes down to Cassandra, deciding that taking
part in a bit of bonding with her dotty mother wasn't on the
cards after all. The thing that makes me boil is the *way* in
which she let me down.

We'd agreed to meet at the Screen Cinema in Dublin.
We both wanted to see *Moulin Rouge* and we both like
Nicole Kidman. We had also agreed that, after the cinema,
we would go and have a meal somewhere nice. At the time we
made the arrangement, she seemed to quite like the idea.

I got there five minutes before the agreed time and I
waited outside. I waited and waited until I felt that, at any
moment, the bronze statue of the man with the torch would
tap me on the shoulder and tell me to get a move on. Ten

minutes after the film was scheduled to start, my mobile vibrates like a trapped bluebottle in my trouser pocket. My daughter informs me that she's been 'held up' and would I mind terribly if we did this another day? Taken aback, like an idiot, I mutter something about it being rather late to cancel an arrangement when she starts to conveniently 'break up'. Like hell she did! When I tried to ring her back, her mobile was apparently switched off.

The more I thought about it, the angrier I got. All thoughts of going to see the film evaporated. I loathe eating out alone and I won't go to the cinema by myself either. Although it's never actually happened to me, I imagine there are creepy men in macs waiting to slide into the seat beside me and start making ludicrous and obscene suggestions. In an effort to calm myself down, I stumbled into a nearby café and swallowed an over-priced Caffè latte and a Rice-Krispie-type sticky biscuit – an evergreen treat even if I *am* forty-six. Unfortunately, the girl taking my money was so sour, I emerged into the street just as cross as when I went in. I stomped around for a bit until I caught a glimpse of myself in a shop window, scowling. Not a pretty sight! So I went back to the multi-storey carpark, paid what seemed like an absurd amount of money for the privilege of parking in its unfriendly concrete guts, and drove home, trying my best to avoid committing any act of road rage.

I really haven't a clue how to approach all of this. If I'm honest and tell Cassandra what I think about her behaviour, I know exactly what she'll do. While I'm busy exploding, she'll listen with lowered eyelids and that frozen expression she puts on when she's feeling got at and then she'll walk out on me, after giving me some sort of feeble excuse – that both of us know has been concocted to silence me while she edges closer to the door. If I try and insist that she stay and talk it through, she'll throw a tantrum before banging out of the room anyway.

But, on the other hand, it's downright *bad* for her to get away with this sort of carry-on. I can't just say nothing. I want my daughter to be happy and reasonable and generous-spirited and tolerant. I would like it to be possible for us to share our thoughts with each other. I want to be friends with her . . . Am I expecting too much?

Joan's coming tomorrow. I'll talk to her. She'll say something sensible, I'm sure. After all, she's managed to bring up three daughters on her own since her husband died over ten years ago and they sound like reasonably well-balanced creatures. I've certainly never seen her tearing her hair out over any of them.

* * *

It's now nearly midnight and I'm tired, tired, tired.

Cassandra eventually appeared at about nine o'clock. She was all casual, as though nothing had happened. When she didn't even mention the aborted get-together and announced that she was going to bed because she was knackered, I'm afraid all the promises I'd made to myself about being mature and calm in my dealings with her went up in smoke. To be blunt, I lost the plot.

"So, you're just going to sail up to bed as though nothing's happened," I said, letting off the first, unwise salvo.

She gave me that look that she's perfected – a sort of mixture of injured innocence and complete bafflement, tinged with disdain. "What's the matter?"

"What do mean, *what's the matter?* Don't you think you at least owe me an apology?"

"For goodness' sake, Mum! Do you mean the film?"

"Yes, I do mean the film."

"It was just a trip to the cinema. Why do you have to make such a drama out of everything?"

"I am *not* making a drama about anything. I just think it wouldn't be unreasonable for you to say what it was that was so urgent you had to cancel going to the cinema with me and *why* you thought that getting in touch twenty minutes after the time we'd arranged to meet was apparently OK with you." I think it was the irritated sigh, combined with a rolling of eyes in the direction of the heavens that really made me see red. "Don't you *dare* pull faces at me!" I all but screamed at her.

When she made for the door, I surprised myself by sprinting over and beating her to it. Even she looked a little taken aback at my sudden burst of speed. I've been in slow motion for so long, I expect she'd forgotten that I used to be quite quick on my feet when necessary.

She stared at me for a moment. "Why are you standing there like that? You don't seriously think that you can stop me from going to bed, do you?"

Trying hard to keep my voice calm, I said, "I'm standing here like this because, this time, you are not going to get out of it by doing a disappearing act. We are going to sit down and talk. I want to know what's going on. I want to know why you are behaving so very badly." She muttered something under her breath as she turned away from me. "What did you just say?" I demanded, following her into the middle of the room like some well-trained hound, walking to heel.

She spun round. "Perhaps I don't always behave the way

you want me to but at least *I* don't parade around in the street in my nightclothes!"

It was as if she'd punched me. I could feel myself trembling. I collapsed into a nearby chair. There was a horrible silence. The sort of silence when the static of recrimination and anger in the air is almost tangible. I felt shaky and slightly sick. Cassandra knew that she'd gone too far but she apparently couldn't find the appropriate words to extricate herself. And I was too stunned to try.

After a little while, I looked up her. She was standing, as though frozen to the spot, pale with her long blonde hair hanging over half her face so that I couldn't see her properly. Both hands were dug deep into the pockets of her jeans.

"I couldn't help it if I behaved a little strangely when I was ill." I said, as calmly as I could. She didn't respond – just stared at the floor. "But that's all over now."

"But it's not, is it, Mum?" she said, in a low voice that was almost a moan.

"What do you mean?"

She looked at me. "The reason for everything bad that's happened over the past year started when Pandora died. And *nothing* will ever be the same again. How could it be?" She shook her hair angrily off her face, her eyes brimming with tears.

"But darling, we have to make the best of things. I know that losing your sister has had a terrible effect on all of us but we have to go on. You must believe that, although we'll always miss her, things *will* get better." I reached out and touched her arm. "It won't always be like this, you know."

Cassandra moved away. She didn't actually shake off my hand but just placed herself out of reach.

"You mean, everything will get back to normal, that we'll get on with life, pretending that it's all really OK?" She shook her head violently. "Maybe that's possible for you but I can't."

"But you *have* to, darling. It's the only way to move forward."

"Don't call me that! Pandora was your real darling, wasn't she, Mum?" I looked at her in astonishment. But before I could say anything, she continued, "Admit it, she was always the favourite."

"How can you say that?" I gasped. "How could you even *think* it?"

"Because it's true. She was always so much better behaved than me. I was the one who got into trouble and she was the one who baled me out and made excuses for me." Her voice sounded rough with emotion. "Don't think that I didn't love her, even though I knew you and Dad thought she was the nicer of the two of us. I *did* love her and I miss her – more than you'll ever know. I don't blame you for preferring her but just don't pretend that you feel the same way for me as you did for her."

"What did I ever do that made you think such a mad, shameful thing?" I stumbled to my feet and moved towards her. She turned away and buried her face in her hands. "But it's *not* true," I almost shouted at her. "We always loved you both – equally. How did we treat you any differently? Give me just one example."

Still turned away from me, she raised her head and spoke in a muffled voice. "In little ways, in the way you used to look at her sometimes, in the way Dad always stopped listening to me when she walked into the room. Oh, in a dozen ways. You didn't do it on purpose, I know that. But I watched and I saw how you treated her. And it was different from the way you were with me."

She moved towards the door, tears streaming down her face.

"Please, please don't go like this, Cassandra. *Please*," I begged.

She turned and looked at me. There was no sign of her earlier belligerence or offhandedness. In a quiet voice she said, "You just don't understand, do you? Even now you're not really listening to what I'm telling you. Dad . . ." She closed her eyes for a moment before turning away from me again. Then she said in a voice suddenly stripped of emotion, "Anyway, I couldn't talk any more tonight, Mum. Please leave it. If we must, we can talk again tomorrow but not now. I'm really sorry if I upset you."

She looked exhausted. I took a step in her direction. I was going to kiss her but she avoided that by moving into the hall and closing the door behind her. I was tempted to follow her upstairs. Not to go on talking. I wanted to take her in my arms and hold her and kiss her. I wanted her to let me be close to her in the way we were when she was a small child.

But I didn't. I stopped myself from opening the door and running upstairs and insisting that this was no way to end a day, with tears and bitterness and misunderstanding. Because, she was wrong. *Wasn't* she? All that stuff about her being treated differently?

I suddenly thought of Pandora's box and how my own Pandora's death seemed to have released so many previously hidden secrets and fears. Her dying had let out all those unspoken terrors into the public domain to be looked at and agonised over. I was beginning to realise that the full impact of what had happened was perhaps only now being felt. And I was frightened.

As well as being frightened, I suddenly felt desperately ashamed of my own anger. I had over-reacted in a ridiculous way. The fact that I'd let the missed film assume such proportions just proved Cassandra's worries about my stability to be not so far off the mark after all. I wasn't as balanced and together as I'd led myself to believe.

* * *

Saturday.

I had a call from Maggie this morning.

"Hello! This is your very own special agent calling! Do you feel up to a little chat, Hebe?"

She sounded so cheerful that, in spite of just having had one of the worst nights of my life, my spirits lifted several degrees.

"Hello, Maggie. In fact, you couldn't have called at a better moment," I told her.

"Why is that?"

"Oh, I was considering my options. Which would be best? To anaesthetise myself with alcohol before sticking my head in a plastic bag – or to just jump off the nearest tall building – preferably timing it so that I land on Owen's bloody mother. Our house is too near the ground for a worthwhile suicide attempt." Immediately I'd said it, I regretted it. Four months ago, I might just have got round to killing myself out of sheer confusion and misery. "Don't worry! I'm not seriously considering doing either," I reassured her. "It's just that I thought when I got home that I had achieved some measure of stability and I was beginning to feel I was making progress. Funny how a ten-minute row can change all that."

"Whom did you have the row with? Or shouldn't I ask?"

"Cassandra. She seems to think that I don't really love her, that she was always second-best to her sister and that nothing I do will ever change that. She also seems convinced that her sister was Owen's pet and that he always preferred her."

There was a pause at the other end. Then Maggie gave a sigh. "Oh, dear! You poor thing! No wonder you sounded rather down when you answered the phone. I sometimes think that I'm a very lucky woman to be unfettered by the bonds of marriage past or present – and even luckier that I never succumbed to the uncivilised practice of having children." She hesitated and then said, "Now, tell me if you don't feel up to this but I have an idea that might just cheer you up."

"Well, unless you can supply me with a personality transplant, a new brain and a re-charged battery, I wouldn't be too sure," I said, wondering if there were anything anyone could do to make me feel cheerful at that precise moment.

"Have you heard of Sam Ellis?"

"I've had a minor breakdown not a total memory loss," I said, laughing in spite of myself. "Of course, I've heard of him! He's all over the place. You can't go into a bookshop without seeing his face plastered on the walls and windows. Why? Is he one of yours?"

"He most certainly is," said Maggie, not making any attempt to hide her satisfaction. "And what's more, he's one of the most unbelievably reasonable men I've ever worked with. Not only is he charming without trying to be, he's also handsome and funny and *nice*. I'd begun to think that nice men didn't exist any more – especially the ones who write books!"

"I'm confused! You sound as though you've fallen for him but I thought you were more into Sapphic relationships."

"I tell you, if I fancied any man, he would be my number one choice." There was a chuckle from the other end of the phone. "But as things stand, I'm far too busy furthering your career to have time for any of that nonsense!"

"So why the eulogy?"

"Because, dearest Hebe, he's going over to Dublin in a couple of weeks' time and is doing an interview on *RTE*, a couple of readings in Waterstones and Hughes and Hughes and there's a big bash for him in the Shelbourne on the first night. The press will be there in large numbers. And I want *you* to be there too!"

"But why on earth? I don't know him and I'm absolutely sure he's never heard of me in his life."

"You'd be surprised! Anyway, I'll be there too and it'll be nice for him to meet some of my other clients. Celia Lacoste is coming and possibly one or two others of my writers as well. It will be fun! So, be good and tell me that you'll be there."

I haven't mentioned the fact to Maggie, but Celia Lacoste is not one of my most favourite women. There's something extraordinarily calculated and tough about her. You get the feeling when you meet her that she only smiles at you (minimally) if she thinks you might be of use. Otherwise, forget it! And I don't like predatory women. OK! She's quite a good writer but I prefer my books. I wasn't the least surprised to find that my beloved mother-in-law (ex) never reads anything by me but is amused and entertained by Celia's novels. Probably because they tend to be about the sort of women who would die rather than develop smile lines around their eyes and think that the smelly, sweaty, not so attractive side of life should never be alluded to. In her books, orgasms, if mentioned, are accompanied by a slightly raised eyebrow and a delicately flared nostril at most – certainly not with yodels of delight! Her female characters never sweat. They sail around in a positive cloud of expensive perfume and I'm willing to bet that they never wear white underwear that's gone a bit grey with dodgy elastic.

"So will you?" Maggie asked again.

"I don't know, Maggie. I haven't been out to any do's of any sort for so long I'm not sure I remember how to behave properly. I might let you down."

"Don't talk rubbish! I want Sam to meet you. He's read your last one and he thought it was very good."

"Good gracious!"

"Well, don't sound so surprised. It's not only women who enjoy your work. So, will you come?"

"All right! Which day, what time?" I asked. I still felt reluctant. Was I ready to appear in public and rub shoulders with the glitterati of Dublin? Everyone would be sure to know everyone else and they would all be far more poised, better dressed and up to date with what was going on in the world than I was. I'd been more or less incarcerated for the last few months and I hadn't felt like listening to the news or reading newspapers. Actually, that had been one of the more enjoyable aspects of life in the clinic – not bothering to find out what was going on outside its walls. It was bound to be depressing – whatever it was.

We talked for a few minutes more. Maggie said that she might have some good news for me when we met. I was dying to ask her what sort of good news but I could hear another phone ringing in the background and then her mobile started up too. I noticed that she's now got *Take Five* as her ring tone. (Which reminds me, I think I've lost mine – my mobile, not my ring tone.)

"I'll have to go, Hebe! But I'm looking forward to seeing you. Wednesday 30th, eight o'clock at the Shelbourne. Bring Cassandra if you think she'd enjoy it. Go out and buy something exciting to wear. And don't let me down!"

After she'd rung off, I sat for a while with the phone still in my hand. What was the good news she might have for me? I wondered. Was my not very exciting writing career about to take off in a spectacular fashion? And what about Sam Ellis having read one of my books? I couldn't help feeling a little glow of pleasure at the thought. A long time ago, I'd found myself studying his photograph in a bookshop window. I remember thinking that he looked darkly attractive and that his mouth was sensual-looking, and yet the ironic expression in his eyes made you think that he was amused at the very thought of being photographed.

I'd read and enjoyed several of his novels. Usually I'm rather cautious about reading other people's work – especially when I'm in the middle of writing something myself. I suppose I'm worried that, if I like the way they write, it might influence my own work. I'm afraid that it might stop me from finding my own 'voice'. Critics often use that phrase I've noticed. A *unique voice*, it says in the blurb on the back cover of many a book. But that's what I hoped I was beginning to find. I want to beaver away until I unearth my very own, unmistakable style. Wacky, weird and uneven though it may be! Certainly that's what they might say about my work if I tried to write anything now. *If* they bothered to review it in the first place!

I liked Sam Ellis' books because he is a great storyteller. His plots are always very different and you can't pre-guess what will happen next and that's intriguing. He also has an extraordinary ability to write from the point of view of a woman. I think that's *very* clever. I'm not sure that I could do the reverse! I don't even understand me all that well. And when I look at my relationship with Owen, what strikes me most about our marriage was my inability to fathom out just what was going on in that man's mind. I never was able to understand how he could see things from a totally different perspective to my own. The times when I thought I'd got it right, he used to completely stun me by doing or saying the complete opposite of what I was expecting.

Like the time I told him not to make a fuss about my birthday – meaning that I knew he was busy and didn't want him to feel that he had to go over the top and spend a lot of time on it. So, when I found out that he'd arranged a business trip that meant he would be away for five days, including on my birthday, I couldn't help feeling that either I would have to be more concise about what it was I wanted or he'd have to learn to use his imagination a bit more. We never did manage to get it right! He once accused me of expecting him to be a top-of-the-range psychic to fathom what was going on in my brain. However, as time went by, I gathered from listening to other people that we weren't too different from thousands of married couples. Perhaps the secret is to learn to laugh at those misunderstandings – not get annoyed by them. And to remember not to expect too much and then you might be pleasantly surprised – occasionally!

I eventually put the phone down. But I sat for some time, thinking about the bash at the Shelbourne. I wondered if Cassandra would consider it too boring or would she like to come with me? I asked myself if she would ever want to do anything with me ever again after the other evening. And then Busby mountaineered up my front and cuddled me. I cuddled him back and had a cathartic weep into his fur for a little while and then went and made myself a cup of herbal tea with him draped around my neck like an electrically heated wrap. As I waited for the kettle to boil, I reminded myself that if I was going to be seen in public, I'd better stop sitting around feeling sorry for myself and stuffing my face with sugary biscuits and drinking unlimited cups of strong coffee.

Over the past few days, it's dawned on me too that, if I were going to be around for the next thirty odd years and if I were going to be of any use to Cassandra – or anyone else, I'd better start living my life again. Only this time, I was going to do it better, if not completely perfectly. It doesn't pay to get too fanciful.

Busby was still purring companionably when I sat down at the kitchen table to drink my mint tea.

Chapter Six

I can't remember what the date is but I do know that this is the first time for days that I've got round to doing my scribbles.

And I only remembered that today was Wednesday because, when the bell rang and I opened the door, Joan was standing on the step, beaming at me. She looked the same as ever, although perhaps a little heavier than when I'd last seen her – but with the same tight perm in her suspiciously raven black hair and with the same hectic colouring in her cheeks that always makes me wonder if she has high blood pressure. Not that you can ever winkle out any information about the state of her health. She always insists that she's fine and then immediately starts asking how I am. I think she would win the prize for being the woman least likely to feel sorry for herself.

She gave me an enormous hug. "Hebe! It's grand to see you! How are you feeling, my dear?" She closed the door behind her and stood for a moment, giving me the once-over. "Well, you've lost a lot of weight but you look as gorgeous as ever."

Those were her actual words. *No one* has ever called me gorgeous but, for some reason, she seems to think that it's not a totally inappropriate description.

I couldn't help laughing. "You are so good for my ego! I think you'll have to come and stay for a few weeks. I just might end up believing I'm irresistible!"

She poked me in the arm with a finger. "I wouldn't say it if I didn't think it. You've never realised just what a fine-looking woman you are. Maybe it's time you started." She fished out a covered dish from a large shopping bag. "I've brought you one of my rhubarb pies. I know how much you and Cassandra like them."

We went through to the kitchen and, before she did anything around the house – which was still in relatively good nick after her previous session – we sat down at the table with a cup of tea. Busby immediately jumped on her lap and went into mountaineering mode up her front, purring like a chainsaw.

Joan stroked him energetically, scratching him behind the ears so that his eyes closed with pleasure. "The reason I'm a little late is because your ex-mother-in-law came round."

I did my best to keep my expression neutral. "Oh!" I said. Then, because curiosity got the better of me – as it usually does, I added, "Any special reason?"

She chuckled. "That lady don't need any special reason to call! I think she just likes to check on things, to make sure I'm looking after the house properly. She's very particular about keeping up standards."

"I would think that it's time she realised that you do a marvellous job. She must have been bored. Perhaps one of her bridge games was cancelled."

I know I sounded catty but Dervla brings out the worst in me. Even Busby can't stand her and *he* likes everyone – including the moth-eaten Labrador down the road. Apparently, the feeling is mutual (between Dervla and Busby, not the Labrador and Busby!) so, on the rare times that their paths cross, they just ignore each other. I don't blame him. She doesn't have a decent bosom up which to climb. Her boobs are like hard little acorns. I've never actually seen them – thank goodness – but that's how I imagine them to be. Unlike Joan's marvellous torpedo-like superstructure!

"Well, she didn't find anything wrong but she held me up discussing a menu for some entertaining Mr Sayer's doing at the end of the week."

"I would have thought Lucy would have been the one doing that," I said.

Joan looked momentarily surprised and then she nodded. "I see Cassandra's been filling you in."

"Well, as you can imagine, she's not too happy about this girl moving in to live with him. I rather think she's hoping that Dervla will frighten her away."

"I don't think Mrs Sayer has quite as much power over her son as she likes to think," said Joan. "Mind you, Lucy isn't just a pretty young thing with no brains. I'd say, if it came to the crunch, she might surprise herself and give as good as she got."

"Well, I don't want Cassandra caught in the middle of anything. It's hard enough that the girl is the same age as she is. I would hate to think that her grandmother might use her to try and get rid of Lucy."

We talked for a while about Cassandra. Joan was shocked when I told her about what she'd said to me about not being loved as much as Pandora.

She sat in thoughtful silence for a moment before lowering her mug and putting it down.

"Whatever gave the silly girl that idea?"

"She says that we never gave her the same amount of attention. She seems to think that her dad only took what Pandora said seriously and that she was always second-best." I stared at Joan, hoping that she might make a suggestion on how best to deal with the situation.

But she shook her head slowly. "I don't know what to say. Poor child! To carry that burden . . . on top of everything else that's happened. It's not fair."

"I know it's not fair but is it *true?*" I asked her. "I keep wondering now if we were guilty of favouring Pandora."

I hadn't got any further with my daughter. In spite of her saying that we could continue our discussion, Cassandra had somehow managed to avoid being alone with me since that particular conversation took place and she'd slipped out of the house early the next morning when I was having a shower. But she had left a note on the table in the hall in which she repeated that she was sorry for upsetting me – which was something.

What Joan said next worried me. "I was with you for several years before you split up with your husband but I can honestly say that I never saw you being any different with the girls. I think you were always the same with both of them. But . . ." She hesitated, looking uncomfortable. "You know I don't like to talk out of turn but I think Mr Sayer might have had an extra soft spot for Pandora. I'm not saying that he doesn't love Cassandra," she added hastily. "It's just that I always thought her sister had a special place in his heart. And perhaps her dying is one reason that he took up with that Lucy one."

"But I never saw him treating her any differently! And if he did show more affection towards Pandora it was because Cassandra wasn't very affectionate herself. She used to get impatient if you wanted to give her a hug. She wanted to be doing things, not sitting around being cosy. But that didn't mean that Owen loved her any the less."

Joan leaned forward and took hold of my hand. "Now, don't you go upsetting yourself. I know how hard it is to step back and see things clearly when you're in the middle of it all. And it's not always easy to hide the fact that one of your children is a favourite – however hard you try to hide it."

"I'm sure *you* love your three daughters in the same way."

"I've never told anyone this before but, Hebe, I've done my level best to treat them all the same but my youngest pulls at my heartstrings just that little bit harder than the other two. I don't know why. I didn't want to have a favourite and I hope I've managed to hide the fact that I feel the way I do – from all three of them. But there's a special feeling I have for young Paula that I can't explain. It's just there."

I found myself looking at her in surprise. She'd always seemed to be so on top of things – as though nothing got to her. She was wise and tapped into that wisdom when it was necessary. I certainly never for one minute imagined she felt more for one of her daughters than for the others.

"Do you feel guilty about feeling like that?" I asked her.

She gave me one of her wide smiles that make her whole face crinkle into a hundred folds and creases. "What would be the point in that? I love them – even if they can

93

be a right pain in the arse some of the time. I do me best and you can't do more than your best, can you?"

I had to agree with her that you couldn't!

* * *

I felt a lot better by the time Joan went home, promising that she would be back on the following Wednesday. It was a good thing that I did because tomorrow is scheduled for another visit to see my mother. What is left of my mother.

After supper I got out an old photograph album and reminded myself of how she had looked before the illness started to take hold of her. There weren't all that many photos. My father and Dr John had been the ones who had wanted to take the occasional photo. Mum never bothered. Not unless I put the camera into her hand and insisted!

I realise now that she used to vanish if there were talk about her being included in a picture. Her shyness meant that she was quite happy to stay in the background. I can see that, in many ways, her shyness has been one of the reasons for us not getting close. She never wanted to talk about her relationship with my father, even when I was a grown woman, who could have understood and appreciated much of what she felt and thought. In the same way, it stopped her from telling me about the facts of life – except in the most rudimentary and hurried fashion. In desperation, by the time she got round to it, I had already gleaned enough from school-friends and magazines to get a rather basic if not very accurate idea about the whole birds and bees scenario. I do remember though that, for a long time, I thought the phrase 'sleeping together' automatically meant you got pregnant if you fell asleep near a man. I was very careful to make sure that I never dozed off anywhere near any boys when I went on school camping trips. I just hoped that the tent was substantial enough not to allow impregnation to occur.

There was one photo that a friend of theirs must have taken of her and my father, sitting together on the old wooden seat near the sundial in the garden before I was born. My mother's posture is rather prim. She's sitting up very straight with her knees together, her hands resting in the lap of her patterned summer dress. Her hair is swept off her face and she's wearing smart, high-heeled sandals. But it's obvious that she'd been caught off guard because she's glancing at my father rather than at the camera. The expression on her face makes her appear unexpectedly soft and feminine. I looked at the photo for a long time, wondering what had been going through her mind at that exact moment. Whatever it was, it made her look sweet-natured and almost pretty.

A later photo, taken when I must have been about two, shows her with me on her lap. Again, the same formal posture and the way she's holding me is stiff, as though it didn't come naturally to her.

Perhaps she never wanted any children because she knew that she wasn't maternal. Is it possible that I was a mistake? Or did she have me to please my father? I'll never know. Perhaps, afterwards, she realised that she'd not been as warm as she could have been towards me and she made up for it when Cassandra and Pandora came along.

If I, in my mid-forties, can still be perplexed by what I see as things lacking in my relationship with my mother, how long will it take Cassandra to overcome and deal with her own feelings of us having let her down?

I wish I could do something that would help and know that what I was doing was right. It's terrible, the realisation that loving her isn't going to be enough. Loving her won't make me wise or guide me into making the best choices.

Hell! I'm getting all maudlin. I sound like some pathetic old biddy, who's had a few too many G and T's! I think I'll make myself another cup of that camomile muck. Perhaps the smell of it will help me pull myself together!

* * *

Next day. Late evening and in bed, thank God!

It's late and I'm almost too tired to write anything but I find that when I start, it does have a sort of cathartic effect. I still haven't felt like going anywhere near the computer. I haven't even checked to see if there are any e-mails waiting to be read. Anyway, the way things are with my mother, she has to take priority for now.

When I went to see her this morning, I sat in the car for ages before summoning up the courage to get out. I found myself almost in agreement with Cassandra. What is the point? She doesn't know who I am. Her poor, shrunken body may still be there but my mother is long gone. Even if she were *compos mentis*, I wondered if she would be pleased to see me. Then, realising that I was indulging in unhelpful, negative thoughts, I pulled myself together and went inside.

There was a different nun on duty. She looked at me questioningly and I told her I was Molly Forde's daughter. She didn't seem very interested in the information.

"She's in the –" she began.

"I know where she is. Thank you," I said, cutting her short.

As I walked along the corridor, I hoped that the nun I'd talked to on my previous visit was more typical of the sort of person entrusted with caring for my mother now. I hadn't remembered seeing either of them on earlier occasions before I became ill. Perhaps that was because I had been too busy concentrating on trying to break through the gathering fog that was seeping into her brain. I remember that I was still feeling full of guilt at her being left in the place.

Almost from the start of her being in the nursing home, it had not been possible to hold a conversation with her – even a disjointed one. She kept getting up from her chair and leaving the room. I'd find her pacing backwards and forwards in the hall, looking anxious. It seemed impossible for her to stay in one place for more than a few minutes. It was as though she had got up to go and search for something but then she didn't know what is was she was looking for or why she had left the room. That had been distressing enough but what had really got me down was the same question being repeated again and again. No matter how many times I answered, a couple of minutes would go by and then she'd ask the same thing yet again. I must say, I was overwhelmed by how patient nearly all the staff were. And she wasn't the most difficult to care for by any means. I saw that too.

She was in the same place as on all my previous visits: beside the window – only today it was closed because the weather had changed and the day was cool and cloudy. Today, my Mum was wearing a navy blue skirt and cardigan over a pale pink blouse. I remembered her in those clothes. She'd always taken trouble with her appearance and she always looked well turned out – neat, like the way she kept her house. But now her clothes are several sizes too large for her. They don't look smart any more. She seemed to be asleep, her head turned to one side, resting on the back of the armchair. Her wheelchair was parked beside her.

It's hard to take in how much she's changed in the months that I've been in the clinic. Her hair has become so thin. She'd always had very fine hair but plenty of it. Now, I can see her scalp, showing white between the untidy grey strands.

I suddenly had an urge to lean forward and stroke her head but I didn't because I didn't want to disturb her. And I suppose I didn't want to have to see that look of puzzled non-recognition in her eyes when she did wake.

She was wearing the tiny pearl earrings that she'd always worn. Those and her watch and wedding ring were the only items of jewellery she'd taken in with her to the nursing home. When we were packing her things to go there, in a moment of clarity, she'd handed me her jewellery box.

"You'll have to look after these," she said.

"But, Mum!" I remonstrated. "It might be nice for you to hold on to them for a bit longer. And they're yours anyway," I ended, lamely.

She gave me a suddenly direct look. "I won't be needing them, Hebe. They belong to you now."

Like on previous visits, I pulled one of the chairs over so that I could sit opposite her. I keep thinking that if I am the first thing she sees when she wakes up, it might just jog her memory for an instant.

She started to fidget and her eyes fluttered under the lids as though she were dreaming.

"Mum?"

Suddenly they opened and she slowly turned her head. She looked straight at me and I could feel my heart thumping. Then her eyes slid away from me, unfocussed. I realised that she hadn't the slightest idea who I was. She muttered something I couldn't catch. I repeated her name several times, calling her Mum and then Molly. But she just stared at me with that wide-eyed stare that held no recognition – just bewilderment.

When her hands started plucking at her clothes and she began to give little moans of distress, I didn't know what to do. I went and found a nurse.

"There's something wrong with my mother. She needs something but I don't know what it is."

The girl came back into the room with me. She watched Mum for a moment before shaking her head.

She turned to me. "She's like that some of the time. Nothing to worry about."

"But there must be something wrong. Why is she looking so distressed? Surely there's something we can do to make her calm."

"She'll go back to sleep in a minute. There's nothing we can do, I'm afraid. It's all right. She's not in pain, you know."

I just bit my tongue in time. I felt like snapping at her. *How would you know she isn't in pain? She can't tell you what's wrong.* But I didn't. And, after a few minutes, with me holding her hand, she drifted back to an uneasy sleep again.

I sat until the pins and needles in my leg got too bad. Easing my hand carefully from her age-spotted one, I stood up and looked down at her. There were deep frown lines etched on her forehead and her lips looked cracked and dry.

I went over to the nurse on my way out.

"I think my mother's had a bit of an accident. There's a very strong smell coming from her," I said carefully.

"Don't worry. I'll deal with her in a minute," was the reply.

I know she was in the middle of retying someone's bandage but I wanted to shake her and tell her that I didn't want my mother *dealt with* in a minute – my mother, who had never in her life smelled of anything more than soap and hand cream and, on special occasions, a light spray of *Chanel No 5*.

* * *

In bed, early morning. Saturday 20th September.

I'm feeling like a rather battered tennis ball, ricocheting from A to B and landing in places where I'd rather not be. At school, my tennis balls always ended up in forests of giant nettles or puddles covered in green slime. So, being a battered ball is the metaphor for today!

What I would like to be doing is making a better stab at getting on with Cassandra and for Mum to be with it enough to know that I'm there for her. *That's* probably selfish because, maybe, she's less miserable not knowing much about anything.

Still, I would like to feel more in control of my life. Anyway, Dr Scheller said I was to write down my moans. So, that's them done – for today!

Now, what about the good stuff? I'm back in my house. I'm more aware of everything than I was before. I know I'm lucky to be alive. I love my daughter – even if she *isn't* the easiest person in the world to love at the moment. I'm not pregnant. No one is trying to drop bombs on me. I'm in better nick than perhaps I have any right to expect to be. I can't think of any more just now but that's seven of them. Not bad going!

Cassandra is still giving me the impression that she's not convinced I'm really cured and tends to give me a wide berth if she can. I think Keith has decided to try and make things easier by taking her along with him anytime he's going anywhere. That way, he believes he's making it easier for us both. Really I can't help thinking that it's just putting off facing up to our relationship, warts and all.

Knowing that the Shelbourne thingie is looming, I've decided to pluck up my courage and go and do what Maggie suggested. I'm going to buy myself something fun to wear on that Wednesday night.

* * *

Later, feeling geriatric with much-needed cup of tea and feet up because of aching legs and sore back.

I spent hours hunting through racks of unsuitable clothing. Either unsuitable in their price or in their style. I didn't want an almost completely transparent garment with a drunken hemline or slits down to my navel. Neither did I want something staid and boring in lilac that made me look like a respectable middle-aged woman up from the country for a wedding. I don't think of myself as middle-aged and I don't particularly want to be all that respectable. Law-abiding – yes. A slave to doing the correct thing at the correct time in the correct manner – absobloodylutely not! What I wanted was a dress that would make me feel special and that was different – a little Bohemian perhaps, but well made. At least I do realise that I'm passed the stage where I can get away with wearing things that are falling apart at the seams and still look great in them.

Eventually, when I was ready to drop, in a tiny boutique in a side alley off Grafton Street, I found the answer to my dreams. But when I looked at the label, I nearly had a coronary. Four hundred and fifty euro! I *know* that the smart women who know about clothes wouldn't think twice about spending that on a pair of shoes. But I grew up in a household where extravagance was frowned on. Even during my years of marriage to Owen, I tried not to waste money. I know he used to get irritated sometimes when I refused to splash out on something I coveted.

"For God's sake! If you like it, buy the damn thing!" he'd say.

"But . . ."

"What's wrong with you, Hebe? You weren't a war baby. Stop wasting time and make up your mind."

After a little while, we stopped going shopping together. It was better that way and I didn't feel pressured into buying things I wasn't comfortable with.

But today, as I looked at myself in the mirror, turning this way and that like some young one in her first evening dress, I thought of all the reasons why I *had* to buy it. I can't remember what reasons I conjured up now but it worked amazingly well because I bought it!

It's utterly beautiful! Shocking pink and bright red and floaty without making me look as though I'm Ophelia about to take off down the river. It has long sleeves that are wide at the bottom and a neckline that shows just a tiny bit of cleavage – nothing too *risqué*. And it will look gorgeous with my heavy gold earrings and my one and only pair of scarlet, spiky-heeled *Prada* sandals (given to me by Owen before we separated and hardly worn). Because my skin is so sallow and I've done quite a bit of sitting around in the sun since I got home, I think I will look a bit of all right! That's if I can camouflage these damn blue bags under my eyes.

I arrived back at the house feeling knackered but exhilarated and a little guilty. But it did me good, that bit of retail therapy. I can't remember when I last indulged myself like that. Before I became ill, I think I'd got rather lazy about my appearance. Until Pandora died, I was writing flat out and, what with one thing and another, there never seemed the time to go off and buy clothes. I had a wardrobe bulging with stuff, so why bother?

I suppose the fact that there hasn't been a man in my life since Owen also made a difference. There wasn't anyone to dress up for. Also, I knew that it annoyed the hell out of Dervla when she bumped into me and I was looking scruffy, bordering on bag lady. Even if I was her beloved son's ex, I was letting the side down and it wasn't good for the extended family image! If she thought I hadn't seen her, she'd scuttle into a shop until I was safely out of the way. Once or twice, I followed her in and then greeted her effusively, all the while hoping one of her well-heeled coven was around to witness her being accosted by this mad woman in jeans and a T-shirt with the unlovely Gallagher brothers' mugs splatted across the front. Not nice behaviour – but worth it just to see the look of horror on her face as I homed in for the attack!

As I get stronger, I realise that I've got to do everything I can to make myself whole again, content, calm. Only when I've got myself together will I be in any position to really help Cassandra. And I'm going to have to be strong about Mum too. It's no good if I go to pieces again. I'm no use to anyone like that and *I refuse to let it happen*. I must say though, when I wake in the night, the idea that I might go under again does frighten me. If anyone had told me a couple of years ago that I'd have some sort of nervous breakdown, I'd have roared with laughter. I wasn't the type. I was cheerful. I didn't worry about things. So, how could that happen to me? That was for vulnerable, over-sensitive introverts – not happy, grounded Hebe Sayer. And how wrong I would have been! It just goes to show that you never know what lies around the corner and, on the whole, you're better off not knowing. Make hay while the sun shines because tomorrow you could well be squashed like a rasher by a 46A bus! Either that or end up in a straitjacket.

As a child, I used to have great faith in gypsy fortune-tellers and I loved it when the circus came on its annual visit. I'd always save up my two shillings, or whatever it was in those days, so that I could cross her palm with silver. The last time I went – I think I was fourteen – I was told that I would be married twice, have two children and make lots and lots of money. Only she said: "You will a make a lotta lotta money." She got the two children bit right. But I think she fell down on the married twice part of things. I think once is possibly all my system will take.

I remember feeling disappointed that I wasn't apparently going to become famous as well. What really put a dampener on the proceedings though was that, when I got up from the rickety chair to leave, I saw the pair of dirty, off-white plimsolls sticking out from under her dark red velvet skirt. That and the fact that, when I'd left the tent, I heard her calling to someone on the other side of the canvas in the broadest Dublin accent. I wanted my gypsies exotic and Dublin didn't quite fit the bill!

To return to the subject of the new dress – it is hanging on a padded hanger from a high cupboard handle in my bedroom. It's crazy, I know, but I keep having to go and look at it and run my fingers over it. The material is so silkily light, it's rather like picking up a cobweb.

I've bought a tube of lovely hand cream for Mum and some lip-balm for her poor, sore lips. I'm going in again to see her tomorrow. I've decided that visiting every day is not a good idea. I have a feeling that day runs into night seamlessly for her and if I go on alternate days it will be a little easier not to let myself get pulled down. I'm sure many daughters would be able to manage every day – would want to – but I have to be honest with myself and admit that I don't. And I don't think that makes me an uncaring daughter. I hope not, anyway.

Chapter Seven

Sunday after supper. I spent the whole of this afternoon hacking my way around the jungle that was once our back garden. To my surprise, Cassandra agreed to help. She stuck it for twenty minutes and then decided she'd had enough and disappeared into the house, looking aggrieved and sucking at an invisible thorn in her thumb.

Up until now, I've never taken much interest in the garden. It was just there. I knew the names of perhaps half a dozen of the poor plants struggling to grow in it but somehow never felt motivated to do anything about increasing my knowledge. It all seemed a rather uphill battle, what with aphids, snails and slugs and that nasty mildew thing. Why on earth were they all invented? I can't imagine Noah taking the time to scoop up that lot into his ark. And I could have sworn that the plants that were supposed to be there grew at half the speed of the ones that weren't. Every now and then we cut the grass and pulled out the tallest chunks of willow herb and thistle – and that was about it.

But since I've come home, I've found myself standing on the small, uneven terrace at the back of the house and wondering what botanical treasures lay under the coils of bindweed and tufts of couch grass. I noticed for the first time that the buddleia was covered in glorious purple flowers that were so dark they almost looked black in contrast to the dozens of butterflies smothering them. I saw too that thick fingers of ivy were beginning to choke some of the smaller shrubs. It's almost as if I'd gone round with only fifty per cent of my faculties working before I went into the clinic. What a lot I didn't really look at or smell or hear or touch – or treasure – before then! It sounds a bit soppy, I know but when I stand out there in the bee-filled sunlight I can't help thinking how bloody marvellous nature is – or whatever it is that's responsible for all this colour and texture and smell. It's just amazing!

Anyway, the garden is now part of my plan for the renewed, recharged Hebe Sayer. I know! This all sounds too optimistic and good to be true. If my friend Suzanne were here, I can just imagine her wide grin and see the quizzical look she'd be giving me right now. "Steady on, old thing! Don't overdo it!"

I *wish* she were here. Right now I'd give anything to hug and be hugged back by her. Although I've known her only since I moved here eight years ago, I feel that we've shared a lifetime of experiences. We have a lot in common, she and I: similar backgrounds, similar taste in books and films – and, sadly, we both have failed marriages behind us. Before she went off on her 'sabbatical' to Australia, hardly a week went by without us seeing each other.

It's suddenly hit me that we always greeted each other

with a quick, affectionate hug and, since Cassandra is out of bounds at the moment from the point of view of anything more than a fleeting smile if I'm lucky, I realise I'm probably suffering from touch deprivation. *Is* there such a thing? If there isn't, then I've invented it and it's *very* real.

It's been so long since Owen made love to me, I've almost forgotten what it is like to be stroked and caressed and aroused by a lover. For now, I can manage without that but I really, really long to be held by a friend, to feel their warmth and affection and to experience that lovely feeling of just being close and at one with a person I am fond of and who is fond of me. I know there's always dear Joan but she's so busy and if it weren't for her Wednesday afternoon visits, I probably wouldn't see her more than once a month.

When I say that Suzanne is on a sabbatical, that sounds as though she's an academic taking a well-earned break from academia. Whereas in reality all Suzy is doing is taking a break from her current boyfriend. He won't leave his wife even though they've been leading totally separate lives for the past five years and yet he says he can't live without Suzy. So, after telling him that she was giving him a year to get his act together, she upped and went, plus eighteen-year-old son, to Australia to paint, swim, walk, lose weight and sort *her* thoughts out. That suited son admirably as he's a lazy sod and, as far as I can make out, isn't the slightest bit interested in third level education or finding a job. It's not that he's stupid. Far from it. But the trouble with Luke is that he's a lotus eater. What he really wants to be doing is lounging around on a Gauguinesque sort of beach, fondling dusky maidens and addling his brains with dope, smokes and drink. To be honest, there was a time when I might have been tempted to do a little of that myself – just substituting dusky maidens with eager, dark-eyed youths! It's sad and a sign of my times but I see now that it's not really the answer if you want a full and satisfying life.

Although I was really sorry to see Suzy go, I couldn't help admiring her guts – as well as envying the fact that she was well enough off to be able to just up sticks and leave like that. Even if I could have afforded it, I couldn't really see me transplanting myself into a strange place, knowing no one and determined to make a new life there – even if it were only for one year. Amongst other things, when I think of Australia, funnel web spiders and large, poisonous snakes, *Jaws* patrolling the reefs and aggressive kangaroos – who will knock you out with one punch if you annoy them – come to mind. And don't they have a problem with millions of single-minded rabbits, whose sole purpose in life is to pile up against and then demolish the wire fences put up to keep them out?

I know I've mentioned the fact several times that, basically and when I'm being normal, I'm a laid-back, easy-going kind of woman. But I'm afraid that I am also an out-and-out coward. I don't *want* to be around biting, stinging, buzzing thingies. I loathe the idea of climbing mountains or potholing, scuba diving or parachute jumps. And, quite frankly, I find the idea of meeting and greeting a whole bunch of total strangers alarming. What happens if you go to the other side of the planet and find that they all loathe you? You'd be well and truly stuffed then, wouldn't you?

This is where writing thoughts down is invaluable. If I'd stopped to think about all of this in the normal course of events, it would have been in my mind one second and gone the next. But, when I take the time to write about it, I consider it more carefully. At this rate, I'll have to buy another exercise book. *Volume Two of The Invaluable Meanderings of Hebe Sayer!*

* * *

Monday, late, in garden with large and beautiful moth batting around the place for company.

When I got back from visiting Mum this morning, Cassandra was in the kitchen, making herself a mug of coffee. Earlier, she'd turned down my offer of coming with me to the nursing home and had been monosyllabic and remote. So it was a nice surprise when she gave me a smile and offered to make a mug for me too. I sat down at the table, wondering whether talking about her gran would be a mistake. I've got like that recently. It's so easy to upset her and so very difficult to defuse an atmosphere once it's been created that I'm nervous about saying the wrong thing. But, when she'd handed me the mug, she sat down opposite me and gave me another, tentative smile.

"How was Granny Molly?"

"Not good," I told her. "They seem to think that she's going downhill fast."

"Well, isn't that better than going on like she is?"

"Yes – of course, although part of me still doesn't want her to die."

"I know she's your mum, but . . ." She looked uncertain, as though she thought I might be offended by what she'd just said. "I mean, it's not *living,* is it?"

"No, you're right. It's no life for her. And yes, I do hope that it won't drag on for too long. But, I wish she knew who

I was when I'm sitting right beside her and I wish I could say goodbye to her."

Cassandra gave me one of her funny looks. "But you and she were never all that close, were you?"

"No, I suppose not," I said, wondering what was coming next.

"So, I would have thought that you'd be pleased that she *is* going downhill so quickly. It will be easier on you."

She sounded so sensible and pragmatic about the situation. How could I begin to explain how I felt about my mother dying? Cassandra was right in that Mum and I never had a close relationship. I'd always felt that she was critical of me and, perhaps, as I got older, she felt that I distanced myself from her. Oh, I know I always made sure that she was all right and was careful to see that she didn't want for anything. But we never enjoyed each other's company all that much, never shared good quality time. She was too occupied being busy and being irritated by my *laissez-faire* attitude to life. And her fussy perfectionism made *me* impatient. Both of us cared about the other. But not enough. That special mother-daughter closeness I've observed other women having was always missing. In spite of this lack, and with her death approaching, all sorts of unexpected emotions have started to force their way up from the depths – like bubbles rising to the surface of a pond. Each time one bursts, it releases some surprising revelation or other about our relationship: good things as well as all the old, well-worn resentments and dissonances. I wanted Cassandra to understand how I was feeling.

"It's difficult to explain," I told her. "I think part of the problem is that she can't understand what I'm saying and I want to tell Granny Molly that I'm sorry I wasn't a better daughter to her. I want to say *thank you* for all that she did for me. It can't have been easy with your grandfather dying when I was only ten. I think that, in many ways, she was a rather lonely woman. The only time I think I ever saw her look happy after he died was when she was working in her garden with you and Pandora belting around the place. I don't know what it was, but being outside, surrounded by her flowers, seemed to somehow iron out all the wrinkles on her forehead. I remember commenting on that once."

"Did Granny Molly laugh when you said that?"

"No, I think she thought I was being fanciful and rather silly," I said, feeling a sudden rush of sadness.

Cassandra stretched out and grasped one of my hands. "Would it make it easier if I came with you next time?" She sounded really concerned.

I know I must have looked surprised. "That would be lovely. Are you sure you want to?"

"Not really but I'd like to come if it would help."

That was the nicest thing she's said for a long time. I was so pleased, I started to get up. I was going to go round to her side of the table and give her a hug. Nothing over the top – just a grateful and affectionate squeeze. But, suddenly, the moment was over. She too was on her feet.

"So I'll come with you next time you go to visit her then. I must dash, I'm meeting Keith and I'm going to be late. I'll see you tonight, Mum."

I sat for a long time after she'd gone, listening to the uneven tick of the clock on the wall. The kitchen felt suddenly terribly empty and colourless. Even Busby seemed to have gone AWOL. I told myself that, at least she'd made the offer – even if she'd then immediately fled, pre-empting any intimacy.

A thought occurred to me just now: I wonder if Cassandra has a good dollop of Molly Forde genes in her and takes after my mother and I just never realised it before. It's possible, I suppose. There's a coolness there that reminds me of Mum. And yet, when I think back, Cassandra used to show affection when she was a child – just like her sister did. When she reached puberty, I realised that she'd become a little different but I put that down to adolescence and the fact that her parents had separated.

I remember that, up until they were twelve or so, neither of them minded me seeing them with no clothes on. And I was the same with them. They would often perch on the edge of the bath and chat – sometimes even scrub my back for me. And we used to sunbathe in the back garden completely starkers. And then, all of a sudden, with Cassandra anyway, it was all locked doors and violent objections if anything to do with the naked body were mentioned. It was almost as if, overnight, she'd turned into a raving prude. I remember thinking that it was just as well that we weren't living in Victorian England or she'd have insisted on covering up the piano legs!

Come to think of it, I don't think I *ever* saw my own mother naked. In fact, I know I didn't. I find that sad. Or is it me who's being abnormal here? *No!* Nudity is a good thing. I don't mean that we should all trot around wearing no clothes – it's a no-no in this climate anyway fifty weeks out of fifty-two – and I certainly don't want to sit in public places in my birthday suit where others have sat before me. How unhygienic can you be? But surely, one's body and how one uses it is all part of the whole person, the way one is? I don't care if people have droopy boobs or saggy buttocks. You don't get all upset if someone's nose is an odd shape or their ears resemble door handles.

I do remember that when I tried to talk to Owen about Cassandra's new-found modesty, he barely listened, telling me that I was making a fuss about nothing.

* * *

Tuesday afternoon.

When I got to the clinic to see Dr Scheller this morning for the first of my check-ups, the receptionist told me that he wasn't there and that I would be seeing someone else. My heart plummeted. All of a sudden, all my smiling pretence at being a nice, reasonable, civilised woman evaporated and this unattractive, wild-eyed, bolshie female took her place. I wanted Dr Scheller, not some watered-down stand-in. I could feel my face getting flushed and my voice, when I next spoke, sounded higher and louder – even to me. I know it made one or two people in the waiting room glance up from their *Woman's Way* and *Homes and Gardens*. I could see them wondering if I was going to supply a bit of light entertainment to alleviate the boredom while they waited.

"But I have an appointment with Dr Scheller," I said, stupidly, staring at her.

The only excuse I can give is that I was in shock. The thought of his not being there had never crossed my mind. I hadn't realised how much I still felt I needed his advice; his approval of my attempts at getting back to some semblance of a normal life again.

She gave me a pitying look, accompanied by an understanding smile. "You'll be quite safe in the hands of Dr Simmonds-Frawley."

Simmonds-Frawley! I mean, with a name like that, I doubted anyone who wasn't a blue-blooded duchess would be safe. No one with a name like that would want to deal with a peasant like me.

"But he doesn't know me," I muttered, feeling like a mutinous teenager, whom no one understands.

The rest of them were pretending to read their bloody magazines but I knew they had their antennae pointing in my direction and were well and truly tuned in and listening intently.

"Dr Simmonds-Frawly is a *lady* doctor," she replied with a broad smile and a smug look as she looked down at the papers in front of her, apparently terminating the conversation.

As if that clinched it. The doctor was of the female gender and no sane person could have the slightest doubt that all was well with the world.

One of the things I find really hard to take is being patronised or being humoured – even if my behaviour deserves it.

"Well, if Dr Scheller isn't here, I will come back when he is," I snapped.

"Ms . . . er," She looked down at the list in front of her again. She didn't even know who I was, for God's sake. "Ms Sawyer . . ." She compounded it by managing to get my name wrong when she did find it. "Ms Sawyer, I do think you should sit down and wait – like everyone else."

If I hadn't turned and nearly run out of the room, I

swear I'd have thumped the idiot woman. Couldn't she see that the one and only person who understands me, to whom I've confided my innermost thoughts and who's been there for me day after day for the past three months is Dr Scheller?

Instead of leaving the building, I took the lift up to the first floor and went in search of a friendly face. After all, it was only three weeks since I'd been released, let out, whatever. Surely someone would be able to tell me what was going on. I eventually tracked down one of the young nurses who had looked after me from time to time.

She smiled when she saw me – a nice, big genuine smile that immediately made me stop and try to get a grip on myself.

"Hello, Ms Sayer! How are you?" she said, coming up to me.

"I'm fine," I lied, at the same time attempting to smile back. "Though there seems to be some sort of mix-up downstairs. Perhaps you could help. I have an appointment to see Dr Scheller at eleven this morning and I've just been told he's not here," I gabbled. The moment the words were out of my mouth, I can only say that her face fell, making me wonder just what was going on. "What's the matter?" I asked. "Why isn't he around?"

She gave a quick glance along the corridor – probably to see if my starched apron-wearing nemesis was on the prowl and then she came up close to where I stood.

"Dr Scheller's on extended leave," she almost whispered. "Family problems."

"What sort of family problems?" I demanded to know.

She leaned closer. "It's Dr Scheller's son. He died last

week. Leukaemia. He was only twelve. He'd been ill for a long time. I think it was expected."

I felt faint with remorse and shame. She must have seen me looking odd because she reached out and took hold of my arm to steady me. I don't think she would have been so sweet if she'd witnessed my bad-tempered altercation with the receptionist downstairs a little earlier. I knew that I didn't deserve her sympathy.

I've no idea what she said after that – only that she offered me a cup of water and tried to get me to sit down. I remember feeling that I had to get away as quickly as possible. Somehow I managed to get myself out of the building. I went over to one of the seats in the garden, where I sat for ages, neither hearing nor seeing anything around me. That poor man. How *could* I have been so insensitive, so demanding?

I'd always known that there was something profoundly sad about Dr Scheller even though, every time we met, he smiled and made jokes and never, never let his attention wander from what I, the patient, was saying. As if everything else for that moment was unimportant. Yes, I know that I have a very real reason to be sad. But all the other absurd little niggles and complaints that I poured out to him now seem so irrelevant. And all the while he listened to me droning on, he knew that his twelve-year-old son was dying.

Even now as I write this, I'm finding it difficult to come to terms with the way I behaved at the clinic. All things considered, I can't think why that receptionist didn't lose her temper with me. I think if I'd been her, and knowing why Dr Scheller wasn't there for the wretched appointment,

I would have told me to get lost in no uncertain terms. Yes, she was rather unprofessional and horribly patronising, speaking to me as if I were a badly behaved child (a more accurate description than I want to admit) but I can't help feeling that she's in the wrong job.

The only thing I can think of doing now is to write a letter to him. A short one. What can you say at a time like this? I suppose, to the bereaved father, a tiny measure of comfort comes from the fact that people *do* take the time to clumsily write how sorry they are. And I'm sure my letter will be as clumsy and inept as all the others. But what else can I do?

* * *

Tuesday night and feeling disheartened.

This afternoon, I searched out the large brown envelope containing the letters I received after Pandora died. I hadn't realised how many there were. They are all pretty much the same but each one, in its own way, is touching and I'm infinitely grateful that so many people took the trouble to hunt for the right words in a generous attempt to salve the unspeakable pain of those first weeks.

After I'd posted the letter to Dr Scheller, I read what I'd written earlier on today. I realise that, however much you try to avoid clichés, they are sometimes the only things that fit the bill. The particular cliché I was thinking of was *Time heals*. And I realise, to my surprise that the ache of Pandora's death *has* lessened. There was a time, at the beginning, when I would have been angry if anyone had told me it would happen. But now, there are whole hours that pass by without my thinking of her or at least, that pass by without my feeling distressingly sad. Instead, I've started to remember the funny, silly, outrageous times that, while we were living them, I never knew were so precious.

I've come to a decision. I don't know if Dr Scheller will come back to the clinic and if he does come back, when that will be. But, in spite of the way I let myself down this morning, I know with absolute certainty that I don't want to see anyone else. If he never comes back, then so be it. But, deep down inside me, I feel I have changed. Perhaps not in any way that is obvious but there has been a shift, a readjustment – I don't know how to describe it. All I do know is that I am different to the Hebe Sayer of six months ago – or even of six weeks ago. I also know that I intend to try and make the rest of whatever journey I'm embarked on on my own. That's clumsily put. You can tell I have pretensions to write, can't you?

There was a special synergy with Dr Scheller. He has a true gift for healing and, knowing me, if I went to someone else now, it would be a disaster. I know it would because, all the time, I would be comparing them with him – and that wouldn't be fair on them, apart from anything else. I want to do this on my own – perhaps with a little help from my friends. I don't think that's being arrogant. After all, one of the things I learned from being in that comfortable, posh clinic is that, although you can be encouraged and prodded along the right road, you're basically on your own and it's ultimately up to me to get it right. And I'm determined to have a bloody good try at doing just that. So, Hebe Sayer – stick that in your laptop in bold and underline it!

* * *

Same day, later on.

I bumped into Dervla this afternoon on my way back from posting the letter to Dr Scheller. I don't know why that should surprise me. Dalkey is a small village and I was bound to sooner or later. She hasn't been near me since I left the clinic. She's probably wary of being seen in my company, frightened that I might start gibbering at her or climbing a lamppost while frothing at the mouth! And of course, she didn't visit me when I was inside. For which I was grateful.

Anyway, we literally bumped into each other. I was coming out of the bookshop and she was tripping along the pavement outside looking as elegant as ever in a moss-coloured linen suit that looked incredibly expensive. She's one of the few women I know who can get away with wearing one hundred per cent linen and not looking as though she'd slept in it. I've tried it and after half-an-hour I ended up with ferocious creases across my stomach and at the elbows and looking as though I'd had a bad shopping day in the Oxfam shop.

She couldn't pretend she hadn't seen me so she gave that slight twitch of the lips that passes for a smile, meanwhile looking me up and down with those cool grey eyes of hers. She's taller than me – damn it – so that means that she literally looks down on me.

"Hebe!" She made my name sound as though she'd just stepped in something nasty.

"Dervla!" I replied, trying my best to sound every bit as calm, cool and detestable as she was.

"And how are you feeling today?"

That sounded as if, yesterday, I lay down in the street

and stopped the traffic and quite possibly tomorrow I'll turn into an axe murderer but today? Who knows what I'll get up to?

"I'm feeling well, thank you," I said in my best tea-party voice. "And how are *you?*"

Her eyes narrowed very slightly. She never had a sense of humour and the idea that I might not feel at a disadvantage talking to her was not on the agenda.

She looked pointedly at her Dior watch. "I'm going to be late for an appointment if I'm not careful. Take care of yourself, Hebe. Don't overdo things."

I knew *exactly* what she meant by that. Don't behave as though everything isn't perfect in your life. Keep up a front and don't let the side down by behaving erratically and embarrassing me even more than you have already. For a moment I was tempted to ask her if she'd seen Owen and his latest acquisition lately and didn't she perhaps think Lucy was a little young for a man of his age? But I hadn't the energy. And, quite honestly, what he gets up to is really of no interest to me any more. I just wish his behaviour didn't have such an upsetting effect on Cassandra.

She set off at high speed, giving a slight royal wave of the hand as she turned away from me. It was obvious that she wanted to put as much distance between us as quickly as possible. I did notice that, in her haste to make her get-away, she narrowly avoided treading on a broken pavement drain. That would have been fun, seeing her fall flat on her back! Although, knowing her, she'd probably have timed it so that she landed gracefully in the arms of some gallant passing male, who would be overwhelmed by her plight. Oh, well! The fact that I live around the corner from her

NICOLA LINDSAY

must be a constant source of annoyance. Though not half as much as the irritation I feel, knowing that she lives around the corner from me!

When I got back here, Cassandra was in her room. Her door was open so I knocked and waited to be invited in, or not. But she was in a better mood than I'd seen her for some days.

"You haven't changed your mind about coming with me to see Granny Molly, have you?" I asked, tentatively.

"No, I said I would," she said, changing a CD.

The sound of David Gray filled the room.

"I've just got back from posting a letter to Dr Scheller."

She immediately looked up from the pile of CDs scattered around on the carpet. "Why? Is there something wrong? I thought you were seeing him this morning."

"He wasn't there. His twelve year-old son died of leukaemia a few days ago."

She suddenly went very still. Then she leaned over and turned off the music. Slowly she got up and went over to the window where she stared unseeingly out into the garden, fidgeting with the curtain, twisting and untwisting it in her fingers.

Then she turned, her face contorted. "Why do these things keep happening, Mum?"

I knew that she wasn't just thinking of her sister. Two friends of hers, young men in their early twenties, had been killed in a car crash at Easter.

"People die, Cassandra. It's part of life and you can't always guard against it, I'm afraid."

"But *twelve!* That's even worse than –"

"I know," I said quickly. "It's terrible and somehow it

seems especially cruelly ironic when Dr Scheller is such a good man. I can't help feeling that he, of all people, doesn't deserve this."

"Does he have any other kids?" she asked, her voice sounding husky.

"I think the nurse told me that he didn't."

"Oh, God! It's all so unfair."

Then she started to cry and, for the first time since I've come home, she let me hold her – properly – with no sense of wanting to break away as soon as she could.

We didn't say anything. I held her to me, stroking her hair and eventually wiping her hot cheeks with a cold flannel. At first, she clung to me like a small child but as the sobs subsided, she released her grip a little and laid her head against my shoulder with her eyes closed as if she were utterly exhausted.

I could hear the sound of the occasional car in the road outside but apart from that, the house was quiet. The feeling of being there for her was uppermost in my mind. The relief that, after all these weeks of distancing herself, she had finally turned to me made me feel as though I wanted to cry too. But as I looked down at her closed eyes, wet lashes and trembling lips, I realised I hadn't a clue about what was going in her mind.

I found myself thinking of Dr Scheller. Did he have a loving wife who would put her arms around him and comfort him or was her grief so great that he would have to try and stifle his own feelings and be strong for her? I know that sometimes you hear someone say that they want to cope on their own. But I think it is too much to ask of a person. No one should have to deal with real loss and grief alone.

I think that was one of the things I found hardest after Pandora died. Even though there were people around, I felt that I had to go through it all on my own. Owen bottled his feelings up and refused to let me anywhere near him and Cassandra was so shattered by what had happened, instead of wanting to be comforted, she put up a wall that she hid behind, refusing to talk or eat. She walked around the place like some sort of alien creature, unable to communicate with anyone and who didn't understand what was going on around her.

I tried so hard not to show how I was feeling. I was like a house, with all its walls covered in almost indiscernible hairline cracks. I didn't know then that they would become more and more visible until the whole edifice collapsed into a heap of rubble. Because my remaining daughter needed me, I did my best – and I know now how shaky a best that was. I remember how she locked her bedroom door and wouldn't eat anything, how I would hear her in the middle of the night, pacing backwards and forwards in her room. When I begged her to let me in, she eventually opened the door and I couldn't believe that the pale, unhappy looking girl with the black circles around her eyes was my daughter. All the light seemed to have gone out of her. Her eyes looked dead and she seemed to be looking through me rather than at me.

I remember when I pleaded with her to talk to me, to tell me what she was thinking, all she said was, "This is all his fault – and yours too."

Then she said she didn't want to talk and shut the door and locked it again. I was left, standing on the landing, shaking, with my heart thumping so violently I felt it must burst. I don't remember going downstairs but I know that I sat on the bottom step, my head in my hands, asking myself if what she'd said contained a grain of truth.

Yes, I'd had a rare argument with them both before Pandora and Cassandra went out on that last evening. Yes, I did lose my temper – but not so much at Pandora as at her sister. I felt that it was she who was the ringleader in insisting they go to that dive. I didn't want them to go to 'Spike's'. It had a reputation as a place where you could get drugs and where the bouncers were involved in selling all kinds of dope and so it was in their interest to see that all the wrong people were allowed in. Cassandra had admitted to me months before that it was the sort of establishment where they turned off the water in the cloakrooms so that the young ones, high on Ecstasy and dying of thirst, were forced to buy bottled water at vastly inflated prices. I'd gathered from something Suzy said, worried about what her own son got up to when he went there, that the management turned a blind eye to a fair amount of sexual activity in the darker corners of the place. She made it clear she wasn't just talking about intimate fumbling and French kissing.

So, yes, there had been an atmosphere when they left. Cassandra had had that look in her eye that I knew meant that she intended doing exactly what she wanted and anything I said made not the slightest difference. Pandora too, unusually silent all that day, had been swept along by her sister's gung-ho bloody-mindedness and left without giving me her usual parting kiss on the cheek.

Looking back afterwards on that awful night, I couldn't help feeling that there should have been some sort of portent, a sign to warn me that I would never see her alive again; that the next time I looked at her face, she would be lying on a stretcher in the A and E department of St Vincent's Hospital. So that silent departure was to be my last memory of her alive: flushed, uneasy at leaving in the way she was but feeling she'd better not incur Cassandra's wrath by giving in to me like she usually did. I'd watched them turn out of the gate into the street, their long blonde hair lit by the street lamps, their tall figures moving quickly out of sight, Pandora's head slightly tilted downwards while her sister – still angry – gesticulated beside her.

* * *

Later on this evening, I managed to persuade Cassandra to come downstairs and have something to eat. I cooked us omelettes while she washed lettuce and made a salad, covered in a pungent dressing. She's started to become interested in cooking, having fallen for Jamie Oliver, and she's also decided that you can't eat too much garlic. With the result that, after this evening's meal, we will both need to be given a very wide berth. Even I can smell my own breath – even though I've just cleaned my teeth and gargled with mouthwash.

When we'd finished eating, we took our glasses of wine out into the garden and watched the evening sky darken to the deepest navy blue with a pale apricot streak where the sun had gone down over the Dublin Mountains.

It was lovely. The air was gently warm, with just the slightest breeze that stirred the trees into fitful whispering in the background. There was even the sound of a cricket. We listened to the unaccustomed creaky noise with enjoyment. We didn't talk all that much but our silences were companionable and, in spite of the fact that it was difficult not to keep thinking of Mum and of the unknown, twelve-year-old boy, I suddenly felt unexpectedly happy – a sharp, poignant sort of happiness that almost made me dizzy.

And then I made the stupid mistake of asking her if she was happy too. I'd meant not happy about everything but happy just at *that* particular moment with us being quietly together.

Her face immediately clouded. "I don't know how you can say that," she said, looking puzzled.

"I said it because it's good being here with you like this. We haven't done anything together for so long."

"Well, that's hardly *my* fault." Suddenly, her voice had all the old bitterness back in it.

Before she could say anything more, I interrupted. "Isn't it time to stop blaming me for everything?" She turned away her head so that I could only see her profile in the light from the house. "I know you think that I should have let you go to the club with Pandora that night and I know that you think that because I made a thing about it, she's dead. I know you think I shouldn't have become ill and that I wasn't there for you." I took her hands in mine. I could feel the resistance but I held them tightly, forcing her to look at me. "Cassandra, that's not fair. I wasn't the one who insisted you go to that place. I was trying to protect my two nineteen-year-old daughters, trying to make them understand why it was no place for them to be. And after your sister died, you've no idea how hard I tried to hold everything together. I know I failed and I'm truly sorry for that but please acknowledge the fact that becoming ill was the last thing I wanted to happen."

"Are you saying that what happened is my fault then?" Her eyes glittered.

"No!" I said, giving her hands a shake. "What I'm saying is that, for the last year, you and your father have both blamed me. He blamed me for not controlling you better and you blamed me for losing my temper that night. And I think that's one of the reasons I became ill. And I'm not accepting all the blame any more. We all have to understand that the three of us contributed to what happened and then we have to let go and accept that it's in the past. We can't change anything but we can make sure that we don't make the same sort of mistakes in the future."

"So, what do you want me to do?" There was a slight tremor in her voice.

"I want you to be gentler with me, with your father and above all, with yourself." It was then that I saw the tears sliding down her face. Full of remorse, I knelt beside her on the damp grass. "Darling! I didn't mean to make you cry."

She looked down for a moment before raising her head again and looking me straight in the face. "It isn't as straightforward as you think, Mum." When she saw me looking confused, she added, "But I know what you mean about being more gentle. I'm sorry! I'll try. I really will."

And before I could say anything more, she had slipped back into the house, leaving me alone, wondering what on earth she'd meant by it not being as straightforward as I'd thought. I do know that, every time her father is mentioned, her face clouds over as though she doesn't even want to hear his name. I've been racking my brains to try and think of a time when all was right with them and I'm starting to think that, perhaps, there was often some sort of tension between Owen and herself as soon as the girls reached their early teens. But I don't remember the same thing happening with Pandora. I know that, because Cassandra quite often tended to be confrontational, it was hardly surprising that it was her sister Owen used to look at with an affectionate smile during the increasingly infrequent occasions when we were all together. I suppose it's understandable. Pandora never had that edgy awkwardness of her sister.

I'll have to leave it for a while. I can't upset her any more. She's had enough upset and turmoil to last her a lifetime.

So, I picked up Busby and brought him inside and he followed me upstairs and he's now sleeping like a baby at the foot of the bed. I'm going to turn the light off and try and go to sleep – hopefully without lying awake for hours wondering and worrying. At least she said she would try and that's good enough for now.

Chapter Eight

Next day – which means there's only a week to go before I officially launch myself into the Dublin social scene! Although perhaps launch is too positive a word – paddle gingerly in the shallows might be more appropriate.

On the way to the nursing home this morning, I asked Cassandra if she'd liked to come with me to the reception for Sam Ellis next week.

"You mean *the* Sam Ellis? Sam Ellis, the writer?" she said, turning around to look at me, wide-eyed in amazement.

"The very one."

"Wow!" There was silence while she digested the information. "How come you were invited?" she asked with a puzzled look.

"That's not very flattering!" I couldn't help laughing. Why is it that one's children think that no one interesting or famous could possibly want to have anything to do with their boring, battered old parents? "Maggie invited me, if you must know. He's one of her writers."

It was on the tip of my tongue to tell her that the said gentleman had read my last book and liked it. When I say last book, I know it sounds as if I'd dozens published but there are only two – so far! But Maggie's a great confidence builder and I know she'll not let on that I'm hardly a well-seasoned or established writer unless it's absolutely necessary. Bless her!

"Really?" Cassandra sounded impressed. Then reality struck. "Did you say next Wednesday?"

I nodded. "Yep!"

"But that's like in one week's time!" she said in a strangled voice. "I don't have anything to wear."

"Cassandra, you have a room stuffed full of clothes I've hardly ever seen you in."

She gave an impatient shake of her head. "That doesn't mean I've got the right thing for a reception at the Shelbourne. Mum, the press will be there and stuff!" She sounded so panicked, I relented.

"Well, I know you don't much like clothes shopping with me. Would you like some cash and you can go and choose something you think is appropriate. And I mean appropriate," I warned her. "I don't want me paying through the nose so that you can wear some skimpy number that will distract everyone's attention. Don't forget that the photographers will be there to take pictures of the celebrity guest, not you!"

It was obvious from her expression that she hoped otherwise!

"Thanks, Mum!" she said, her face glowing.

Suddenly, all the light had come back into her, like a lamp that's been switched on, transforming a cloudy day and making it golden.

Although, as we got nearer the nursing home, her high spirits subsided. By the time we arrived, she was subdued again.

As we walked up the steps, I took her arm. "Would you rather wait for me outside?"

She hesitated a moment before replying, "No, it's OK. I'll come in with you. I haven't seen Granny Molly for well over a month."

"You know she's very frail now, don't you?" I warned her as we walked along the corridor to the residents' sitting room.

"Yes," she said, with a nod. "Don't worry, Mum. I'll be fine."

We went into the room together and stopped short. The armchair by the window was empty. Anxiously, I scanned the room. My mother was nowhere to be seen.

"Nurse!" I hurried over to a uniformed figure bent over a medicine trolley, while another handed pills and a glass of water to an old woman, whose head shook so violently I wondered how she would ever manage to swallow them. "Nurse, where is Mrs Forde?"

The girl barely lifted her eyes from the chart in front of her. "She's along the corridor. Turn right, room twenty-three."

Cassandra gave me an anxious look as we hurried through the door. "Do you think something's happened?"

"I don't know," I said, walking as fast as I could, checking the numbers on the doors. I felt suddenly breathless. Mum had always been in the sitting-room on my previous visits. Something *must* have happened for her to be in her room today.

The door to number twenty-three was closed. My hand felt sweaty as I nervously turned the handle and pushed it open.

The bed was on the other side of the room, opposite the door. My mother was lying on her back, snoring. They had put cot sides up on the bed and I was disturbed to see that her wrists had been bandaged with one end of each bandage tied around the bars of the cot sides. I also noticed that she was wearing a white cotton gown rather than one of her own nightdresses.

She looked so pathetically small lying there I found I had a lump in my throat. I glanced over at Cassandra, who seemed as thrown as I was, her eyes taking in the scene, darting from the restrained wrists to the pale face on the pillow.

"Why have they tied her wrists like that?" she asked in low voice, as though she were frightened her grandmother might hear her.

"I'm sure it's for her own safety. Perhaps they were worried she'd try and get out of bed on her own and hurt herself."

As I got closer to the bed I saw that there was a tube leading down into a plastic container of urine hanging from underneath the side of the bed and that there was also a drip stand on the other side. I was aware of a cold feeling in the pit of my stomach. In the space of a couple of days, she'd been catheterised and put on an infusion of some sort. Surely it wasn't necessary to restrain her as well?

I bent over my mother and looked into her face. It seemed as though she'd shrunk even more since my last visit. Her cheekbones seemed to protrude more noticeably than before and her closed eyes were deeply sunk in their sockets. Her lips were cracked and flaked.

I opened my bag and took out the lip-salve and hand cream. "Would you like to put some hand cream on her?" I asked Cassandra.

I think I thought that she might not want to touch the small dry hands that were more like some fragile bird's claws than human hands.

But she silently took the tube of cream from me and unscrewed the top. I wiped away the spittle from the side of my mother's mouth and smeared her lips with the salve, while Cassandra gently massaged her hands.

"Can you smell the cream?" Cassandra asked me, working more cream into the desiccated skin. "It's like the roses that Granny used to have in her garden when I was little."

"Yes," I said. "Do you remember the time she baked you and Pandora a birthday cake and decorated it with sugared rose petals that she collected from her favourite roses?"

Cassandra nodded. "And she made a special drink in her best glasses. It had pineapple and apple and orange and she decorated the top with tiny mint leaves. And do you remember, Mum, how she froze nasturtium and borage flowers in ice cubes to put in at the last minute?"

I smiled at the memory, remembering the look of sheer delight on the two children's faces as they were handed their rainbow cocktails in the long-stemmed glasses with the twist of gold in their stems.

She suddenly leaned forward and, with the back of her hand, stroked the sleeping face. The way she did it was unusually gentle. I don't think I'd seen her being so restrained or careful with another person before. For a moment, all her attention was focussed on her grandmother. Gone was the usual self-absorption. She was oblivious of anything else and the expression on her face was suddenly sweet. It made me think of the French word *douce*. I remembered coming across some poems of courtly love in my battered copy of the *Anthologie de la Poésie Française* years earlier, in which the beloved was often described in this way and represented virtuousness, sweetness of spirit, generosity and womanliness. But seeing her looking like that also sent a fierce dart of pain through me. Just for a moment, it was Pandora leaning over the bed.

"Her cheeks are so soft!" she exclaimed in a low voice, glancing up at me.

Then she stiffened and looked down as, suddenly, my mother's eyes opened wide. I too leaned closer and I was suddenly struck by what pretty eyes she has – a sort of light hazel colour with speckled darker brown around the iris. I hadn't realised that until now. It dawned on me that I'd not really looked at my mother's eyes before – not properly. For a long time they had been half hidden behind glasses. She gazed up at the face above her, frowning with concentration. It seemed as if she were struggling to say something.

Then, out of nowhere and quite clearly, she said, "Cassandra! Good girl!"

And then her eyes flickered shut.

Cassandra stood, frozen like a statue, staring down at her grandmother. I went around to the other side of the bed and put my arm around her shoulders.

"Did you hear that? As clear as a bell!"

"She knew who I was, Mum. Just for a moment, she knew it was me," she said, her voice cracking with emotion.

I was so glad for her. I know that it's probably too much to expect it to happen again – for Mum to recognise me, to say something – however brief. But, even if that's it and my mother never says anything more, I'm happy that she spoke those words to Cassandra.

I left her sitting beside the bed while I went in search of someone who could tell me more about Mum's condition – although I don't really think I needed telling. It's obvious that she's not far from death.

Writing those words, I feel a quiet sense of inevitability. I think that when she does die, I'll be as prepared as I can be. And I suppose that seventy-four is not too bad a score. I know that she wouldn't want to go on like this a moment longer and I'm just so thankful that she seems not to be aware of how bad she is.

When I spoke to the doctor, he confirmed what I'd been thinking, that there wasn't anything more they could do for her, other than making her as comfortable as possible. He said that they'd had to restrain her because she'd become very confused during the previous night and had tried to pull out the drip from her arm. He was vague about how much longer she has but he reassured me that, when it does happen, it will be a gentle death. Oh, I *hope* so. I don't want her to be frightened. I don't want to see that confused, anxious look in her eyes like before. I want her to slip out of this world easily and peacefully. And I want to be with her when it happens.

* * *

One week later. I've not had the time to write anything for days because of spending every available minute I can manage at the nursing home.

When I went to see Mum yesterday morning, there was no change and, although I talked to her, remembering things that might give her pleasure if the words got through, there was no reaction. She just lay, looking almost as if she'd already died. They don't seem to know if she can hear what I say or not. The doctor seems to think that she probably can't and that, even if she could, it wouldn't make any sense to her. But, it's worth a try. And, actually, it helps me to talk to her. I talk about everything – about her garden and the picnics we used to have on the beach at Killiney and the journeys in the train to Bray when I was a child to ride the dodgems and eat ices decorated with a chocolate flake plunged into the middle, about swimming in the icy water off Brittas Bay and shivering, blue-lipped, in the sand dunes, squinting eagerly at the darkening sky, trying to convince ourselves that the little patch of blue on the distant horizon *was* getting larger. I even talked about Dad, although he's just a shadowy memory to me now, made a little more permanent by looking at the few photos of him that still exist. For I'm sure, after he died, she destroyed some of them.

I remember the day I found the charred remains of photos lying, mixed up with garden rubbish that she'd burned. I was horrified. I thought then that she did it because she didn't love him, that she didn't care that he was dead. To my ignorant child's eyes, she was treating him like unwanted clutter. Now, instead, I think that she kept only a few of the better ones because she did love him and only wanted to save the best as a reminder of how he'd been and what they'd shared in a marriage that had been so cruelly cut short.

Now that it's too late, I keep thinking of things I want to ask her. It's awful that there are so many gaps that I will never be able to fill in. But then again, she never talked much to me when she was well, so I suppose it's foolish to think that, even if she were able, she'd tell me all the things I'd love to know.

I stayed with her until they had to come and change her sheets. Apparently, she's doubly incontinent now – hence the catheter. Poor Mum! The indignity of it all. Thank God she seems to spend most of her time sleeping.

Why can't your body just close down without any fuss or mess when the time is right? I once read about some of the North American Indians who chose the time and place and the manner of their dying. And that was after a life lived in harmony with the natural world around them. Somehow they managed to maintain the right balance between what was taken from their environment and what was given back. It seems to me that we really have got it dreadfully wrong, the way we approach most things – the important ones, anyway.

After I left her, I went and sat on the wall of the tiny harbour near the house and watched a couple of men working on their small trawler and listened to the gulls and to the sound of rigging tapping its metallic Morse code out against the masts. I breathed in the nicely pungent smell of old seaweed and fishy leftovers on the minute crescent of sand nearby. It was especially welcome after the smell of disinfectant and decaying old age I'd just left behind.

* * *

It's late Wednesday night. Well, actually it's not, it's Thursday morning and, even though I'm completely wiped out, I've got to let off steam and write about the Shelbourne bash or I won't be able to sleep!

When I left Mum this morning, I had been going to have my hair done but, somehow, I couldn't face the thought of going from the nursing home straight to that busy, noisy hairdresser's with its very nice but very inquisitive girls, who were sure to ask me how I was and how she was, how was Cassandra managing and what was I doing these days? etc etc. It was too late to book an appointment somewhere else. I usually give hairdressers a wide berth. Before she went away, Suzy used to hack bits off for me when I thought it needed attention. I don't like the smell of the lotions and potions they use and which you inhale whether you like it or not. Nor do I relish having my head bent back at an impossible angle over a basin while I'm hosed down with scalding or luke-warm water – depending on how thick-skinned the trainee's hands are. And while I'm 'giving out', I might as well also mention the fact that, at some point, they succeed in scalding your scalp with the hair dryer because they're eyeing the neat bum of the male trainee who's sweeping the floor. And another thing; they have a nasty habit of managing to nearly rip my ears off with the comb. I've lost a couple of earrings that way. They were sent flying into a pile of someone else's shed mane, lying in unappetising-looking drifts on the floor. It took several minutes of hairy rummaging before they were retrieved.

So, after a quiet sit on the harbour wall and a spot of deep breathing, I went back to the house and found Cassandra, holed up in the bathroom, deep into preparations for the evening. When I pointed out it was only just after two and we didn't have to be there until eight, she said she was doing a bikini wax. Having seen the outfit she's planning on wearing, I had no difficulty figuring out quite why that was necessary. I hadn't realised that her dress, even with a shift underneath, was quite so thin, requiring her to wear a G-string.

"So as not to spoil the line," she told me firmly when she finally emerged, waxed, lacquered, golden body lotioned and scented all over with my precious *Dune* shower gel.

I must admit that she did look gorgeous when she appeared in my bedroom later on and did a twirl. Her dress was the softest greeny-blue with a hint of gold thread in it – like the colour of early morning mist over blue sea when the sun is starting to rise. It made her look even more tall and slender than usual. I could quite see why she was wearing the G-string. Although I suppose the dress wasn't too revealing, but it did rather cling to her. She'd done something to her hair with rollers so that it was slightly springy-looking and fell around her shoulders, framing her face in soft waves. I don't know how she does it – all that stuff with rollers and a gadget that hisses steam at you like an angry viper when you press the handle. I find the whole thing a giant mystery – and one that I'm not prepared to grapple with. Or, if I'm writing proper English: one with which I am not prepared to grapple. (I think I prefer the first way best.)

My own hair was bunged up in a sort of loop at the back. I tried to fix it so that I wouldn't have hairpins slipping down the back of my neck if I turned my head suddenly. And actually, the grey streak in the front doesn't look all that bad – you could almost say it makes me appear just a tiny bit distinguished!

When I'd finished dressing and looked in the mirror, I must say I was quite pleasantly surprised at the finished article! I don't wear much make-up but I did add an extra smudge of green eye-shadow as well as lip-gloss and mascara. There's no doubt that *Prada* shoes do a lot for your self-image too!

Cassandra appeared as I was filling my bag with the usual emergency supplies: paper hankies in case they've run out in the loo – hardly likely where we were off to – pretty hanky liberally splashed with perfume, small pencil in case I need to take down the name and number of someone interesting, comb and plastic card – very crucial to a sense of well-being!

"Mum, you can't go looking like that," she disconcertingly announced.

"Why? I thought I was looking rather good. What's wrong? Is it the dress?" I asked, in a sudden panic.

She came towards me laughing. "No, the dress is gorgeous! It's just that your hair is starting to collapse at the back."

"So soon?" I groaned, peering into the dressing-table mirror.

"Sit down and I'll see what I can do," she said firmly.

A few minutes later, she'd taken out most of the hairpins I'd jammed in and done the whole thing again.

I looked at myself in the mirror. "Wow! Thank you, Cassandra! I don't know how you did it but it looks marvellous."

She bent down and gave me a light kiss on my cheek. "You look lovely, Mum. You look like you did before you got ill."

When I looked in the mirror again, I could see what she

meant. I was still a little gaunt but I could detect a brightness in my face that had been missing for an awfully long time.

When we went downstairs, I rang the nursing home and was reassured that Mum was sleeping peacefully. There had been no change in her condition. Then we headed off, in a cloud of perfume, for the bright lights of Dublin. I can't remember when I last had that feeling of anticipation – a sort of tingly feeling that was half nervousness and half expectation – I don't know quite know what it was. Cassandra too was all bubbly and talked more than she has for months. It was lovely to see her looking so animated. I certainly noticed a lot of heads turning to look at her when we went into the foyer of the hotel.

It was obvious from the noise where the reception was being held. We made our way into the room and took our glasses of champagne from a very dashing waiter, who looked as though he should have been cavorting in front of adoring fans in a bull-ring, cape over one shoulder, rather than circulating with a drinks tray in a Dublin hotel.

There was a sudden shriek of, "Hebe!" and I caught a glimpse of a hand, frantically waving above the sea of heads. Then I saw Maggie, clothed in a very smart suit of electric blue, her halo of fair hair shining in the evening sunlight that streamed through the windows as she pushed and shoved her way through the crowd. It was like watching a determined swimmer, battling her way against a strong current that, at any moment, might sweep her off her feet, making her disappear from sight.

"You terrific woman! You made it," she said, giving me an enormous hug and then kissing me on both cheeks.

"And Cassandra too! How lovely!" She gave Cassandra a kiss as well. Then she looked us up and down approvingly. "I must say you Irishwomen certainly scrub up well! You both look absolutely smashing!" She moved closer and said in quieter voice, "How are you? Are you up for all this?"

"Perfectly! I'm feeling fine," I assured her.

"Good! Because I want you to enjoy this evening." She grabbed one of my elbows. "Come and say hello to the man himself before all the droves of photographers get their hands on him. He's looking forward to meeting you."

I caught a glimpse of Cassandra's face beside me as we surged through the throng. She was looking impressed again!

He had his back to us when we finally fought our way to the other side of the room and onto a sort of raised platform. To my horror, I realised that two of the women crowding around him were two of my least favourite. *That* sounds as though there are dozens of women I don't like. Actually, the opposite is true. I like most women rather a lot. On the whole, I find them good to be around, supportive, brave, capable and interesting. But there *are* a couple of exceptions. One is Celia Lacoste, writer *pas extraordinaire*. The other, as you've probably guessed, is my ex-mama-in-law. I suppose I shouldn't have been surprised to see them really. It happens all the time in a small place like Dublin. Decide you desperately want to avoid some one and you'll spend the next month tripping over them every time you turn a corner. As a friend of mine once remarked, "If you want to have an affair, for God's sake, don't try and hide away in an intimate hotel in the Dublin or Wicklow mountains. You're sure to bump into everyone you know if you do. Just brazen it out and book into the smartest Dublin hotel he can afford and you might just get away with it!"

I don't think I've set eyes on Celia for well over a year and to find the pair of them in the same room at my first big social engagement in I don't how long was a bit of a comedown, to put it mildly. Luckily, they were so engrossed in what Sam Ellis was saying, I spotted them before they saw me. They made me think of a couple of scrawny birds of prey with their sharp little eyes not missing a thing and their pointy beaks ready to stab to death any interesting morsel that might have the misfortune to wander in their direction. The fact that I saw them first gave me a few seconds to metaphorically gird my loins and take several deep breaths. Then, armed with metal ball covered in spikes and helmet visor well down, I put on my widest smile and joined the group, with Cassandra forming a rearguard action.

Maggie slid between the women and Sam Ellis with a deft movement.

"Sorry to interrupt, ladies, but I have someone here who I want to introduce to Mr Ellis." She gave the *ladies* a beguiling smile. "So, if you'll just excuse us for a moment."

I was aware that both Celia and Dervla were watching in sour amazement as Maggie spun him around to face me. I swear that she gave me an enormous wink as she did so.

My first impression was slight disappointment that he wasn't as tall as I'd imagined and he looked tired and, just possibly, a little bored? But, on the upside, there was something of a gypsy about him that I found immediately attractive. The long, dark hair, tied back into a ponytail, and the sallow skin, I recognised from studying the posters of him that were plastered on the walls and windows of practically every bookshop you went into at the moment. But it was his eyes that held me. They were the darkest brown, under dark eyebrows and when he caught my eye, something *went* inside me.

I've just read that bit through – and it sounds like something out of a trashy love story for schoolgirls. But, damn it! That's what happened. It was as if some sort of internal knicker-elastic gave an almighty ping, causing everything to collapse in a floppy heap on my pelvic floor! It took an immense effort on my part not to let him know what had happened, I can tell you.

"Hebe, this is Sam. Sam, Hebe and her daughter, Cassandra," murmured Maggie, smoothly, before making some sort of excuse and disappearing into the multitude again.

We stood for a moment, clutching our rapidly warming champagne, and looking at each other.

Then he raised his eyebrows slightly and gave a rather crooked smile. "In her element is our Maggie. Nothing she likes more than the roar of the crowd and the smell of success."

"Well, you've certainly been very successful, so far," I said.

"So far?" He looked suddenly amused. "That sounds as though you think I'm about to come a cropper."

I laughed, feeling clumsy. "I hadn't meant it quite like that – more that you've been successful in what you've done to date – as it were," I said, lamely.

There was a definite twinkle in his eye as he said,

"Maggie tells me that she thinks you could well outdo me in the success stakes, once you get into your stride."

That took me by surprise. "Did she really say that?"

"Yes, she said that your last book was a massive improvement on the first and that the first wasn't all that bad. That's high praise indeed from a woman who knows all about books."

"Indeed," I said. "I feel rather overcome – if it's true," I couldn't help adding suspiciously.

"You'd better learn to accept praise graciously, Hebe, especially when it's the real thing. So much of the time it's just a load of bullshit." He tilted his head a little to one side and gave me a searching look. "Do you do this sort of thing often? Do you enjoy coming to this sort of literary circus?"

"Hardly ever – and not much. On the whole, the writers I've come across are really rather ordinary. They just seem to carry more than their fair share of angst about their job than other people do and they tend to be rather too self-absorbed and oversensitive to make them relaxed company. Most of my friends have proper jobs." I stopped, embarrassed. Now he would think I was describing him as self-absorbed and oversensitive and not good company – and possibly without a proper job as well. "I didn't mean to say that *you* were like that. After all," I added, "I don't know you, do I?" I was making such a hames of it all. I could feel Cassandra twitching with frustration beside me. "This is my daughter, Cassandra," I said hastily, shoving her in front of me and quite forgetting that Maggie had already told him who she was. I thought that, perhaps, if he got talking to her, I could observe him in silence while rearranging my scattered faculties.

They shook hands and exchanged a few pleasantries. But all the time he was talking to her, I got the feeling that he was watching me out of the corner of his eye. When Maggie suddenly resurfaced and dragged her off to meet someone, he immediately turned his attention back to me, much to the chagrin of Dervla, who at that moment had tried to manoeuvre herself into his eyeline.

Taking my arm, he led me away from the posse of waiting women, towards one of the long windows overlooking St Stephen's Green.

Pointing to the window seat, he said, "Let's sit while we still can."

He signalled to the dashing waiter, who dutifully replenished our glasses. He swallowed a mouthful, watching me all the time in a way that I found unnerving.

"Do you realise that you're staring at me?" I said.

"I know! But, in that frock, you are most definitely worth staring at. It must have cost a packet. It's lovely. May I?" he asked. I nodded and he ran his fingers lightly over the end of one of the floaty sleeves. "What is it made of? It's almost weightless."

"I've no idea. I bought it especially for tonight and I've never spent as much money on a dress before in my life. I'm still feeling a bit guilty about it."

"Well, I think it was money well spent. You look really spectacular in it."

He sounded as though he meant it too!

The evening went a little downhill after those few heady minutes we spent together, perched on the window seat. But not before he had scribbled down my telephone number with a borrowed biro on the back of a paper napkin he retrieved from the floor. He was soon dragged off to have his photo taken and to be interviewed. The dinner Maggie had been hoping to arrange never materialised as she and he were being wined and dined by the bronzed boss of some film company, who wanted to talk about screenplays and contracts and other exotic-sounding stuff.

"Sorry about this, Hebe." she whispered in my ear. "It's not going as planned, I'm afraid. I'll ring you in a few days, when I'm back at my desk."

I couldn't help noticing that she didn't say anything about having good news for me.

Still, Cassandra enjoyed herself. Her dress had been much admired and she'd even been approached by someone from a modelling agency, asking if she would be interested in having some studio pictures taken. Of course, she's tickled pink by the thought.

"I can't wait to tell Keith," she said, excitedly, in the car on the way home. She also commented on the fact that I'd had Sam Ellis to myself for a full five minutes. "You should have seen the expression on Dervla's face! Bitter lemons wasn't in it. She was well put out, Mum. And that Lacoste dame you don't like, *she* looked as though she'd like to plunge a blunt dagger in between your shoulder-blades."

"Then I shall obviously have to start wearing a rucksack when I go out in future," I said, I thought rather wittily.

But Cassandra gave me one of her pitying looks. "I think you should keep off the comedy, Mum. It doesn't suit you."

"Is that in my books or in real life?" I asked, rebuked.

"Both probably." And then she laughed as though she hadn't meant it. "Don't take any notice of me. I'm just dead jealous. That Ellis bloke never took his eyes off you. Even when he was talking to me!"

At this point, if I were sixteen again, I would probably be jumping up and down, punching the air with my fist and shouting *Yes! Yes!*

I just couldn't resist the temptation of asking her what she'd thought of him.

"Did you think he was nice?" I enquired, in a casual voice.

She considered me for a moment, head on one side, a slight smile on her lips as though she was going to say something outrageous.

Instead, all she said was, "That man is drop-dead gorgeous!"

Chapter Nine

Feeling a bit strange. Can't remember the date but I know it's Thursday night because yesterday was Wednesday!

After all the euphoria of last night, I woke up this morning feeling a bit hung-over. It can't have been the drink. I only had two glasses of champagne before I moved on to the orange juice. It's more likely to be because last night was rather a shock to my system. I haven't done anything like that for so long – got dressed up and all hot and excited and all the rest of it. I suppose the way I feel now is just reality kicking back in.

The first thing I did was ring the nursing home. There's been no change.

I didn't set eyes on Cassandra until nearly one o'clock today and only then because Keith arrived to take her to some gig or other somewhere down in the depths of the country. She wasn't on particularly good form when she did appear. After some rather one-sided exchanges with me making most of the effort, they left. She was being so nice yesterday. Perhaps, seeing me sitting at the table, looking a bit bleary-eyed, brought her down to earth too. I think she doesn't know how to be at the moment. Keith looked back over his shoulder as they went out of the kitchen and rolled his eyes expressively. I couldn't help smiling. As usual, her moodiness didn't bother him one bit. He was going to enjoy the day. If she didn't, then, the choice was hers. Marvellous to be so unruffled! I think the old me was a little like that. I wonder if I'll ever be that way again.

I spent a couple of hours sitting with Mum this afternoon. She was much the same, although looking a little less like a small wraith now that they'd taken off that awful white hospital garment and put her into one of her own nightdresses. She sleeps most of the time, every now and then opening her eyes and staring around her as though she's lost. It's heartbreaking, seeing her looking like that. It doesn't seem to matter how much I talk to her or hold her or stroke her hands – I don't seem to be able to reassure her.

After the other day when I got such a shock because she wasn't in her usual place in the day room, they've promised me that, if there's any deterioration, they'll ring me, no matter what time of the day or night. Part of me dreads that phone call, but the other part wishes that it would happen soon so that it will all be finished and this awful waiting will be over. And yet, I can't imagine a world in which she won't exist. When my mum dies, I'll sort of step into her shoes and then it will be me in the front line. I hadn't thought of that before and it's a bit scary.

When I woke this morning, although I was feeling rather the worse for wear, there was also this tiny kernel of warmth inside me. The Sam Ellis factor, I suppose. I can't get over the fact that he seemed to genuinely like me. Knowing that he's asked me for my phone number boosted my morale no end. But when I'd woken up a bit more and focussed my brain and eyes, I had to accept that the likelihood of him having the time, let alone the inclination, to actually get in touch was, at best, remote. And then, as soon as I was up and dressed, my thoughts were full of Mum.

I didn't think about him again until much later in the day when I'd got home and was sitting down having a cuddle with Busby, who wasn't going to be refused. He really is the limit. When he wants attention, he stalks me in such a single-minded fashion. And he doesn't give up staring and stalking until I give in, stop whatever I'm doing and pick him up. Then he goes into overdrive and does his demented loving bit. It's rather uncomfortable, wearing a fur collar when it's as hot as it was today! But I know I'd miss him dreadfully if he weren't around! And it's very comforting having an animal that's warm and purrs as it snuggles up to you. It's remarkable that, after leaving him to Cassandra's tender mercies all the time I was in the clinic, he didn't become highly offended and give me the cold shoulder when I came home again!

Owen rang this afternoon to ask after Mum. He always sounds very distant and business-like on the phone so that even when he's inquiring about her, he makes it sound as though he's asking about some dodgy shares that aren't performing too well and really he's just anxious about the state of the stock market.

"And how are you managing?" he said, when I filled him in about how she was.

"I'm doing all right," I said. I've always tried to sound as cheerful and positive as possible on the few occasions that he gets around to asking me that. It's especially important after what's happened to me over the last year. I don't want him thinking that I'm not coping properly. He'd only tell his mother and then she'd be at him to do something about me before I become a danger to myself and others *again*. "How are things with you?"

"Fine, fine," he replied quickly. He hesitated and then added, "Lucy wants to know if you and Cassandra would come to dinner on Wednesday next week, if you're free."

"Oh!" I said, rather dumbly. But *that* bright suggestion came out of nowhere like a Scud missile on a sunny day. "Why on earth would she want to do that?" I couldn't stop myself. I mean, *really!* He knows perfectly well that Cassandra has a major problem over the Lucy thing. I don't know the girl, having only seen her from a distance, filling up with petrol as I drove past the local garage. Cassandra, who was with me, went into overdrive at the sight. And he wants us to go and have dinner with them?

"I knew you wouldn't want to," he said, rather snappily.

"Well, do *you* want us to come? Don't you think it might be a little . . . awkward?"

"Hebe, Lucy is an extremely sweet girl and she wouldn't have asked you unless she really wanted to meet you and see Cassandra again. There's no hidden agenda here, no ulterior motive – just a thoroughly friendly gesture, that's all. But if you want to read something sinister into it, then perhaps, we should just leave it." He sounded thoroughly irritated.

"Sorry! Of course, I've nothing against the idea of

meeting Lucy. But, Owen, you know that Cassandra finds the whole situation very difficult."

"It's time Cassandra stopped behaving like a spoiled brat and got on with her life. And let me get on with mine," he said, testily.

"But, come off it! Lucy and she are practically the same age! Surely you can see that she finds that a little difficult to deal with."

"I don't see how age has got anything to do with it. She's just jealous that she doesn't have my full attention every time she sees me."

"So, if Cassandra leaped into bed or started living with a man who was the same age as you, you'd have no qualms?" Definite ace! Thirty-fifteen, I thought to myself when I heard the silence from the other end of the phone.

Then he lobbed one back. "Don't be absurd, Hebe. That's hardly likely to happen and if it did it's not the same thing at all."

"How come?"

"What do you mean, *how come?*"

"I'm genuinely interested in understanding the logic – or rather the lack of it – in your argument."

"Look, I'm not going to waste time explaining it all to you. You're just being obtuse. Do you want to come to bloody dinner, or not?"

I had to take myself in hand at that point. It's a good thing neither of us owns one of these super-phone gadgets that allow you to see the person you're talking to! After making a few violent throat-slitting gestures in mid-air, I steadied my voice and tried my best to sound reasonably sane – or sanely reasonable. Take your pick!

"Why don't you leave it with me and I'll mention it to Cassandra when she gets back. Or I'll have a word with her tomorrow. She'll probably be late getting in tonight."

"Why? Where is she?" His tone implied that he thought I'd probably allowed her to go somewhere she shouldn't.

When he reacts like that, there is always the same, unsaid accusation mixed in with the spoken words. If I'd kept better control of Pandora, she could still be alive. When I confronted him once about it, he denied laying any blame on my shoulders – but I'm pretty sure that's how he feels.

"She's perfectly safe. She's with Keith at a concert down in . . . Cork." That sounded better than a gig down in the middle of goodness knows where. And she *was* safe with Keith. At least that bit was true. I'd trust that young man with my life. I just know he wouldn't do anything that would mean Cassandra came to harm. Owen doesn't like the fact that he's a musician. He thinks that he's not the right sort of young man for his daughter. He hasn't realised yet that it doesn't matter that Keith sometimes has to go on the dole. I doubt if he'll ever cotton on to the fact that he is just the sort of funny, reliable, intelligent person his daughter needs to be around.

"Well, get back to me tomorrow about it. I don't want Lucy kept hanging around, wondering if you are or aren't coming." He rang off, after a mumbled, "Have to go."

How did I ever fall in love with that man? There's no graciousness, no gentleness in him and his manners leave a lot to be desired – even if his mother thinks the sun shines out of not just one orifice but the whole bloody lot of them. My falling for her son must have been just another case of sheer lust, combined with the misguided notion that he would give my life direction and purpose and there was nothing we couldn't achieve, working as a team – caring, sharing and supportive into our dotage. Sad that I got it so wrong.

I suppose one good thing about a typical phone conversation with my ex is that I get so cross. It's splendid cardio-vascular exercise! I'm sure my blood pressure goes up and my heart-rate increases. It must get all the old corpuscles circulating at high speed. Come to think of it, I suppose it's really quite energising!

When I'd got off the phone, I wondered if Owen's unexpected invitation stemmed from an idea to try and improve things between Cassandra and himself. Or was it Lucy who was attempting to do some bridge-building? I can't say that I'm particularly looking forward to relaying the invitation to Cassandra. Although, what her father said about getting on with her life and letting him do the same sounded a bit brutal, it's true. Isn't that what I'm trying to do myself? So, what is the point of not giving Lucy the benefit of the doubt? Surely, lack of graciousness is one of the things I accuse Owen of. Aren't I just as guilty? Oh, if only life were more simple. Or is it just that humans can't resist buggering it all up and that there *is* a divine plan, which would work just fine if we only let it? What was that silly but apt rhyme I learned years ago? Something along the lines of:

God's plan had a hopeful beginning
Till man spoilt it all by his sinning.
They tell me God's story
Will all end in glory
But, at present, the other side's winning.

I like that!

I took the car down to Wicklow after tea and went for a long walk along the beach at Kilcoole and watched the geese on the marshy land on the far side of the railway track. It's rather like being on the other side of the perimeter fence at an airport and watching the planes land and take off. You can tell the old pros from the learner drivers. Arctic terns were swooping over the water's edge and there was a scattering of sandwich-munching fishermen, sitting on camping stools beside their fishing lines. I wonder if they ever catch anything? I've never seen anyone jumping up and down, waving a fish in the air.

I used to go down there a lot after Owen and I first separated. You don't meet all that many people once you get away from the families clustered near to the entrance to the beach – just the odd nice dog with its doggy owner, who usually greets you with a cheerful smile as they stride past – the owner, not the dog. They just sniff and wag.

I walked for a long time, thinking, trying to sort out my thoughts. At one point, feeling tired, I sat down on the shingle beach and watched the light change on the water as the clouds came and went. I love watching the sea. I love its smell and the magic sound it makes. I was miles away, brain in neutral, when I suddenly realised I was only a few feet away from a pair of bulbous brown eyes and some rather splendid whiskers. The seal watched me for a few seconds and then, obviously unimpressed, it resubmerged as silently as it had surfaced.

By the time I got back to where I'd parked the car, half buried in a hedge, heavy with blackberries, I found that everyone else had gone home. Hardly surprising as it was beginning to get dark. I leaned against the bonnet and helped myself to the berries, taking care to shake off the odd creepy crawly. Once you've ended up with half a maggot in your mouth, it makes you wary of repeating the experience! The blackberries were extremely juicy and tasted delicious. I ended up with my fingers stained purple and a matching splodge on the front of my shirt. As I got back into the car, I found myself thinking of how, when I was pregnant with Cassandra and Pandora, I'd always seem to manage to splash things on the bump – much to the disgust of Dervla. I can still remember the pain in her eyes after she'd noticed the splodges of chocolate ice cream adorning my front!

I'm glad I went to Kilcoole. It was very quiet there, with just the faint sound of the waves and I felt content and peaceful. I hadn't made any remarkable decisions or discoveries during my walking and thinking but it had done me good all the same. I've noticed that, as each day goes by, I'm feeling less tired – and that's good too.

Before I came to bed tonight, I sat down at my computer and opened a file and stared at the screen. I had got about a third of the way through novel number three when Pandora died. I started reading it from the beginning but it left me cold. The story is based around two people, who seem to have a real vocation for the work they are doing but who fall in love and the love is so all-consuming and obsessive that they lose interest in their jobs and lose their way emotionally and spiritually. The original idea had been to do a sort of modern version of the Abelard-Héloïse story. It sounds an utterly daft idea now. I don't know how I thought of it or even how I imagined I could do anything with it. My second novel had left me feeling a little panicky. Maggie, everyone, said it was so much better than the first and they all seemed to be expecting even better from the next one. If I was worried about delivering then, that's nothing to the way I feel about writing *anything* at the moment – anything the least bit worthwhile, that is. It hadn't occurred to me until just now that, as I'm back home, I could be using the computer to write my progress notes but there's something nice about writing it all down on a pad with a good, sharp pencil.

So, as I sit here in bed with my exercise book on my knees, I'm doing my best to convince myself to keep calm and not to behave like a neurotic writer, suicidal because of a prolonged attack of writer's block. (The sort of sad individual I mentioned to Sam Ellis when I was falling over my words the other evening!) I tell myself that I *will* write again when I'm ready; that the time isn't right. I know that I couldn't get involved in starting anything new at the moment. There's Mum and Cassandra and Joan's coming tomorrow to help – and I want to get the garden looking more like it should.

I was going to include Sam Ellis in my list but that's just me being silly. I checked the answering machine when I got home this evening – twice. Not a dicky bird.

* * *

Next day.

My conversation with Cassandra after breakfast this morning went something like this:

Me: "Dad suggested that you and I go and have supper with him some night next week."

Her: "Not a chance in hell – especially if that blonde bimbo is going to be there."

Me: "You might as well accept the fact that she exists and, unless you want to lose touch with your father completely, you might as well make the best of it and be pleasant. You never know, she may only be a passing fancy," I tacked on the end, hoping that might cheer her up and take the stubborn look off her face.

But it didn't.

Instead, she rounded on me. "Why are you taking her side all of a sudden? I thought you didn't approve of her either."

"I'm trying extremely hard not to take any sides. I haven't met the poor girl, Cassandra. It seems to me to be rather unfair that you've taken against her purely on the grounds of age. You get furious if people judge you without giving you a chance first. Has she, at any point, done or said anything unkind or spiteful to you?" She looked taken-aback and then there was a mutinous silence. "Come on! Be honest. Has she?"

The "No!" sounded somewhat constipated. (The opposite of verbal diarrhoea, I suppose.) "But that's not the point," she muttered angrily.

"You sound just like your father," I said, remembering my conversation with him on the previous day.

That really annoyed her. "I do *not!* I'm not one bit like him."

"Yes, you do! When he hasn't got a leg to stand on and knows quite well he's being unreasonable, he always pretends that *I'm* 'missing the point'."

That silenced her for a good few moments.

One of Cassandra's nicer qualities is that, however furious she gets during an argument and however unreasonable, afterwards she does go away and think about what's been said.

So, I wasn't all that surprised when she followed me outside into the garden after lunch. "I was thinking about what you'd said, Mum. If you think we should go, I'll go. But I just want you to know that it's not going to be easy and I'm doing it for you, not him."

I gave her a hug. "You know, I think you can probably help make the occasion easy by just relaxing and not looking for difficulties. Remember what I said about being more gentle? You wait and see; it won't be nearly as bad as you think."

She raised her eyebrows and gave me an unconvinced look. "You reckon?"

"I do," I said, firmly.

She shook her head as if there were no point in even trying to explain to me what was so awful about going. "OK, Mum! I can't wait!" she said, with heavy sarcasm.

"I just hope that we can *both* be pleasant and reasonable and that the evening won't be too awful," I said, with a cheerfulness I didn't feel.

Owen sounded quite surprised when I rang him and told him that she had agreed to come.

So, now there's an entry on the kitchen calendar for next Wednesday night at eight o'clock. Help!

* * *

Late, Saturday night.

I was just getting myself organised to go to the nursing

home when the phone rang. Cassandra picked it up, listened for a couple of seconds and then turned towards me, while doing a sort of crazy semaphore, pointing at the receiver and mouthing, "It's him! It's him!"

"Who?" I mouthed back.

She thrust the phone into my hand. "It's *Sam Ellis*," she whispered in an excited voice.

For a moment, I was completely taken by surprise. I almost had to think who Sam Ellis was. I was aware of Cassandra, standing inches from my elbow, obviously with the intention of listening into the ensuing conversation. But I needed to calm my thoughts and I didn't want to sound like an idiotic, flustered female, whose prayers had just been answered. And I most certainly didn't want an audience.

With a hand over the receiver, I flapped the other one at her. "Go away," I hissed.

Reluctantly, she wandered out of the room, moving in slow motion and leaving the door open behind her.

I counted to ten before speaking. "Hello?" I said, as casually as I could.

"Hello, Hebe." His voice sounded good – not BBC 4 exactly but quietly cultured – and in strange contrast to his rather gypsy looks. "I hope I haven't caught you at a bad time?"

"No," I said. "Perfect timing in fact. Another five minutes and you would have missed me." I wasn't going to go into an explanation about where I was going in five minutes' time. Keep it simple, I told myself.

"I enjoyed meeting you the other evening." There was the slightest of pauses and then he continued, "I wondered if you would mind if I dropped in to see you later on today."

"I thought you were going back to London today."

"I decided to stay on. I don't know Ireland at all and book signings and interviews take up so much time, there's none left for anything more than a quick glimpse. And I like what little I've seen so I'm not flying back until next Thursday."

"Oh, I see."

"Look, if it's not convenient, that's fine."

I gave myself an almighty mental shake. What was I doing? "No, that would be lovely if you dropped in. What sort of time were you thinking of?"

"How about after supper? Nine? Half past nine?"

"Nine would be fine," I mumbled – at the same time thinking that, at least I wouldn't have to cook him anything to eat.

I gave him directions on how to find the house and we said goodbye. When I put down the phone, Cassandra emerged almost immediately from the shadows.

"Were you listening?"

"Yes, I was. And, Mum, you were *pathetic!* I thought you liked him."

"I do!" I retorted, stung. "What do you mean, I was pathetic?"

She lifted both hands in a gesture of hopelessness. "You made it sound as though you wished he hadn't asked if he could come round to see you. Like you'd have preferred to spend an evening having red hot needles stuck in your eyeballs."

"Was it that bad?"

"Yes!" she said, with an emphatic nod. "It most definitely was."

I sat down on one of the kitchen stools with a thump. "Oh, dear! I didn't mean to be offhand with him. It's just that he took me by surprise."

"Well, you'd better be nice to him when he does come. You won't get another chance. Men like him don't hang around if they feel they're not wanted."

"Is that right?"

"Mum! He's gorgeous and famous and –"

"Stop right there!" I said, holding up a hand. "Don't try and make something out of this that isn't there. We enjoyed talking to each other the other evening and he's at a loose end and probably just wants the opportunity to get away from all the publicity so he's using us as a bolthole for a few hours before he takes off to do a spot of sightseeing. That's all! And I don't need you making a grand production out of it. So, this evening, I suggest you go out with your mates and leave us to have a cold beer or a cup of coffee, or whatever the man wants, in peace."

She shrugged. "Well, I just hope you do better than you did just now, that's all I can say." I gave her a warning look.

"OK! I'm going," she said, exiting the room swiftly.

Chapter Ten

Sunday 4th October. It was well after midnight by the time I crawled into bed. I was too exhausted last night to finish writing up my day, which is why I'm doing it the following morning, sitting up in bed with Busby watching me from the windowsill with a sort of 'shall I, shan't I' look on his face. I know that look. He's wondering if I'm in the right frame of mind for an early morning cuddle.

Sam arrived at nine on the dot yesterday evening. I don't know why but his punctuality surprised me. Probably because my time-keeping is generally crap, as Cassandra would point out with her usual delicacy. I managed to get her out of the house before he got here. She used all possible delaying tactics that she could think of, including deciding, at the last minute, that she wasn't happy with what she was wearing. This necessitated a complete change of wardrobe, even a different hair style. She eventually left at ten to nine and I wouldn't put it past her to have lurked in the bushes in the front garden, mounting a lookout. But at least she was being cheerfully and pleasantly slow-motion. I get the feeling that she's more pleased than she's letting on about Sam Ellis wanting to visit her mother!

When the doorbell rang, I have to admit that I was feeling incredibly nervous. As I made my way to the front door, I found myself wondering if I shouldn't have taken a little more trouble with my own appearance. I'd not wanted it to seem as if I had tried to look especially smart, so I had gone for the understated look. But perhaps I shouldn't have left my hair a bit wild after a last-minute blow-dry, on top of jeans and a loose white shirt and bare feet (it's still hot – even though we're into October). As I grasped the door handle, I was aware that I probably looked really rather scruffy. Comfortable, yes. Attractive, not really.

When I opened the door and saw him standing there, a bottle of wine under one arm and a paper bag in his hand, my insides started to do funny things. It felt as though my internal organs were in the process of rearranging themselves. He looked browner and darker and more gypsy-like than ever in his open-necked terracotta-coloured shirt and faded jeans. He had a cream-coloured sweater tied loosely around his shoulders and I couldn't help noticing that he was wearing a pair of creamy-coloured leather moccasins that looked extremely expensive. But his feet were bare inside them. He smelled good too.

The taxi that had just delivered him drove off as I let him in. I realise now that I must have looked catatonic, staring at him without saying more than a rather mumbled 'Hello'. But, thinking back, I find it reassuring that he too was looking at me in a somewhat similar fashion – taking me in as if he were reassuring himself that I was the same person he'd talked to two nights earlier. (A sort of ball-gown to rags scenario – rather like Cinderella in reverse!) The difference being that I'm sure he wasn't as bowled over at what he saw as I was. Jeans and bare feet could be considered quite a comedown after long, dangly earrings and diaphanous evening wear in hectic colours! There was something about him that was so compelling, attractive . . . I don't know. Perhaps it's just my hormones out of control. I'd forgotten I had any. His pheromones, or whatever he exudes, have a serious effect on me. Or is it only randy moths that secrete those? Perhaps it's testosterones. Whatever it is, it's deadly dangerous.

"Do you like olives?" he asked as we walked towards the kitchen.

"Yes, if they're not salty," I said, immediately wondering why his being so attractive seemed to have the result of making me the verbal equivalent of a cavewoman. I'd be grunting my responses next if I weren't careful.

"Well, I think you'll approve of these. They're black and meaty and not one bit salty. I got them in Temple Bar this morning. Do you have a dish I can tip them into?"

Without thinking, I handed him a small saucepan that happened to be sitting on the draining-board and, without batting an eyelid, he decanted the olives into it. Definite brownie point! After my initial few minutes of cretinosity, I settled down and, by the time we'd taken our wine out into the garden, I was starting to behave like a normal human being. I think.

I was glad that I'd worked so hard to make the garden look better. I'd put the backdoor light on so that it shone out over the 'terrace' (all six square feet of it). The lavender bushes were doing their bit and so were the late roses. In fact, their evening scent was heavenly. He noticed it too.

He stood for a moment, taking it all in and then he suddenly tipped his head back and sniffed in the air. I couldn't help noticing how brown and smooth the skin at the base of his neck looked.

"What a lovely smell! It's almost like being in the Mediterranean." He pointed to the rather tatty cordyline at the corner of the house. "Very exotic! I didn't think they grew west of Bognor!"

Then we sat down and we started talking. We finished the bottle of wine and the olives – which were indeed meaty and delicious and not one bit salty. I got out some bread and cheese and we opened another bottle. And we went on talking. We discussed topics from families to good places to go on holiday, the theatre and what films we liked – and dozens of other things besides. It was *so* nice to be around an interesting, interested adult, who was a good listener as well as a thoroughly entertaining raconteur. I enjoyed his rather dry sense of humour and his refusal to accept the sham or trite aspects of being a celebrity. But most of all, I was drawn by a feeling that he cared deeply about things. He didn't make observations that you felt he'd culled from someone else. It was obvious that he'd made his own mind up about Tony Blair (or Tony Blur as he called him) or George W or the Palestinian-Israeli war or fundamentalist Muslims or how the West treats the countries of the Third World.

I've been grappling for so long with my own internal world and my immediate family that I feel appallingly ill-informed and out of touch with a lot of what is going on. But not for a moment did he patronise or monologue in that way so many men do – leaving you feeling that they are being extraordinarily kind to impart their wisdom, which ignorant little you should lap up and for which you should be undyingly grateful.

He told me about his mother, dying five years earlier and how it had knocked him off his feet and how, with no communication with his ex-wife, he still missed picking up the phone to ring her and tell her what he was doing when something good happened for him with his writing. I told him quite a bit about Mum and he was sympathetic, asking non-intrusive and sensitive questions and seeming to understand the mix of emotions I am feeling at the moment about our relationship. I began to understand why the female characters in his books are so rounded and real. He really listens.

I don't know how much Maggie has told him about me. She's pretty discreet, on the whole. I didn't mention my incarceration in the clinic and I didn't tell him about Pandora. I just felt it wouldn't have been appropriate. Even though we were getting on so well and seemed to feel a similar sense of accord with each other, somehow, that was something I wanted left to one side and kept private – for the time being anyway. Does that mean that I'm not doing as well as I thought? *Should* I be able to talk about my lovely daughter, who died when she was only nineteen, taking a part of me with her? All I know is, it still takes a lot of effort to accept that she won't ever come back, that I'll never see her again or feel that sensation of brightness that she carried around with her so that, even if you'd been feeling down, you suddenly felt cheerful again. And anyway, Sam Ellis is still pretty much an unknown quantity. I hardly dare believe that he is as nice as he appears to be after only two meetings.

Busby took an immediate shine to him. When, only ten minutes after us sitting down, he landed with a thud in Sam's lap and made a move to climb up his shirt, I offered to take him.

"No, he's fine. I like cats." A few minutes later, with Busby's paws on either side of his neck, giving an affectionate if rather manic chin-rub with his head, Sam burst into laughter. "What an extraordinary animal! Does he usually carry on like this?"

"If you let him, he'd be at it all day long. I've never met a cat who needed cuddling so badly."

"Perhaps he was ignored as a kitten and he grew up feeling that his mother didn't love him," he joked, stroking Busby along the ridge of his spine so that the lunatic cat's purrs took on a sort of three-dimensional sound – like the thing they run in the cinema before the main feature – to illustrate the *Dolby* surround-sound effect.

We were still talking when Cassandra reappeared. She looked surprised to see us sitting there, a bottle and a half drunk dry and Sam draped in the Great Busby.

Her arrival prompted Sam to get cautiously to his feet and squint sideways at his watch as he tried not to drop the cat.

"Blimey! I didn't realise how late it was. I must go." He turned to Cassandra. "Would you mind off-loading this mad creature for me?" When the reluctant cat had been deposited in a chair, Sam asked if he could ring for a taxi.

"Where are you staying?" I asked him.

"The Shelbourne."

"Oh, I'll run you back. It won't take more than twenty minutes at this time of night."

"Are you sure? I can easily get a taxi."

"It's no problem," I insisted. "I'll just go and get my shoes."

I knew that Cassandra was looking at me oddly. Taking care not to catch her eye, I left the two of them there while I went for a much-needed pee and my shoes. (And a quick squirt of perfume. Well, it was hot and I didn't want to seem sweaty as well as crumpled, did I?)

In fact, the journey seemed to be over almost before it began. When I drew up outside the hotel, he leaned over and gave me a kiss on the side of my cheek. His lips were warm.

"I really enjoyed this evening. Can I see you tomorrow?"

I felt weak with relief. I think that if he hadn't asked me that and I'd had to come back home, not knowing if I would ever see him again, I would have expired in a puddle of sheer desperation and desolation.

Blasé went out of the window. Without even *trying* to sound as though I were surprised that he'd asked, I immediately said that it would be very nice.

"I know that you want to see something of Ireland," I added. "How about if I pick you up after I've visited Mum, say twelve-ish? We could go out to Glendalough."

"Is there somewhere nice there where we can eat?" he asked. "I'd like to take you out to lunch."

"I'm sure there is," I said, at the same time racking my brains, trying to remember where the best place was.

I drove home in a cloud of happiness – to be met by Cassandra, now in nightgear. She was still wearing her quizzical, you-can't-be-serious look.

"Well?" she asked casually.

"Well what?"

"Did he kiss you goodnight?"

I tried fixing her with my most unapproachable stare. "We are not going to have a post mortem of my evening."

"I don't know why not. There's nothing you like better than dissecting *my* evenings out."

Sometimes she's just too smart for her own good, that one!

I couldn't help laughing. "Let's just say that I can't remember enjoying talking to anyone as much in a long time. And, yes, he kissed me politely – and chastely – on the cheek when we said goodbye. Happy now?"

"Hmm!" was all I got for my efforts.

"Why are you still looking at me like that?" I asked.

"Mr Ellis must have had quite an effect on you, Mum."

"What do mean?"

"Have you ever heard the term 'drink driving'? You must have been over the limit but you disappeared off into the night before I realised how much you'd had."

I suddenly felt cold. This was just the sort of thing I would have warned her about – and been furious over if she'd done what I just had. How could I have been so irresponsible? I was behaving like a delinquent teenager, letting myself get so bowled over by a man that the rules had gone out of the window.

She must have seen the look of alarm in my face because she came over and laid her hand on my arm for a moment. "Don't look so upset, Mum. He probably drank more than you did and you didn't sound or look the least bit drunk."

"That's hardly the point, is it?" I replied, shamefaced.

I was pretty sure that I'd not had more than three glasses of wine but they had been fairly large glasses. I couldn't remember how many points you were allowed before you were over the limit, neither could I remember how many points there were in each glass.

She did her best to convince me that I wasn't a witless criminal, before giving me a kiss and disappearing off to bed. As I sat, drinking a very small glass of whiskey, I wondered why Sam hadn't turned down my offer of a lift. They had the points system in England, I was pretty sure. On the other hand, perhaps I'd had an effect on him too and he wasn't thinking straight either.

* * *

Next day, late.

I realise that I've been writing more now about what I'm physically doing rather than grinding on about my thoughts. Not as many moans either, which can't be bad! If I ever make the time to read all this through from start to finish, no doubt I'll be covered in embarrassment. But then, I suppose that, basically, most people's lives are not so very different from mine, now that I'm home again. Most of us live lives filled with all the hundreds of unremarkable, necessary, daily tasks we perform, almost without thinking.

Something Sam said yesterday has been resonating at the back of my mind. He said that he didn't believe in God but he believed the spirit could live on. He said that was

173

the only way he could explain the feeling of his mother's presence during the first weeks after her death. That has made me ask myself – yet again – what it is I really believe. The trouble is that I'm still not sure. All I know is that, when Pandora died, I never felt the slightest sense of her being around me or anywhere nearby. I didn't feel close to her when I visited her grave or, on the few occasions when I went into her, still untouched, bedroom. When I was in that room, the only sensation I had was one of unspeakable sadness and regret that it couldn't have turned out differently. Sam said that he found the experience comforting. I don't know if I would. I think I might find it more disconcerting than anything else. I wouldn't like to think of her still being a wandering presence in this world. I want her spirit – if there is such a thing – at rest and to be at peace.

I went and saw Mum straight after breakfast. I do think that she's being well looked after – considering that they say they're impossibly short-staffed. They had just finished turning her and rubbing her back with something that stops her getting pressure sores. A couple of nurses were with her when I arrived. I caught a glimpse of one of my mother's slim, white thighs. The skin looked so smooth and, well, so surprisingly young. I found myself looking quickly away. I knew she wasn't even aware of my being in the room but I also knew how she would hate it if she knew I could see her like that, with her nightdress hitched up. I went over to the window and waited until they'd finished.

When they'd left the room, I got out the hand cream and started to gently massage one of her hands. It's become a sort of ritual. The scent of roses helps to mask the nursing home smell of old age and disinfectant and floor polish. I spend a long time on her hands. She doesn't seem to mind and it helps me to feel that I'm doing something – even if it's small. When I've finished her hands, I put the lip-balm on her lips and dab a little lavender water on her forehead and behind her ears. Then I comb her hair. After that I sit beside her, sometimes just lightly holding her hand, sometimes talking; still hoping that some of what I'm saying is getting through to her. The nurses come and go and the shaft of sunlight that falls across the foot of her bed from the long window creeps onto the polished floor and lights up a rectangle of wall beside the door. The room is very quiet. Sometimes I find myself going into an almost trance-like state where time stands still.

When it's time for me to leave, I don't kiss her goodbye. She didn't like me being demonstrative when she was well so I feel I should respect the fact that she almost certainly wouldn't want me to start kissing her now. It's one of my regrets that it should be like that.

Driving out through the nursing-home gates, I'm struck by what a very separate, other world it is in there with its elderly, sick and dying inhabitants. Each time I emerge, I feel a sense of relief that I can go back into the real world again, immensely grateful that it isn't my lot to remain there. It always takes me some time to adapt back into this other dimension. It's not that I want to stop myself from thinking about my mother, lying in that hospital bed with so little time left to her. It's that, to become positive about my life and to do the things that need doing, I need to be different from the way I am when I'm with her. I suppose that makes sense.

Cassandra went into town to meet some of her friends

from college. She's putting off visiting her grandmother again and I know she feels guilty about it, even though I've told her I understand. But she does have a genuine reason to go into Dublin today. University life grinds into action in a few days so she has some sorting out which of her room-mates will bring what in the way of furniture and extras to make their rooms more comfortable for the coming term.

I don't know if she'll stick at this Media Studies course of hers. She did well enough in her first end-of-year exams but I sometimes get the feeling that she's not all that pushed about it and wouldn't mind switching to something else. It's just that she hasn't really got a notion what that something else might be. Keith says that she has a lovely singing voice and that it's not too late to do something about having some lessons. (That's another thing she and Pandora shared but it was usually Pandora who won the prizes because she put in the work.) I suspect that Cassandra might find the grind of daily *vocalises* a little trying. Come to that, so might I! But, on the other hand, I'd be more than happy to put up with them if she were really enthusiastic. I suspect that she's hoping that something will come of the photos she plans to have taken (a result of her discussion with one of the photographers at the Shelbourne the other night). I'm not so sure that a modelling career would be the right thing for her but I daren't even hint that I think that or she'll immediately move to Milan and sign on with some agency. I keep getting the feeling that she's unsure about a lot of things at the moment although we seem to be closer than we've been for a long time. Every now and then, I catch her watching me with a kind of undecided expression. I don't know whether it's because she's still waiting for me to show that I'm not really on the mend or if it's because she can't make her mind up about how much she wants me to know about what's going on in her mind – how she is *really* feeling.

I've just realised that one of the things that's changed since her sister died is that she isn't as self-confident as she used to be. She's lost some spark, some intangible ingredient she used to possess that made her rave about a project she was involved in or some idea she'd just had. Before, she couldn't wait to get stuck in. Now, that's not there any more. She and I are getting on so much better but there's still that slight reserve in her, as though she doesn't completely trust me. I keep asking myself, is that because of my illness? Or my part in the argument with Pandora? And, although she's agreed to this dinner at Owen's on Wednesday, she doesn't seem to want to spend any time in his company. On the few occasions that he rings, she'll usually make a face and hand the receiver to me immediately she hears his voice. It's as if she doesn't want to spend time on him – as if she doesn't take him seriously any more. I've tried remonstrating with her over this but she gets so icy and difficult, it's easier not to make too big a fuss over it. She refuses to discuss it with me. I've tried all sorts of different approaches. Nothing works. I just hope that she'll get over whatever it is that's bothering her. I would like to see her getting on with her dad again. Daughters need their fathers. Almost as much, I suspect, as fathers need their daughters' love and respect.

* * *

It was a shame that the weather decided to break just as

Sam and I set off from Dublin for the Wicklow Mountains. A shame in a minor way only. I've always thought that Glendalough was at its most magic when the skies are a bubbling cauldron, full of racing clouds, and the lake is dark one minute, silver bright the next. I love the way the lake-walk snakes along the side of the water, through tall pines with the odd squirrel suddenly darting from branch to branch. Your footsteps are cushioned by decades of fallen pine needles so that you move almost noiselessly along the water's edge.

Sam was spellbound by the place. He inspected the ruined churches and round tower with interest, running his hands over the old stone crosses with their ancient Celtic designs, doing his best to decipher the weatherworn script.

"Can you imagine what this place was like in the twelfth century with hundreds of mud and wattle huts and a thriving university?" he said, in an awed voice. "I can just see it."

In a sudden attack of not wanting to get too carried away, (which I must have inherited from my mother) I replied, "Yes, with the valley being regularly plundered by bloodthirsty Vikings, while the monks all scarpered into the tower, dragging their ladder up behind them, leaving the rest of the poor peasants to have their throats slit. It must have been really lovely."

"*Did* that happen?" he asked.

"Yes. Don't tell me you're surprised. Nothing's changed. Well, I haven't noticed too many bloodthirsty Vikings around lately but we do have more than our fair share of dodgy politicians, clutching brown-paper bags instead of spears – and the Catholic Church still protects its own first –

however bad the ensuing publicity."

"I gather from your tone that you are somewhat disenchanted with Mother Church."

"Not just the Catholic one. Pretty much all of them. In the past, it was a way of controlling the ignorant populace. They're having trouble, now that people are better educated and won't kowtow. They don't like it and instead of reforming, they're just withdrawing, while spewing out the same old dogmas."

"Good Lord!" said Sam, looking surprised. "And I thought you liked living here."

"I *do*. And this place is especially moving. It's extraordinary, but every time I come here, it's different from the time before. I've been here on days when there isn't a cloud in the sky and the sun glints on strands of floating spiders' webs, drifting over the water. I've been here when it's under a blanket of snow and the place is covered in a frosted maze of fox and deer tracks. Quite often, I've been the only person here on a day when there's not the slightest breath of wind and the silence is like a roar at the edge of your hearing. I find myself searching for new words to try and describe what I see. I've spent ages here at odd times, looking for a fresh, different way of saying what it's like." I laughed, realising that I had got somewhat carried away.

Sam gave me a sudden, intense look. "I see now why you had to be a writer."

"Why? Because I get all wordy at the sight of something beautiful?"

"No. Because you look and you feel and a lot of people don't make the time to do that. And they should. It's important." He smiled. "You were 'giving out' – I think that's the correct expression – about the Church. Don't stop!"

"Forget Christianity for a moment. There's a more ancient magic in a place like Glendalough that makes it so very special. A magic that goes back long before that misogynist St Kevin and his merry band of followers arrived on the scene."

Sam looked interested. "*Was* there someone called St Kevin? I always thought Kevin was just one of those silly names that the Brits sniggered at on the telly."

"Oh, yes. And it is said that some poor woman followed him up to his mountain hide-away in a cliff overlooking the lake and he was so miffed that she'd tracked him down he pushed her in. How's that for Christian good manners?"

"Not too hot! Although, mind you, there has been the odd occasion since I became better known when I might have been tempted to copy him. That's if there'd been a lake handy."

"I meant to ask you about that. I noticed the coven surrounding you at the Shelbourne gig. Do women always behave like that when you appear in public?"

"Not always," he grinned. "I met this lady just a few days ago, who was refreshingly underwhelmed by all my star qualities."

"Oh, really! And what might those be?"

"I can't think of a single one at this precise moment."

We both laughed.

And that was how the rest of the day was – relaxed, pleasant and good-humoured. We had a delicious meal in The Roundwood Inn before making our way back to Dublin through the mountains.

I left him with a mutual kiss on the cheek, promising to

meet the next day.

"Are you sure that I'm not being a pest?" he asked, leaning into the car. "I wouldn't want you to think that I'm taking up too much of your time."

"Well, to be honest, it's a bit of a bore – on a par with changing loo rolls and unplugging blocked sinks but I think I can just about cope. And I did get the impression that Maggie would be terribly disappointed if I didn't do my stuff and entertain you properly. She's a good friend and I wouldn't want to let her down."

"That's all right then," he said, shutting the door. "I'll ring you tomorrow morning!"

As I drove off, I realised that both of us were wearing silly grins – as if we'd just been engaged in the most incredibly witty, sophisticated repartee of our lives. And that just goes to prove that most adults don't grow up at all. Which, when you think about it, is really rather nice.

Chapter Eleven

Late on Tuesday night.

I will never forget today. It was one of those days when everything came together and was perfect. I was woken by the phone.

"So what have you got planned for us?" asked Sam.

"I don't know yet. What time is it?" I croaked, squinting at the bedside clock.

"Do you mean to tell me you're not up? I've just had my morning constitutional. I wandered downtown to see your famous Dublin spire. And most impressive it is too! It's a heavenly day – all mist and early morning sun and the smell of autumn in the air. It's eight o'clock, by the way."

"Oh, God! Just let me get my brains in gear and I'll ring you back in twenty minutes when I've had a shower and I know which way is up," I said.

Amazingly, Cassandra was in the kitchen when I went downstairs. She looked up from rummaging through a pile of recently tumble-dried clothes, heaped on the kitchen table.

"I can't find any clean knickers but I did find this." She handed me my mobile phone.

"Where was it?" I asked her.

"In with the washing," replied Cassandra, as though that were quite normal.

I suppose, in a house where I'm quite likely to track down writing paper in the larder or my bag in the cupboard where the Hoover is kept, I shouldn't be too surprised.

She picked up, then quickly replaced one of my shirts that had once been white but that now had an interesting blue streak down one sleeve. "I suppose you and the great man will be spending the day together – again?" she quipped.

I suddenly thought that she might be feeling left out. It's bad enough with her dad being so taken up with Lucy. She might really feel abandoned if her mother keeps doing a disappearing act as well.

"I was thinking of taking Sam down to Kilkenny. Would you like to come with us?"

"Can't, I'm afraid. I've got things to do. I've got to have another go at making sense of desktop publishing. Graphic design isn't my strongest point," she observed with a grimace, while still rummaging through the heap of clothes.

"Can't these things wait until next week? I'd love it if you could come."

She uncurled her legs from under her and got up from the chair, picking up her mug from among the jumble of clothes. "It's OK, Mum, I'm not miffed or feeling left out. I think it's great that you're having a bit of fun at last." She suddenly smiled so that her blue eyes creased at the corners. "You deserve it." And then she came over and gave me a kiss. "I really *have* got things to do for the start of term. And

Keith's taking me out somewhere this evening to meet some singer friend of his who, he says, has an amazing voice. So go and have a nice time with the gorgeous Mr Ellis. I'm as jealous as hell but I'll be just fine!"

Reassured, and after checking that all was well at the nursing home, I rang Sam back and arranged to collect him at ten.

As he'd said, this morning was the best sort of October morning with the birches and chestnuts beginning to change colour and the Kildare fields half hidden with ribbons of mist, tinged a soft rose colour by the strengthening sun. The sky above was cloudless and the air felt cool and fresh. We drove as far as Moone, where we made a detour so that I could show him the famous – not so very high – High Cross and then we stopped for an eleven o'clock cup of coffee beside the river in Loughlinbridge.

We did the full tourist thing and toured the castle at Kilkenny behind a group of camera-festooned Japanese visitors and then explored the Design Centre on the other side of the road. While I wandered around looking at things in the shop, I was vaguely aware of Sam having a long and rather conspiratorial conversation with a madly helpful sales assistant. Judging by the way she was fluttering her eyelashes at him, she'd sussed who he was. (I don't much like young women who think that by sticking out their boobs and bottoms as far as they'll go like a malformed Coca-Cola bottle, they immediately become infinitely desirable.) By the time I'd investigated all the pottery, the woollen wear and the rugs and throws with their lovely earthy colours, he'd finished and I went over to join him as he examined some pieces of silver that had caught his eye.

I ended up buying Cassandra a chunky, blue jersey that I thought would suit her fair skin beautifully and Sam bought a silver pendant to take back to London for his – as he put it – long suffering, eternally patient, extremely dull but very nice secretary, Sylvia.

"I don't know how I'd manage without her," he confided as we climbed the stairs to the first-floor restaurant, "but I sometimes wish that she'd find some other interests in life."

"You mean, apart from you?" I teased.

"I mean apart from looking after me and a twice-weekly session of Bingo and at least four hours every evening watching the telly. She'd win first prize in a competition on soaps. Knows all the characters, their pedigree and provenance. She's only in her mid-thirties but she behaves as though she's well into middle-age and beyond."

"Nothing wrong with middle-age," I reminded him.

"*You* will never be middle-aged."

"No, I won't," I replied with feeling. "I shall hurtle from unbelievably adolescent to high-flying geriatric without any intervening period of sanity – to paraphrase Mark Twain."

"Sounds good to me," he said, grinning. "But don't you think that her life is somewhat circumscribed for such a relatively young woman?"

"Perhaps she's happy living like that," I suggested.

"Perhaps. But I'd love to give her the chance to sample something a little more than that. I tried to get her to go to the theatre once. I bought two really good tickets for a show I was sure she'd love and told her to take a friend."

"And did she go?"

"Did she hell! No, only gave them away to a niece. She said that she wasn't a theatre sort of person."

"Well, at least she sounds as if she knows what she wants. An awful lot of people don't."

"I know. You're probably right," he said, in a resigned voice. "It taught me not to interfere but every now and then I catch myself looking at her and wondering if she'd had a different start in life, if fate had dealt her a better and more exciting hand, would she still be the same? It doesn't seem much of a life – to be typing for me and organising my diary, before going home to solitary microwaved suppers on her lap in front of the telly. I feel she deserves better than that. There must be something or someone that would make a difference. You know, to inject some colour into that rather grey existence of hers."

No wonder he writes so well about women! The more I get to know that man, the more I like him. This is a *quite* separate emotion from the attraction end of things. I've learned the hard way that being madly attracted without really liking a man is a recipe for catastrophic misery.

I noticed that, several times during the day, people were nudging each other and pointing him out and I heard his name whispered in awed tones. One or two people even peered at me hopefully, wondering if they had spotted two celebrities in one go! A couple of rather elegant women approached the table when we were having lunch and asked him for his autograph, which he obligingly gave but, when they seemed to want to linger, he politely but firmly made it clear that he wanted to eat his lunch in peace – and continue his conversation with me. No wonder one of them gave me a dirty look! Ha!

After they'd drifted back to their own table, I asked him if he minded that sort of thing.

He pulled a face. "Well, yes and no. I have to remind myself every now and then that I was chuffed to bits the first time someone asked me for my autograph. I thought they'd made a mistake. Almost told them they had! But, sometimes, it can get a little wearing. At least I'm not a pop star or they might scream and hurl underwear at me as well!" He gave me one of his lopsided grins. "That's one of the reasons I like you so much, Hebe Sayer. You wouldn't dream of asking me for my autograph."

"Dead right I wouldn't! But I think it really ill-mannered of you not to have asked for mine before now."

He put a hand up to his brow in mock despair. "I *knew* there was something important I'd forgotten to do. Will you ever forgive me?"

I'm not going to go on repeating all this stuff! When I write it down, it sounds a pretty daft way of carrying on but, underneath that rather casual, sophisticated aura of his, he has this lovely, silly streak in him that seems to be utterly at home with my own particular brand of lunacy. And it's so good to be with someone who doesn't stare at me as though I'd lost my marbles when I suddenly go off at a tangent; someone who just joins in! Mind you, a lot of our conversation was quite rational and serious!

We got lost on the way back to Dublin. Or rather, I got lost as I was doing the driving. I think we were so busy talking that I forgot to check the signposts. We ended up miles from anywhere I recognised. Sam didn't mind in the least. He didn't have to clock-watch for another couple of days, he said, and he was thoroughly enjoying it. We somehow ended up in the mountains again at dusk.

The sky was incredible, changing from a rich salmon

pink to lilac to deep purple. We'd stopped the car, high up and halfway along a valley, to watch the daylight fading. The road ahead glimmered in the half-light and a deer suddenly bolted from a group of trees, disappearing into a thick belt of forestry, its white scut bobbing up and down as it vanished into the shadows. All of a sudden, what seemed like thousands upon thousands of rooks filled the skies above and around us. The effect was rather like being in the middle of a swirling mass of giant black flakes of ash from some unseen bonfire. Their cawing was deafening. Then, five minutes later, there wasn't a sign of them – not a single, solitary bird remained in the darkening sky.

"Do you think that happens every day?" Sam asked, tucking his hand through the crook of my arm.

"You mean, would they bother to commute on a Sunday?"

"Something like that!" he said, before leaning over and kissing me on the lips.

That kiss made the whole world lurch and spin. I wasn't aware of anything else. I didn't hear, see or feel anything except the sensation of his lips on mine. I don't know how long it lasted but, when we eventually drew apart, I felt as though all the air in my lungs had been sucked out. I also felt quite dizzy for a moment. I've certainly never felt like that after kissing Owen – even in the early days. Anyway, it was quite the most wonderful kiss of my life. Well, it *was*. I'm not going to apologise for saying it either – because it's the truth – and I felt marvellously light-headed – and *young* – as we got back into the car and headed home for Dalkey.

Because I hadn't been very organised, there wasn't too much of a choice when it came to the food. So, we had scrambled eggs on toast and a banana each and then sat for a while in the sitting-room. I lit the first fire of the autumn and we listened to the crackling and spitting of the logs while we sipped our whiskeys. We sat very close, facing the fire, side by side on the rug, Sam's arm around my shoulders. I'd only switched one small table light so that the flames made our shadows flicker and waver on the walls and ceiling.

I added some turf to the logs and, a few moments later, Sam sniffed the air appreciatively.

"What a lovely smell! So much nicer than the coal fires we used to have at home in the winter."

"If I'd been more organised, I would have bought some muffins to toast," I said pointing at the old brass toasting fork, hanging to one side of the fireplace.

"Followed by marshmallows, all crispy on the outside and runny inside," he said with a happy sigh. He turned to look at me. "Next time, perhaps?" he said, softly.

"That would be nice," I said, fighting back a sudden desire to grab him by the hand and take him upstairs.

We didn't kiss any more. I was partly relieved because I half expected Cassandra to walk through the door at any moment. Not that I think she would have been fazed by seeing us kissing. It was more that I was frightened that if we did start to kiss again, I would have wanted to take it further. I think Sam felt the same. At least, I hope he did.

However, she didn't appear and he called a taxi because, by eleven, we were both tired after all the driving and sightseeing and emotion.

We said goodnight by the gate with one last kiss. "I'll ring you," he said as he turned to get into the cab. "Sleep well," he added, before closing the taxi door.

* * *

Wednesday morning after a really good night's sleep. It's pretty late, but I've taken coffee and toast back to bed and am writing this with cat stretched out, stopping circulation in feet.

Today is the day of the dinner party. God help us! I had a brilliant idea about making the whole thing slightly less awful. I rang Owen and asked him if I could bring Sam with me.

He didn't sound overly enthusiastic about the suggestion. "I wanted this to be a family get-together. I've never met the man."

"Lucy is hardly family, is she?" I said quickly. "And, I've never met *her*. So it will be a level playing field, so to speak."

"I hope you aren't going be awkward, Hebe. It's bad enough having Cassandra playing the fool."

I felt like Miss Piggy, all outrage and quivering snout, when Kermit has just accused her of being affected. *'Moi? Affected/ Awkward?'* He can be *so* pompous sometimes.

But, of course, I didn't say that.

"I'm not asking much, Owen. He's over for a few days. He doesn't know anyone and it might be nice for him." I paused and then added, "If you really feel that Lucy couldn't cope with an extra guest, that's fine by me."

That worked!

There was a sigh of irritation from the other end of the phone. "Oh, I suppose it will be all right! But just make sure that you're not late."

"Of course," I said, demurely.

I did feel a little guilty about landing Sam with an evening chez the ex and his 'bit on the side' as Cassandra will call her, when she's not referring to her as the Blonde Bimbo. Still, I reckoned that there was more chance of everyone behaving themselves with a stranger in their midst. I also thought that he wouldn't want to be on his own for his last night. And he could always say no.

I rang him just now to ask him how he would feel about it, explaining that things might be a bit sticky as Cassandra had taken against the hostess and could become somewhat hostile. I didn't tell him that she is also very anti-Owen too.

"Never turn down the opportunity to get a close look behind other people's front doors. You never know, it might be useful fodder for the next novel!" he said, cheerfully. "I'd love to come – if it won't make a delicate situation worse."

"Please come," I said. "It will be just about bearable if you're there."

* * *

Later, having got sidetracked.

A minute after putting down the phone, having agreed that he would take a taxi out to the house in the next half-an-hour, it rang again. It was the nursing home.

I don't know why I knew immediately that it was one of the nuns speaking, even before she told me who she was and where she was ringing from. They just sound different. She told me that my mother's condition appeared to be worsening and was I going in to see her that day?

"I'll be there in twenty minutes," I told her. I found my hand was shaking when I put the receiver back on its holder.

Then I rang Sam and told him that I was going to the nursing home.

"What can I do?" he asked straight away.

"I don't think there's anything much you can do. I don't

191

even know how serious it is. It may be a false alarm. That's happened before. If she's bad, I'll ring Owen and cancel this evening. I'll keep in touch. I'll have to turn off my mobile in the nursing home but Cassandra will be here all morning, so you could always ring her."

"Hebe?" he said, in a quiet voice. "Before you ring off, I just want to say good luck. I hope, whatever the outcome is, that it goes well for you both."

I felt comforted by his words. That was the best that could be hoped for. I knew that.

When I hurried into Mum's room, I was met by a tall, quietly-spoken nun, whom I hadn't seen before.

"Hello, Mrs Sayer. I'm Sister Paul. I'm afraid we may have got you here under false pretences. Your mother was running a bit of a temperature earlier on and seemed distressed. But, as you can see, she's peaceful enough now and her pulse and temperature are nearly back to normal. I'm sorry if we worried you."

One look at my mother's face told me that she did indeed look very peaceful.

"I'm glad you called me. I'd much rather that than you not phoning and something happening," I reassured her.

She smiled and then started to walk towards the door where she hesitated. Then she turned and looked over to where I was standing beside the bed.

"Is there something else, Sister?" I asked.

Slowly, she came back toward the bed again. "When your mother was admitted, I believe you filled in the form which gave details of contact numbers, all that sort of thing." I nodded. "You put *None* in answer to the question of what church your mother belonged to."

"Yes, that's right."

She looked at me for a moment with her calm, grey eyes before continuing. "Was that because you were following your mother's wishes or . . ."

"My own?" I finished the sentence for her. "No, I talked to my mother long before she came in here, when she was still lucid for quite a lot of the time. She stopped going to church several years before she became ill and she was quite clear about what she wanted to happen at the end of her life. I know she wouldn't have changed her mind. So, please, Sister, don't try and persuade me to have a priest giving her the Last Rites."

She gave me a very sweet, slow smile that made her suddenly look young. "Don't worry, Mrs Sayer. We just wanted to be sure. It won't be mentioned again unless you want to bring up the subject."

She left the room on silent feet. I went and sat down by the bed, taking one of my mother's fragile hands in my own. The skin looked especially transparent in the morning light flooding the room. Her face too seemed more wasted. And yet, I'd been with her only two days before.

I didn't rub cream into her hands like I usually did. I didn't want to do anything that might disturb her in any way. Her breathing was like small, even sighs, her chest hardly seeming to rise under the sheet.

Instead, in a low voice, I told her about Sam. I described him down to the smallest detail I could think of. I told her that I thought that, miraculously, and even though it was early days, I had found the man who was right for me and that he, apparently, felt the same way. I told her that he hadn't actually said it in so many words. He wasn't the sort of man who gave everything away in one go. But, I told her he's made it plain that he thinks that I am different and special. Even telling her that gave me a small shiver of pleasure. I described to my mother how it made me feel to be with him – at ease, happy, contented. I tried to explain how, from the evening when he first came to the house, I felt that I'd known him all my life, that I could say anything to him, that I could let him see the real me and not be afraid that it would put him off.

All the time I was talking, her face showed no trace of a reaction. Occasionally her eyelids fluttered briefly.

It was lunch-time when they came in to turn her. I wasn't sure if I should go or stay. My mother hadn't moved all the time I'd been with her. In the end, after being reassured that they would ring me on my mobile if there were any change, I left her sleeping.

* * *

On the way home, I had a sudden attack of feeling guilty that, in the middle of being a witness to my mother's slow letting go of life, there was a part of me that was full of renewed hope and excitement. It was a feeling that was very real and that made me feel very alive.

I got back to find Sam and Cassandra in the kitchen, sharing a pot of tea and making serious inroads into the biscuit tin. My heart gave a sort of lurch of pleasure at the sight of him.

Cassandra leaped to her feet as soon as I walked into the room.

"How's Granny Molly?" she asked, her voice sharp with concern.

"She seems fine. She was fast asleep when I left." I pushed back some of the hair from her troubled face and kissed her. "Don't worry. I think whatever it was has passed. They don't seem to be bothered and they've promised to ring me if she becomes unwell again. Any chance of a mug of tea? I'm parched." While she fetched a mug out of the cupboard, I sat down and looked over at Sam. "This is a nice surprise. When did you arrive?"

"About an hour and a half ago. I thought it might be company for Cassandra if she was upset and that you might be comforted to have my ugly mug to look at when you got back. Sort of take your mind off things."

I smiled at him gratefully. "It's very nice to see your ugly mug."

Actually, I suddenly felt like bursting into tears. I suppose it was the relief of the worst not happening, combined with the delight of seeing him again. I couldn't have begun to tell him, especially with Cassandra there, just how marvellous it was to walk in the door and find him sitting there, chatting to my daughter in that relaxed way of his. He looked so at home – as if he belonged.

Chapter Twelve

Thursday morning, impossibly early because I've given up trying to sleep. Even the birds haven't started up yet and Busby's curled up, snoring like a small steam engine at the foot of the bed.

Cassandra suddenly announced, half-an-hour before we were due to leave for, in her words, "The Dinner Party from Hell", that if Sam were accompanying me, why couldn't she have Keith as moral support for her? I pointed out that she should have thought of that before and that it was too late now to do anything because, quite apart from the difficulty of trying to track down Keith, who was off recording in some studio or other somewhere in Dundalk, Lucy had presumably prepared dinner for five of us, not six.

She said I was being unreasonable, that the whole thing was a fucking disaster and she was pissed off. It's extraordinary! Just as I feel that she's starting to behave like a reasonable human being and I'm beginning to think I must be doing *something* right, she suddenly reverts to cranky, foul-mouthed six-year-old on a bad day. You know what I mean – *I'll cry and I'll cry until I make myself sick!* or, more likely, *I'll cry and cry until I fucking puke.*

Anyway – with Sam's good-humoured non-interference as a prop, we finally trooped out of the door and into the car. She didn't say very much on the ten-minute drive to Owen's house – which was probably just as well. Sam insisted she sat in the front with me, so at least she didn't feel relegated and forgotten in the back, and he sat quietly, looking out of the window in mild astonishment at cars changing lanes without indicating, their drivers showing a happy disregard for the speed limit. So at least we didn't arrive looking hot and cross and not speaking to each other.

I've always loved the home I lived in with Owen, in spite of it having some rather unhappy memories. I like the way the terrace of houses curves around in a gentle half moon facing the sea. I like its cream walls and long windows with the wrought-iron balconies and the steps up to the front door with its lacy fanlight. I noticed that he'd changed the colour. When I lived there, the door was always a dark blue. Now it's bright red. As we climbed the steps, I wondered if Lucy was responsible for the change. And why not? She's the one living with him now.

Owen ushered us into the hallway, where I introduced him and Sam to each other. I was aware of him being particularly smooth, courteously thanking Sam for the bottle of wine he brought while, all the time, I knew that he was scrutinising him from head to foot. I noticed too that Cassandra made no effort to kiss her father. All he got from her was an offhand, "Hi, Dad". I saw him make a move in her direction and then stop himself. Just for a second I thought he looked embarrassed. Probably because he didn't want a stranger witnessing his daughter's offhandedness. It struck me that there might be more to her attitude than just not wanting to make an effort. She seemed genuinely on edge and I began to wonder if my persuading her to come had been a big mistake.

With misgivings, I made my way into the sitting-room, followed by the others. A fire blazed in the grate. The room was warm and would have been impossibly stuffy if both windows hadn't been open at the top. While Owen got the drinks, I had a quick look around. There were new satin cushions on the couch that wouldn't have been my choice but which were OK, I suppose. There was also a strange new painting over the fireplace, where once had hung a lovely watercolour of the walk through the trees on Bray Head. The new thing was abstract and rather – weird. All ridges and dollops of colour. I tried squinting at it through partially closed eyes but it didn't help me work out what it might be a painting of. But that was probably just me being futile. I never was much good with the really modern stuff. Sam, realising that it was probably a waste of time to try and involve Cassandra in conversation, gave me a reassuring smile and asked when the house had been built and admired the elegant proportions of the room and the sea view from the windows.

Finally, Owen reappeared with Lucy in tow. She was looking very pretty in a short red dress that matched the front door. Her bobbed blonde hair was shiny and beautifully cut. I couldn't help noticing that her nails were amazingly long (how she does any typing with those mandarin-like extensions on the ends of her fingers, I can't imagine) and that they matched the dress. The thing that struck me most forcibly was that she looked so incredibly young. As she approached, I found myself mesmerised by the carefully applied make-up. All that foundation, blusher, eyeliner and mascara and expertly applied blue eye-shadow made me feel as though my own face must look horribly naked. Looking at the lovely smooth skin of her firm young arms and legs, I couldn't help wondering why on earth she would want to smother herself in all that stuff. It must be hell taking it off before going to bed. I bet Owen gets impatient while she goes through the necessary paint-stripping and cleansing process.

"Hello, Hebe," she said. Her voice was surprisingly husky – as though she lived on gin and cigarettes. But I know from Cassandra that she doesn't smoke and hardly drinks. "I'm so glad you could come." Her smile included Cassandra, who managed a rather sickly and fleeting smile back. Lucy shook hands with Sam, who had got to his feet the moment she'd entered the room. "I'm so glad you could come too, Mr Ellis. Please do sit down. Dinner won't be long. Joan's working her magic in the kitchen. I couldn't have done it without her."

For a second, I experienced a quick stab of jealousy. Joan used to help *me* in the kitchen when I had to conjure up meals for Owen's boring business pals. She was *my* friend, and had been *my* much-relied-on help. We had spent many a happy hour mixing and slicing and dicing and chatting together. I hoped my thoughts didn't show on my face. I didn't want her to think I was curdled with middle-aged angst over what I'd lost in so stupidly separating from the handsome, successful Owen!

Actually, I was surprised how someone, only a year older than Cassandra, could be so socially adept. She appeared to be at ease and her smile seemed warm and genuine. I'd made my mind up before going that I wasn't going to make any assumptions about her before we'd even met but I found myself liking her almost from the first minute. Added to the fact that she appeared to be a very sweet girl, I could only look at her and think of her almost as a child, playing at being an adult, in all her finery and careful make-up. She was certainly no hard-faced usurper, who had clawed her way into Owen's affections. I did wonder why he had decided to live with someone who was so much younger than himself. Did he ever get teased by his business cronies for cradle-snatching?

Sam was his usual, easy self and, within minutes, had Lucy laughing over some story about encounters with a famous author, with a vastly inflated sense of his literary importance, in a large London bookshop where there had been a mix-up over which of them was supposed to be there for a book-signing session. I even caught Owen looking amused. Cassandra was wearing her bored, 'don't even think of talking to me', expression. Nothing anyone said was going to amuse her!

I was dying to nip into the kitchen to say hello to Joan but I knew that wouldn't have been appropriate. I had to forget that this was once my home. And I'd seen her last week and we could have a good natter the next time she came over to dispense her weekly dose of help and common sense.

The meal was delicious: a cold gazpacho, followed by chicken casserole with orange and couscous and ending up with my favourite of all puds, *crème brûlée*.

Although Sam, Lucy and I tried, at various stages of the meal, to get Cassandra to unthaw, she stuck firmly to her ice-maiden routine. So much so that I stopped being puzzled by her behaviour and became mildly irritated and, eventually, quite cross. I mean, Sam was being delightful, as was Lucy. OK, I know that she's not going to win the Super-Intellectual of the Year Award and doesn't have anything terribly interesting to say. I probably didn't either at her age. But she was really putting herself out to include my wretched daughter in the conversation. She couldn't have been more friendly or attentive, checking that our glasses were refilled and all the rest of it. She was a far better host than Owen, in fact. He sat there, looking rather pasha-like and knocking back the wine at a steady rate. He was keeping his end up in the conversation stakes though and, although I kept catching him giving Sam sideways glances when he thought nobody was looking, he was doing all right.

I reckoned I was playing the part of well-behaved guest reasonably adequately. I was certainly enjoying myself a lot more than I'd thought I was going to. It was just Cassandra, sitting opposite me like a dark shadow, emanating gloom as though brewing up a storm, that was acting as a dampener on the proceedings. Once or twice, I caught her staring at her father with a look that I couldn't decipher. Wary? Condemnatory? Miserable? I really didn't know. If he noticed, he didn't react. Early on in the evening, he'd stopped trying to get a response from her and, by the time we sat down to eat, was more or less ignoring her.

We'd just finished the meal and had gone through to the other room to have coffee when there was a long ring on the doorbell.

"That will be Mother," said Owen, putting down the coffee pot and hurrying into the hall.

I don't know whose face fell the furthest – mine or Lucy's. It appeared from the speed at which he'd responded to the ring that Owen was expecting his wretched mother. Lucy was obviously not. I saw how her hands involuntarily clenched in her lap. Her smile disappeared and she suddenly looked nervous. There was a pause while we waited. Sam looked expectant, having been filled in the day before on my not-very-good relationship with the woman. I wondered if, after meeting her, he would use her in one of his books or was she too awful to make into a credible character? Cassandra just looked non-committal and bored.

You have to hand it to Dervla. When they'd finished their little *tête-à-tête* in the hall and she swept into the room with her son in attendance, like a well-behaved tugboat, she made a spectacular impression. She was wearing some sort of pale lavender-coloured evening coat that made her eyes look a little less chilly than usual and her grey hair was as immaculate as ever. As I have so often done in recent years, when I looked at her, I found it impossible to believe that she and Mum are the same age. And while she was swanning into the room in a cloud of expensive perfume, I thought of my mother in the nursing home, barely clinging on to the last shreds of her not-so-happy life. And it seemed suddenly unbearably unfair. I couldn't stop myself from checking in my bag for the umpteenth time to make sure my mobile was there and still flashing green.

Her eyes roamed the room, alighting rapidly on Sam, who had risen to shake hands with her.

"I certainly didn't expect to be mixing in such illustrious

company this evening," she said archly. (Seeing her in action like that always made me feel nauseous.)

Like hell she didn't! Owen must have told her that Sam was going to be there – hence the 'on the spur of the moment' appearance.

"I remember you from that evening at the Shelbourne," Sam said, in a suitably intense voice, gazing into her eyes as he took hold of her extended hand – as if he'd been counting the hours until he saw her again.

I fought down the urge to laugh.

She couldn't stop the little tremor of pleasure, sparked by that bit of flattery, from showing in her face.

"Cassandra!" she murmured, reluctantly turning away from Sam with a smug look. "How lovely, you're here too. I haven't seen you for so long." Her words simply leaked reproach, as though the girl had been kept under lock and key – by me, of course – thus denying her loving grandmother access.

She hardly acknowledged Lucy or me. From then on it was downhill all the way.

As the minutes ticked by, it became more and more obvious that the only people Dervla was prepared to talk to were her son and the famous author. I moved so that I was sitting beside Lucy, who looked as if all the fight had gone out of her. I realised that she must have been having a tough time with the old girl ever since she'd moved into the house to live with Owen.

She gave me a grateful smile. "Would you like some more coffee, Hebe? I can easily go and get some."

"No, thanks. I'm so full of good food that there isn't room for any more of anything." I gave a sideways glance at

Owen's mother and then grinned at Lucy. "Don't let her get you down. She can be such a cow sometimes."

I'd spoken very quietly and, if the others had continued talking, no one would have heard what I said. But – there was a sudden and total lull in the conversation and my words floated through the air, unhindered and unmistakable in their meaning.

There was a horrible silence and then Owen spoke in icy tones. "I think that remark calls for an immediate apology, Hebe."

Dervla's expression had gone all glassy. She looked as though she had a frozen mackerel shoved up her backside. Cassandra's posture had suddenly changed from indolently bored to one of rigid attention, her eyes darting from her grandmother to me and back again.

Unfortunately, Lucy compounded my *faux pas* by leaping to my defence with, "It was only a joke. Hebe didn't mean it really."

Before I could say anything, my suddenly – and excessively – pro-active daughter, dived into the proceedings with, "Oh, yes she did! And what's more, Mum's dead right." She suddenly stood up, knocking the side of the coffee table with her leg, making the cups rattle on their saucers. "You're not very nice to people who aren't useful to you, are you, Gran?"

Dervla's head whipped around with such speed I thought her neck might snap. I don't know which she hated more – the accusation of not being nice or being called Gran. For the first time since I met her, she appeared totally silenced, unable to find the words with which to respond to such an appalling situation.

"That's *enough!*" bellowed Owen, his cheeks flushed.

"Oh, *you* can talk!" Cassandra rounded on him. "You're such a bunch of hypocrites! You pretend to be civilised with your fancy clothes and nice manners but underneath you're really rotten."

We all stared at her. Out of the corner of my eye, I was aware of Sam, sitting very still, his face expressionless.

Then, trying to salvage something and feeling guilty that I'd been the one to start the whole thing off, I said, "Cassandra, can you sit down and count to ten or something before this all gets completely out of hand?"

She shook her head angrily and I could see tears in her eyes. "You still don't get it, do you, Mum?"

"Get *what?*" I asked.

"Do you know why he's asked *her,*" she stabbed a finger in Lucy's direction, "to come and live with him? Because he fancies young girls. He doesn't want old, tired flesh. Oh, no! He prefers the young ones, does Dad. He doesn't even know how ridiculous it makes him look." She turned to face Lucy, her eyes wild. "You'd better watch him, you know! It'll be girls in school uniforms next."

Lucy stared back at her, uncomprehendingly.

Owen walked swiftly over to where his daughter was standing. For a moment I thought he would hit her.

"Owen!" I shouted, as I moved towards them.

He ignored me, staring at his daughter, his mouth a thin line of barely controlled fury. "Shut up! And get out of my house."

"My pleasure!" she hissed back at him.

Without any hesitation, she grabbed her shoulder bag and marched to the door, her face red, her eyes full of unshed tears.

And that was it, really. It was obvious to everyone that the evening was unsalvageable. A still silent Dervla retired to another room, looking as though she might faint, where her son fed her brandy and no doubt apologised again and again for her granddaughter's behaviour. I gave Lucy a quick kiss on the cheek and thanked her for the lovely meal. And then Sam and I fled.

It took us some time to find Cassandra. We eventually tracked her down by some rocks at the far end of the nearby beach. She was crying as though she'd never stop. I didn't ask any questions, just held her until she quietened and then we drove home in silence.

When we got back, Sam asked me if he could stay. "I don't want to leave you after all that upset. Can't I stay in the spare room or something?"

"No, Sam. It's better if I'm on my own with Cassandra just now."

"Are you sure?" He looked so concerned I almost said yes, I would love him to stay but I felt that if she wanted to talk, to tell me anything, it would be better if we were on our own.

"Yes, I think you should go. And, Sam, I'm so sorry about this evening. I never should have asked you to come. It was always bound to be tricky but I never, for one moment, thought that it would be as bad as that."

"I know," he said lightly, putting both arms around me and giving me a gentle hug. "Just promise you'll ring me in the morning. I don't have to leave for the airport until midday." Briefly, he rested a hand lightly on Cassandra's arm. "Goodnight, Cassandra. I hope I'll see you again soon."

And then he left to catch the last train back into town.

I hardly noticed him leave, I was so preoccupied in getting her into the house and upstairs.

When she was in bed, I went in to see her.

"Mum, I'm sorry," she said in a tearful voice. "I shouldn't have said what I did – even if it was true. Lucy didn't deserve it anyway. *She's* not that bad really."

I tried to keep the mood as light as possible. I smiled and said, "I know. I think she's a sweet girl. And, although you were really naughty to have a go at Dervla, I did enjoy the look on her face when you called her Gran." She gave a slight smile at the memory. I hesitated before nervously adding, "I'm not surprised that Dad got angry though. What you said about him was pretty awful."

Cassandra looked at me. She hesitated and, for a moment, I thought she was going to tell me what was going on in her mind and why she'd said what she had to her father. But the moment passed. Her eyes clouded and she withdrew her hand from under mine and turned on her side so that she was facing away from me. "Mum, do you mind? It's late and I don't want to talk any more."

So I gave her a kiss and left her to sleep. Although I suspect that she tossed and turned for a long time after I closed her bedroom door.

Sitting here now, writing this, I still can't understand what's going on in her head. Is her over-reaction because she feels that, in taking up with Lucy, who's so much younger than I am, he's being unkind and she sees me as the rejected older woman? I'll have to reassure her that I don't at all mind being the age I am and that I'm happy for her dad to have someone new in his life. Somehow, I've got to convince her that he is totally irrelevant to my life now but that he shouldn't be excluded from hers. Oh, Lord! I must try and make her see sense. I hate to see her looking so miserable and angry. And we can't have any more outbursts like last night. It's too damaging all round.

* * *

Later, Thursday night.

I feel as though I need to catch my breath. So much has happened in just twenty-four hours. Sam has gone back to London.

He phoned as soon as he got home.

"Are you all right?" he asked.

"Yes, I'm all right. Confused, feeling guilty that I was the catalyst for the unpleasantness last night, embarrassed that I should have involved you in all of that."

"Well, don't be, Hebe. It wasn't so terrible really. There were definite moments of divine farce involved."

"You mean, the ex-mother-in-law's reaction to the news that she's not God's gift to mankind – perhaps not perfect?"

"I have to agree that her expression of wounded outrage was perhaps the high point of the evening! And, don't forget, the food was splendid!" There was a pause and then he said in serious voice, "Obviously Cassandra is a very unhappy girl and there are big issues she has to resolve but perhaps she needed to say what she did in order to move on. You never know, it may just be a good thing that she got it off her chest."

"Perhaps," I said, rather doubtfully. "But there's more to it than her just not approving of her father's lifestyle. I know there is but she won't talk to me, Sam, not properly, and I don't know what to do to help her."

"Be there for her, be patient, watch her and listen carefully to her when she does talk, even if she's not ready to tell you everything that's bothering her. It will work out, Hebe. These dramas have a way of resolving themselves. It seems terrible when you're going through it but there will be an end to it. She'll talk when she's ready." He gave a small laugh. "Listen to me! I'm no expert when it comes to solving family problems. You should ask my ex-wife." To me, his voice sounded full of regret. There was no hint of bitterness in his words.

Our conversation cheered me up considerably, although I'm missing him already.

Cassandra shut herself in her room and switched off her mobile, I had a worried call from Keith, asking if she's all right and should he come round? I told him to hold off for the moment and let her cool down. He agreed but I could tell that he was worried about her and didn't understand what was going on between her and her father. As far as I can make out, his relationship with his own parents has always been an open and friendly one. I can't imagine him ever having tantrums or being hurtful. I've seen him, occasionally, when Cassandra has really gone too far, become quieter than ever and very serious. It always makes her sit up and take notice. He somehow manages to defuse difficult situations effortlessly and doesn't seem to let the world's unpleasantness get to him.

There was also an angry call from Owen, saying that he wouldn't have Cassandra in the house until she apologised and accusing me of poisoning her against him. I didn't have the energy to argue with him, just told him that I would speak to her and that I was sorry. He rang off very abruptly. He's probably having a dreadful time with his mother. I can just imagine her, droning on about what a fool he had been to marry me in the first place and, if it weren't for me, Cassandra would be a different sort of problem-free girl etc etc. I just hope he's not taking it out on poor little Lucy. He can be quite vindictive sometimes.

As well as all of that, when I went to see Mum this afternoon, I knew that she had slipped a little further from the world. It's like watching a flower fading, dying in silent slow motion. You are powerless. There is absolutely nothing you can do to stop the process.

The only nice thing that happened today was the arrival of Joan, carrying my jacket that I'd left behind last night in my hurry to escape from the sulphuric atmosphere pervading my old home.

She handed it to me with a questioning look in her eyes. "Don't tell me if you don't want to but what in the name of Heaven happened last night? You seemed to suddenly disappear and then there were a lot of closed doors and serious conversations going on behind them." She looked a bit ashamed at spilling the beans. "Oh, I shouldn't have said that, should I?"

"It's all right, Joan," I said, with a laugh. "You can't be expected to go around with your eyes and ears closed. And anyway you're one of the family, so you're not being indiscreet!"

We sat down around the kitchen table; where so many councils of war, discussions, family arguments and brain-storming sessions have taken place over the last eight years.

I took a deep breath. "To put it bluntly, Cassandra told her dad that he was fixated on young women and that he wasn't a nice person. She included Owen's mother in the not nice part of her speech and she called her Gran, which didn't go down at all well."

"You don't say!" said Joan, her lips twitching slightly.

"But I'm afraid that was after Mrs Sayer had ignored Lucy – and me – but that didn't bother me one bit. The more that one ignores me, the happier I am. I tried to cheer her up by telling her not to take any notice and reminding her that the said Mrs Sayer can be a right cow. Somehow, everyone heard my words of wisdom. Needless to say, neither Owen nor his mother was too thrilled. In fact, I don't think I've ever seen him looking so angry. As you know, we left rather hurriedly."

"Jesus, Mary and Joseph!" For a moment, Joan looked horror-struck and then, slowly, a broad smile spread across her face and she started to laugh. Joan is a large woman. The laughter started like a rumble of distant thunder somewhere in the depths of her and grew in strength until great gusts of it filled the kitchen as she shook and held her sides, tears streaming down her face. It was impossible to sit looking at her without joining in.

While we were both still hiccoughing and wheezing with the leftovers of hilarity, a pale-faced Cassandra appeared at the kitchen door.

"What's all the commotion about?" she asked in a sulky voice.

Still wobbling and wheezing, Joan got up from her chair and went over to her. "Come and give me a hug, you bad, bad child! I've just been hearing about how wicked you and your mother were last night." For an uncomfortable second, I thought Cassandra was going to snub her but her expression softened and she suddenly threw her arms around the woman's broad shoulders and allowed herself to be hugged tightly, her face almost disappearing into the ample bosom.

"I don't know what to do with the pair of you. You're as bad as each other," said Joan, grinning at me over the top of Cassandra's head.

And then the front door bell rang. It was Keith. When I led him into the kitchen, he looked at me questioningly.

"I know you said not to come but I thought I might be able to help." He observed the scene and the three dishevelled females in front of him. "I'm not entirely sure that I timed it right. Is this a wake or a party? I can always go and get my sax out of the car and we could turn it into real session. We might even get old Cass here to give us a song!" He gave her an encouraging glance. "How about it, Cass. Nothing like a bit of music to heal mind and body."

She looked at him for a moment without speaking. Then, pushing the hair back from her face, she went over to him and put a hand up to his face.

"I'm not in the mood for bloody singing." She looked up at him. "You know what?"

"What?"

"You're an awful eejit. But you're very nice too."

At least she got that right!

In the end, he persuaded her to go with him to the local for a drink and Joan and I made ourselves strong coffee with a good dash of brandy in it. We sat in front of the fire and mused over the complexities of human relationships and generally put the world to rights – if only temporarily.

All I need now is Sam, lying beside me on the bed. Not

to make love – just for the sheer comfort of having him here. Although, who am I trying to kid? If I did manage to morph him into my bedroom at this precise moment, I think it might be awfully difficult not to make love. I'm sure he looks even more gorgeous without any clothes.

Chapter Thirteen

Saturday night, in bed with Busby. Well, I suppose Busby's better than nothing!

I've just put the phone down after talking to Sam. He rang last night too. I must say it's nice to have someone who rings up, not because they have anything important to say but because they want to hear the sound of your voice!

I can't remember Owen ever doing that. He was more into the occasional spectacular bunch of flowers, expensive items of jewellery – that I didn't need or want – and meals in posh restaurants, where I had to pretend I was an old hand at dealing with frog's legs, *moules*, artichokes and snails. At the time, all I really wanted was good, wholesome steak or nice, fresh, unmucked-about-with fish. It was an awful shock for him to find out that I wasn't the least bit sophisticated in my choice of grub.

"I'm *really* missing you," Sam said, the first time he rang.

"Surprisingly, I'm kind of missing you too!"

"You're so good for me."

"Why's that?"

"You'll never let me get too big for my boots!"

"I'm sure you're just loving being back in the London whirl, surrounded by adoring fans and living the high-life," I joked.

"At this moment, there is nothing I want more than to be lost in the depths of the Wicklow Mountains with a certain Hebe Sayer. Either that or curled up on your squashy couch in front of a log fire, slurping good red wine and listening to music – and the chiming of your delightful carriage clock that can't tell the time."

That was a reference to the fact that the clock in the sitting-room has a habit of giving one dong more than the actual hour. It's something it's been doing for years and I've somehow never got round to getting it fixed. And now it's second nature when I hear it to just subtract a dong when it's finished donging. It's the same with the clock in the car. For half of the year, I'm out one hour because I never seem to have a handy biro to stick into the little hole to adjust it. But I can't help thinking that, unless you've a dental appointment, it doesn't really matter if it's two or three o'clock. An hour, one way or the other, isn't important. Owen would disagree with me passionately on that one!

"How is Cassandra?" Sam asked. "Have things cooled down a bit?"

"Much better but Owen's not speaking to either of us at the moment."

"I wouldn't worry too much about that. As long as things are better between you and her. I hate to think of the pair of you feeling miserable and her not being able to talk to you."

"It's so frustrating," I told him. "One minute, I think she's ready to open up to me and then, for some reason, she withdraws again. It's almost as though she's afraid that, if she told me what she was thinking, I wouldn't believe her or wouldn't be able to sympathise. I have the feeling that my being in that clinic, not to mention how out of my mind I was before I went in, has shaken her belief in me more than I thought."

Of course, I can't expect Sam to come up with all the answers but it does help to talk – to have someone who is genuinely interested in the ups and downs of my life and who really cares that both Cassandra and I are all right. It's miraculous too, the way in which, when he was with us, he succeeded in never alienating my prickly daughter, who seems to genuinely like him.

Half an hour passes in a flash with these precious conversations of ours. It was true when I said that Cassandra was much better. She has been making a big effort. She's even started to tidy her room – a very rare occurrence and, this morning, she made a half-hearted attempt at tackling the pile of ironing crouching threateningly in one corner of the kitchen. She has started teasing me about my long phone chats, saying that, if I go on like this, we'll have to put a tin by the phone for contributions, like we used to when she and Pandora were young teenagers. They seemed to spend entire evenings with the receiver glued to their ear, like some strange, irremovable growth.

As well as always enquiring about Cassandra, Sam never fails to ask after Mum. It's uncanny how he has managed, in a few short days, to have become one of us in a way that I never felt Owen did, even in the relatively good times

216

when the girls were young. There was always the feeling that he had allotted a specific amount of time to do certain things as a family but wasn't prepared to let the family times extend because that would mean that they ate into his business and social life.

I think he quite liked being a husband and father when everything was going well. But as soon as the girls played up and started yelling at each other or ate too many ice creams and puked, he didn't want to know. It was the same where I was concerned. Not that I puked very often, but I did have a habit of forgetting I was married to a successful man, *who is well known in these parts* – to quote his mother. I think that's where the old devil, Dervla, made the biggest inroads into Owen's and my marriage. She kept pointing out to him that I wasn't elegant enough, well dressed enough, didn't mix with the right sort of people, that I was too spontaneous and lacked suitable gravitas – *and* – almost the worst sin of all – my cooking was lousy! She was right, of course. But, as some famous lady once remarked, 'Life is too short to stuff a mushroom'. I couldn't agree more!

I'm glad that Sam and I haven't made love yet. (Interesting segue from lousy cooking to sex but this *is* a stream of consciousness sort of affair – my writing, not my relationship with Sam – so sudden leaps from one topic to another are completely acceptable.) I expect that we'll both know when the time is right. I know the chemistry is there but, for the first time in my life where a man is concerned whom I really, really fancy, I am content to be patient. We haven't even talked about it. The good thing is, he seems to know how I feel and he understands. Wow! is all I can say when I think about him. Wow! that I had the good luck to meet him and that he apparently feels as enthusiastic about me as I do about him. In fact, I think it's really a case of Triple Wow – with frosting and bells on!

Maggie rang this morning just after I'd got back from visiting Mum.

"What have you done to my Mr Ellis?" she said as soon as I picked up the phone.

"Good morning to you too, Maggie! What do mean, what have I done to him? I haven't done anything to him."

"Oh, *yes*, you have! That man is walking into doors and forgetting meetings – meetings with his literary agent, what's more! He doesn't know whether he's coming or going." There was a pause and then she chuckled, "I gather that you and he had a nice time in Dublin after I left."

"We did." I tried not to sound too pleased with myself.

"Well, all I can say is that I'm delighted for the pair of you. You both deserve something good in your lives, especially after what you've been through. Sam too has had a really tough time over the last couple of years."

"Why especially?" I asked with interest.

"That wife of his has really put him through hell. Didn't he mention her?"

"Yes, he did. But they've been divorced for ages, haven't they?"

"Yes, but he still has to pay her maintenance, even though she's earning a massive amount herself. She's a real taker, that one – the sort of female who gives womankind a bad reputation. She expects Sam to pay for his son's skiing trips and sailing holidays and all the rest of it but, at the same time, she's managed to turn the boy against him. He hardly ever sees James and it really upsets him."

For a minute, I felt disappointed that I'd had to hear it from Maggie but then I remembered I still hadn't said anything to Sam about Pandora. Like me, he is obviously keeping some things to himself for the time being. And that's all right too.

"Maggie, what happened after the press conference in Dublin?" I asked her. "You disappeared back to London before I even realised that you'd gone."

"I know! Sorry about that! But I had something come up that had to be dealt with urgently. In fact that was the reason I was ringing you. I have some good news!" She paused.

"Well? Don't keep me in suspense!" I said, realising that, what with one thing and another, I'd completely forgotten about the previous phone conversation we'd had when she mentioned the possibility of some good news.

"One of the reasons I had to belt back here at top speed was that I had a call from a top executive in *Worldwide Studios*. They want to know if you would be interested in co-writing a screenplay for your second book. They are offering a quite reasonable amount of money for the film rights."

For a moment, I was speechless. "But, I . . ."

"I know! You've never written a screenplay before. That's why they will provide one of their very best to nurse you along and hold your hand while you learn the ropes. There's a first time for everything, remember! Listen, I know that this is a bit of a bombshell and I know you have a lot on your hands at the moment but have a think and get back to me in a couple of days. It will be fun, Hebe. Hard work and an interesting experience *and* I shall make sure that you will make lots of lovely money out of it. Take care. I'll talk to you soon!"

I think I sat with the phone in my hand, staring out of the window at nothing for several minutes after she'd rung off!

Cassandra went into unexpected orbit when I told her. "Oh, my God! You're going to be famous – like Sam."

"Hold on a minute! I happen to know that a lot of screenplays get written that don't get any further than that. So, don't assume that anyone will be making a film and that my name will be on the big screen for all of two seconds because it may come to nothing," I warned her.

Ignoring my brave attempt at staying calm and sensible, she rattled on. "Mum! You're brilliant! I'm so proud of you!"

"Are you?" I couldn't help asking her, in astonishment. It seemed only a couple of weeks earlier that my very existence was a constant source of irritation to her.

"Of *course* I am. I'm going to ring Keith and tell him. He'll be thrilled to bits!"

I thought that might be a little premature, seeing as I hadn't even agreed to attempt writing a screenplay and given the fact that I hadn't written anything for over a year. I don't even know if I *can* write anything that isn't a third-rate garbled disaster. The thought of sitting down in front of the computer on my own, let alone with some stranger, makes my insides go all jelly-like.

Still, I didn't stop her from ringing Keith. Although she's been trying hard not to show it, I know she's still upset about what happened on Wednesday evening. Maggie's call was the first thing that had really energised her. And, now that term has started, I want her to concentrate on her work, not spend time moping around feeling depressed. There still hasn't been a proper opportunity to tackle her about her behaviour towards Owen. And he's so furious with both of us that I'm certainly not ringing him. Quite honestly, I don't mind if he never forgives me for calling his bloody mother a cow but I would like him and Cassandra to be on speaking terms again. I did, however, write to Lucy and tell her how very sorry I was for causing so much trouble and thank her for the meal. Poor girl! I hate to think what the atmosphere was like after Sam and I scarpered, leaving her with Dervla spitting bricks and Owen, no doubt, giving all his attention to patching up her wounded pride. Lucy was probably left helping Joan to collect up half-full coffee cups and trying to keep out of their way.

* * *

Monday, late.

I can't write very much tonight, I'm too tired. Also, I get the feeling that I should try and get some sleep while I can because I know that Mum is very close to dying. I spent nearly all day in the nursing home with her today. Once or twice she opened her eyes and looked at me and sometimes she mumbled a few words that I couldn't quite catch. I leaned close to her and whispered my name into her ear but she didn't react as though it meant anything to her. Am I being foolish in wanting her to know that I'm there with her? I realise that it's probably more for my benefit than hers but it would mean so much if, just once before she dies, she would open her eyes and recognise me. I really would like to have that as a memory in the future.

After one of the nuns found me nearly falling off my chair with weariness, she said that it made sense for me to go home and sleep in a comfortable bed for a few hours. So, that's what I'm going to try and do. I just hope I *can* sleep. Although I can't wait to turn off the light and lie down, my brain is looping the loop.

I keep having flashbacks to when I was a child. They all feature Mum. Mum gardening, cooking, balanced on ladders, painting, Mum irritated, resigned, impatient, withdrawn but always *doing* things – never sitting quietly, at rest. The sitting quietly didn't happen until Pandora and Cassandra were small and she started knitting all those lovely sweaters for them. She *had* to sit then. Even she realised that you can't dash around the place and knit at the same time!

I've been searching my memory for times when she and I were together, just the two of us, in harmony. Sadly, they are very few of them. The one occasion that stands out clearest is when she came to visit me after the twins were born. It had been a long labour and a difficult delivery and I was feeling as though I'd been put through a mincing machine.

She came straight from seeing them in their cots in the hospital nursery. When she approached the bed, I remember noticing with surprise that there were tears in her eyes. I don't think I'd ever seen her cry before. She smiled and leaned over to kiss me – which was also rare – and then she lightly touched the back of my hand, almost tentatively as if afraid that I might not like it, before turning away quickly to pull a chair nearer the bed and to surreptitiously wipe her eyes. When she sat down, we talked for a little while and I was aware that, for once, I had her full attention and that she was glad to be with me and happy that I had got through the births in one piece. I think she was surprised that I'd actually got down to it and produced something so worthwhile after all my years of inconsequential potterings and flitting from one interest to another.

That feeling of being in accord didn't last long though. It was shattered as soon as she found out the names I'd chosen for her new granddaughters. Once again, her features registered the familiar look of disbelief and frustration at my perverseness. With hindsight, I almost wish that I'd called them something that she would have liked, something conventional, unfussy and ordinary. Isn't hindsight a bugger?

It's strange the way that I'm already grieving for her and remembering while she's still alive. Although, in a way, she's been absent for some time now. I keep coming back to the fact that having, usually inadvertently, been the cause of so much disappointment, I can't, at the very end of her life, make up to her a little. I find it distressing to not be allowed the chance to make amends. Surely it would please her to know that someone wants to make a film out of one of my books? Wouldn't she be proud? Or would she just think of it as not being of any importance? After all, generally speaking, books and films don't save lives or feed hungry mouths. Perhaps she would put it into the category of, what she used to refer to as, arty-crafty carry-on, like dressing up to go on stage or taking part in a second-rate soap or splashing dollops of paint onto a canvas. I really don't know how she would react, do I?

Goodness! I sound like a small child, wanting approval. OK, I admit it. I can't help myself. I do want to know that she looked kindly on me at the very end. She's my mother, *God damn it!* The only one I've got. If I'm honest, I would like her to hold me and tell me she's proud of me and that she loves me. Yes, I know I'm asking for the impossible – but there you go.

* * *

A week later. 10 am Sunday morning, 18th October.

My mother died at ten minutes to seven this morning. She was seventy-four years old and had been a widow for almost forty years. She left behind her a few personal possessions – so few they would fit into a small case. There is hardly anything left in her bank account, I do know that. The proceeds of the sale of her house have been used up to pay for her care in the nursing home.

They'd called me at home and I was with her for the last hour of her life. She never regained consciousness. Her breathing changed so that, several times, I thought she'd slipped away and then her chest would rise almost imperceptibly. I sat beside the bed and held her hand and waited. There was nothing I could do for her. She never opened her eyes or spoke. Her leaving was completely unobtrusive. One moment there, and then a sensation of sudden stillness and she was gone.

I looked down at her strangely smooth face. I could see that what I was looking at no longer bore any real resemblance to the person who had been my mother. All the character written in the lines and wrinkles had somehow been erased. What was left was a husk, the remains of a woman called Molly Forde. A woman who'd been as quietly unremarkable as most people are and yet who'd made it through her allotted seventy-four years with no small measure of courage and quiet fortitude.

I looked out of the window at the pale, early morning

sky and saw red and gold leaves swirling through the air in a sudden gust of wind that seemed to come from nowhere. When I looked at the trees at the far side of the garden, not a branch seemed to be stirring.

I can't write anything more at the moment. I feel strangely dry-eyed and empty.

* * *

Tuesday evening.

So much has happened since Sunday, this is the first time it's been possible to sit down and write anything. Funnily, it's not a duty now but more a compulsion – the emergency safety valve of being able to write down some of the jumbled stuff ricocheting around my brain.

It keeps hitting me that the rest of the world is carrying on quite normally around me. Somehow, I feel that it's not quite right; that it should look or feel different. I certainly resented the fact that, when I lost Pandora, there was no cataclysmic global happening to mark the way I felt. It seemed terrible that people could still go on eating and drinking and laughing and carrying on as if nothing appalling had taken place. I suppose most people feel like that after a death. They forget that, in a while, they too will be eating and drinking and laughing – just like the rest. And somewhere, perhaps quite close by, some other person's daughter or mother will be dying.

I can't remember when I had so much to do in such a short space of time. From arranging the service at the crematorium, registering my mother's death, putting notices in the papers, making phone calls, ordering flowers. The list is endless. At least her death was expected and there's no delay because of there having to be a post mortem. I'm also glad to be spared the thought of my mother's poor remains laid out on a table while the pathologist cuts and dissects.

All this week, I've been monitoring Cassandra to make sure that she's all right. All this must remind her of what we were going through just over a year ago. Wisely, she hadn't wanted to go to the nursing home for a last goodbye to her grandmother.

"I'd rather remember Granny Molly as she was before she got ill," she said. "Do you mind, Mum? It's not that I don't care or anything."

I gave her a hug and told her of course I didn't mind and that I thought that was the best way to remember her.

Cassandra's been very sweet over the last couple of days, missing lectures and doing her best to keep an eye on me! Keith has spent a lot of time at the house. He's extraordinarily restful to have around the place. He never hovers, looking uncertain. Quietly and unobtrusively, he washes up and when there is nothing obvious left to do, he folds his wiry frame into a chair and sits at the kitchen table, reading the paper but always ready to talk if he feels that's what Cassandra or I want. The two of them have made me – or offered to make me – umpteen cups of tea. I've caught both of them watching me at different times, Keith with a little frown of concentration, Cassandra with real anxiety. I think she's worried that I might have some sort of relapse and she'll have to cope with me absent-mindedly spraying my armpits with hair spray and squirting my hair with deodorant – like I did only a few months ago when my life was in the process of unravelling.

It was with great difficulty that I persuaded them to go out earlier on this evening.

"For goodness' sake, Keith, take my daughter out and leave me in peace for a while," I told him.

"But, Mum, I don't think you should be left all on your own," said Cassandra.

When Keith saw my look of frustration, he grinned at me and pulled her up from her chair by the hand.

"Come on, babe! I think your Ma's got enough on her plate without feeling that she's in a *Big Brother* style horror epic!"

For the first time since Sunday morning, I took the phone off the hook and soaked in a hot bath and just let my thoughts drift.

I realise that, although I feel very tired, I'm also relieved – grateful that the waiting is over and that Mum died peacefully. There are so many horrible ways of dying. I think that, always, at the back of my mind, I was afraid that she might not make a gentle exit.

I'm not looking forward to the funeral very much, which is, on Mum's instructions of many years ago, to be as quick and simple as possible.

"No flowers, no music, no fuss," she'd said. "And absolutely no one holding forth about what a nice person I was and how I will be sadly missed. It's such a waste of time and money." She also made the revealing remark that the only person who could have spoken about her with any accuracy would have been my father.

I'm afraid that I've disobeyed her on the flowers front. A funeral with no music will seem bare enough but one without a single flower to soften and breathe its scent over the proceedings is too much to cope with. If she's watching me, which I'm sure she isn't, no doubt she'll put it down to my usual ineptitude and inability to carry out instructions.

The one nice thing is that Cassandra will be with me and Sam is coming over for the day.

"I've told Sylvia to put everything on hold for the day. Unfortunately I won't be able to stay any longer on this visit because of various things that she says are utterly unchangeable and unavoidable. I'm sorry, Hebe," he said, when he rang me back to confirm that he was coming.

"Don't worry," I assured him. "It's lovely to know that you will be there for the funeral," I reassured him.

Maggie rang and we spoke for a long time. She won't be able to get over for the funeral tomorrow but she said she was sending flowers and that she'd be thinking of me. She was lovely, not at all sentimental – she'd never met my mother and was well aware of how ill she'd been and for how long – but she somehow managed to say things that were sympathetic and positive and her call left me feeling more cheerful.

Owen rang and was stiffly sympathetic. It will take a long time for him to get over the dinner party fracas. I even got a short, very correct letter of condolence from Dervla. *That* made me feel guilty and irritated at the same time. She and my mother never liked each other. Dervla hated the thought that they were the same age and I think she's secretly frightened about what old age will dish up on her plate. And Mum thought she was an overbearing, bossy snob and would run a mile rather than spend any time in her company. Anyway, I should be charitable and I must make sure to write a letter back, thanking her for hers.

Though it won't be easy after our last meeting! (Especially as I still think I was speaking the truth at the time and she probably suspects that.)

It's a shame that they feel they have to come to the service in the crematorium. So, no doubt, will other people, whom I won't know but who, through some tenuous link with my mum, will feel obliged to appear. I don't think this happens in England, this compulsion to attend funerals. In Ireland, it's a sort of national pastime, high on the list after Gaelic football, greyhound racing, debunking anyone thought to have become too pleased with themselves and socialising in the pub. All the time you hear about whole businesses grinding to a halt for an entire day because the great-aunt of the sales manager has died and they all want to be seen doing their bit. Personally, I think it's rather daft – but nice too, I suppose, in a world that can be cold and unfriendly a lot of the time.

I've noticed that Busby has been even more attentive than usual, following me around, giving little meows whenever I look at him as though he's trying to comfort me. It's a good thing cats don't live as long as humans. He'd probably go into a decline if I suddenly popped my clogs!

Chapter Fourteen

Wednesday night.

Joan, Cassandra, Keith and I have just finished supper. As it turned out, they did most of the clearing up after the get-together when the funeral was over. I must say that the whole day went far better than I'd dared hope.

Sam arrived before lunch. When I opened the door and found him standing on the step, I burst into tears. I hadn't realised just how much I wanted him to be here today. He wasn't the least bit taken aback by all the waterworks. He didn't say anything, just stepped into the house and put his arms around me and held me for a few minutes. Long enough for me to come to my senses and dry my face before Cassandra and Joan saw me.

"Are you all right?" he asked before we went into the kitchen where the other two were buttering bread and making scones.

"Yes, of course, I am. Thank you so much for coming, Sam," I said, kissing the side of his face.

"Wild literary agents and stroppy secretaries couldn't stop me from being here with you today," he said, giving my cheek a gentle stroke. "And, now that I'm here, I want to be useful. What do you want me to do?"

The four of us worked away in the kitchen, preparing the food. Cassandra seemed genuinely pleased to see him again and I noticed with pleasure that she made the first move to give him a welcoming kiss. Joan and Sam took an immediate liking to each other and somehow the next couple of hours melted away in an atmosphere of busy but quiet companionship.

I hadn't the slightest idea of how many people would be at the funeral or how many would want to come back to the house afterwards.

"We'd better do too much rather than too little. I don't want someone to have to rush to the corner shop halfway through the afternoon for emergency top-ups," I said, while trying to slice a cucumber into delicate, even slices – not too successfully. Delicate and even just ain't me, it would appear.

"Especially as the corner shop only stocks cheese and onion crisps, tortilla chips and manky little sponge jobs with electric icing," commented Cassandra dryly.

"Sounds delicious to me," commented Sam, pointing a knife, covered in butter, at her. "I'll have you know, I grew up on cheese and onion crisps and manky little sponge jobs with electric icing – as you so accurately put it. And look where that got me!"

"I wonder, if you'd been fed a proper diet, where you'd be now. There are more important things in life than being a mere novelist!"

"Ouch! That was an evil little dig! I see you take after your mama in your lack of appreciation of my fame."

"Don't you believe it," I interjected. "She's chuffed to bits that she's shared a pot of tea with the notorious Sam Ellis!"

"I think not!" said my daughter, giving him a broad smile.

Glancing over at her, I could see that Joan was amused at the way Cassandra blushed, even as she denied the accusation.

I hadn't gone down the usual route of hiring large black cars to take us to and from the crematorium. All the flowers and Mum's coffin were going straight from the undertakers to the chapel and we were to go under our own steam. Mum would have approved of the money saved by doing things that way and actually, I was glad not to have to sit in the back of a limousine, looking suitably dignified. My grieving is being done in private and I don't want to make other people uncomfortable by parading the fact that I've just lost my mother. Also, I wanted to make it as low key as possible for Cassandra's sake after what she went through at her sister's funeral. Then, Owen had taken charge. No expense was spared and I just remember the whole occasion as a black pageant – a macabre masquerade of some sort, with me, puppet-like, having my strings yanked by my ex-husband and, more often by my ex-mother-in-law as I numbly shook hands and stood and sat when I was told.

When we arrived at the crematorium, there weren't all that many people there. Among the first to arrive were Owen and Lucy, who gave me the sweetest smile from the far end of a pew, and Dervla, haughty and elegant in black. It was obvious from the look on her face that she was shocked that neither Cassandra nor I were dressed in mourning clothes. I wore a blue woollen dress with matching jacket that I'm always comfortable in. Cassandra wore her favourite green dress that *she* was comfortable in. Keith was resplendent in a suit with a rose-coloured brocade waistcoat. I've never actually seen him in a suit before. His wild, curly hair had been carefully combed and he'd even polished his glasses so that they didn't have their usual slightly smudged look about them. As he joined Cassandra, I thought that he looked rather like someone who'd been told that he'd better behave and dress appropriately for an important occasion. I suspect, that if Cassandra hadn't bullied him, he would have worn his usual uniform of jeans and sweater, limp from too many over-hot washes. We'd discussed it earlier and agreed that Granny Molly wouldn't have cared what we wore as long as we looked tidy and reasonably respectable.

I was touched to see that a couple of the nuns from the nursing home had come. Apart from that, a handful of faces, some of whom I recognised as having been friends of my mother's and one elderly couple who had known my parents from the early days of their respective marriages. I suppose, including Keith and Sam, there must have been about twenty of us in all.

The service was ably conducted by the resident chaplain and I found it easy to stay calm. The only time that I felt a sudden lump in my throat was when the coffin started to slide away from us and I had this overwhelming desire to have my mother alive and well and standing beside me. But it passed and the service drew to a close without any show of emotion on anyone's part.

Now, remembering how smoothly it all went, I can't

help feeling sorry that my mother's funeral should evoke no tears or apparent distress from anyone in that small cluster of mourners. But then, I suspect that she would have approved of that. I can see her, shaking her head and saying, 'No fuss, no nonsense, Hebe, thank you.'

When we came out of the chapel afterwards, a tall figure detached itself from one of the groups. Even though he had lost a considerable amount of weight, I recognised him instantly. He must have slipped in at the back of the chapel after the service had already started. Dr Scheller came over to me and took my hand.

"Mrs Sayer, may I offer my condolences? I was sorry to hear of your mother's passing, although I know that she has been ill for a long time." He looked so dreadfully thin and tired, I found myself standing, with my hand in his, silently staring into his eyes, not knowing what to say.

When he withdrew his hand, I somehow managed to pull myself together. "Dr Scheller! How kind of you to come. I was so very sorry to hear about your son."

"Thank you for your kind letter. I received so many I'm afraid that I haven't had the time to reply to many of them." His voice too sounded dispirited, as though it took all his energy to just remain standing. He started to turn away. "I must go. My wife is unwell and is at home . . ." the sentence tailed away.

"I was going to ask you if you would come back to the house and have something to eat and drink."

"No, I'm sorry. That is not possible. But thank you all the same. And I am very pleased to see you looking so well."

He gave a slight smile and turned away, walking slowly back towards the gates. I wondered if he had been back to the clinic and whether he'd heard of my bad-tempered refusal to see anyone but him. I hoped not. As he walked away, I remembered his words of encouragement and all the times that he had assured me that all would be well in my life. I knew I wasn't equipped to return the favour. I didn't have either the facility or the training. But how I would have loved to be able to say just one thing to lighten his grief or change the look in his eyes.

"Who was that?" asked Sam in a quiet voice.

"My doctor when I was ill in the clinic."

"My God! I haven't seen such sadness in a man's face for longer than I can remember," he said quietly, his eyes following the dark-suited figure. "What has happened to make him like that?"

"His only son – a young boy – died a few weeks ago after a long illness."

The look on Sam's face was one of distress as if he understood the other's hell. Then I remembered the words Maggie had spoken over the phone about Sam's only son not being in touch, alienated from him by the boy's mother. So he too had lost a son, not in such a final way as Dr Scheller but I sensed not only a deep compassion for the other man's suffering, but also a sudden surge of regret about his own situation.

As we walked back toward the car, with Keith and Cassandra following some way behind, I said, "Maggie mentioned that you have a son, Sam."

He slowed his pace and turned to look at me. "What did Maggie have to say about him?"

"Only that his name is James and that you don't see him very often," I said, feeling suddenly uncomfortable.

"That was untypically discreet of her," he said with a humourless laugh. "It would be more accurate to say that I never set eyes on him. His mother sees to that." There was more regret than bitterness in his voice.

Cursing myself for bringing up the subject, I squeezed his arm. "It can't stay that way for ever, you know."

"Can't it?" he asked. "There's talk of him going to work in the States and she's planning to move over there too. I think it's going to be very hard to change things if we're not even living in the same country."

"Then, you must make sure that you by-pass her and have it out with him," I said. I don't know how I became such an instant expert on other people's family problems. I was suddenly overcome with embarrassment. "Sorry, Sam! I don't know anything about your situation. I didn't mean to start dishing out good advice. Ignore me! I don't usually behave like that."

We had reached the car at this point. He gave me a wide, reassuring smile and told me not to worry, that things had a way of sorting themselves out. I don't think he believed that for one moment. He was just putting me at my ease, letting me know that I hadn't upset him with my unsolicited and uninformed advice.

Later, when everyone was drinking tea and sampling Joan's lightest of light scones with her home-made raspberry jam, I followed Sam into the leaf-strewn garden, really more in an attempt to evade Dervla than anything else. The woman seemed to be everywhere I looked. I had noticed her sizing up the unimpressive guests (in her eyes anyway), peering at some of the better paintings on the walls, looking askance at my choice of cheerful curtain material and even turning over a fork to check the hallmark on the back. No doubt she was worried I might have done a runner with some of Owen's family silver when I left him. (It did cross my mind to at the time – there was so much of it – but I behaved honourably and even left him the bone-handled carving knife and fork that Mum had given us as a wedding present because I knew how fond he was of them. Definite gold star, Hebe!)

I'd also noticed that Busby was watching her intently from the back of the sofa with half-closed eyes. He looked like a miniature version of an African lion, sizing up a none-too-attractive wildebeest and wondering if chasing it would be worth the effort. The end of his tail was twitching back and forth in a regular rhythm like a furry metronome. I knew exactly how he was feeling. Where Owen's mother is concerned, if I'd had a tail, it would have been twitching too!

"What time do you have to leave?" I asked Sam.

"Around six, I suppose."

"I'll take you to the airport."

"But what about that lot in there?" He gestured in the direction of the gabble of voices coming from inside the house.

"Don't worry, they'll be gone well before then. I've hidden the gin and whiskey. I'm not offering them anything more interesting than tea or orange juice. Anyone who is gasping for a drink can go down to the local and continue the wake there," I told him.

"I thought that the booze always flowed after a funeral in Ireland," he said with a grin. "Isn't there a custom where everyone gathers around and tells grisly stories about their aunties being buried alive and strange knocking sounds coming from inside the coffin, while the fiddler fiddles and everyone becomes increasingly plastered?"

"Perhaps but not today," I replied firmly. "They can go and get merry in the pub. Mum wouldn't have approved and quite honestly, enough is enough. Quite honestly, I don't much enjoy having the place invaded by strangers, nice though they are. I still don't feel quite up to all the noise and I never was any good at being an efficient host and saying the appropriate thing at the appropriate time. I always seem to put my foot in it."

He took my cold hands in his warm ones and stared into my face. "But you're coping all right, aren't you, Hebe? In spite of everything."

"Yes," I said, "I'm coping remarkably well."

I don't think he realised how much his presence here today helped my ability to cope. Of course, I know that I could have done it without him but I'm just glad that I didn't have to.

* * *

We got to the airport well before he had to check in. Sitting in the downstairs bar, we sipped our first drink of the day while we chatted and I people-watched – and quite a lot of people watched Sam. He took absolutely no notice of them. He's developed the uncanny knack of managing not to focus on what's going on around him if he feels he's being stared at. So, when we were talking, it appeared that anything peripheral was blocked out and all his concentration was on me.

"How do you do it?" I asked, fascinated.

"Do what?"

"How do you manage to be apparently oblivious to the fact that there's a fat woman at the table over there, who is only desperate to catch your eye and there are also a couple of rather attractive young ones sitting near the bar, flashing their navels at you? They've been staring at you for the last ten minutes without blinking."

"Easy when you're in the company of a gorgeous woman. Why would I want to look at anyone else?"

He did actually use those words – the gallant and, oh, so foolish, man!

"When will you be able to get over to Ireland again?" I asked, hoping that it wasn't too obvious that I thought next week wouldn't be soon enough.

"I told Sylvia that I wanted a week or two off. She's seeing how she can wangle the diary. Maggie knows I've been working hard on the latest book and she's quite happy for me to disappear for a while." He took hold of one of my hands. "Are you doing anything at the end of October or, possibly, the start of November?"

"Nothing, as far as I know. The only thing that's lurking is the possibility of working on a screenplay but I dare say that won't be for a while – if it comes off."

"Maggie told me about that! Very exciting!"

"I'll have my work cut out to catch up with you. How many of your books have been made into films?"

"I dunno! Four or five."

"Listen to the man! So casual. A mere four or five, he says."

"Listen to me, Hebe Sayer. What I was going to say, before you interrupted, was that I was thinking of taking a couple of weeks off somewhere warm and sunny at the end of October and I wondered if you'd care to spend all or some of that time with me. If the idea isn't too grisly to contemplate, that is."

"I'll have to think about it," I said, buying time.

All of a sudden, all I could think about were problems, reasons why I wouldn't be able to go anywhere at the end of October. There was so much to sort out in the aftermath of Mum's death. And was I up to taking off for a couple of weeks with this man? Was I sufficiently together to embark on the next stage of the relationship? I suddenly felt unexpectedly nervous.

In his usual way, he seemed to understand. "You don't have to tell me now. Think about it and if the idea doesn't appeal I shall take it in my stride." Then he gave me one of his smiles that make my inside plummet. "I shall probably slit my throat if you say no, but I promise you, there's absolutely no pressure!"

I walked as far as the taped-off cattle-pen affair before the security check (where I remember from previous departures, they irritatingly insist on relieving you of the most minute pair of nail scissors.) We kissed and then he started to walk away. Suddenly he turned and came back.

"What is it?" I asked. "Have you forgotten something?"

"I just wanted to kiss you again. It's the nicest thing in the world, kissing you, that's all!"

So, I shut my eyes, breathing him in as we kissed again! And it lasted a long time and was gentle and sweet.

As he stepped back from me, he said, "There was one other thing. You remember when we were in Kilkenny and I bought a present for Sylvia in the shop there?" I nodded.

"Well, I also bought something else. It was for you but I didn't give it to you then. I thought you might consider I was rushing things so I hid it in your house for a future special occasion – or for a rainy day when you might need cheering up." That seemed just about the most romantic gesture anyone's ever made for me. I probably had a soppy expression on my face because he began to laugh. "Don't you want a clue on how to find it or would you be quite happy to ransack the whole house?"

"A clue, please."

"It is said that elephants never forget."

"And that's it?"

"Yep!" He looked at his watch. "I'd better go or, famous author or not, the bloody plane won't wait for me."

Just before he disappeared around the screen, he turned and touched his fingers to his lips and blew me a discreet kiss. Not so discreet that a woman following close on his heels didn't notice. She turned around to have a good gawk at the object of the famous author's attention. Me!!! I could have waggled my ears at her and danced a jig. But I didn't. Just stood there – probably looking rather horribly smug.

All the way home, I racked my brains, trying to remember if I possessed an elephant in some shape or form. I didn't own a painting of an elephant or a figure of an elephant. Then, when I had steam coming out of my ears, I remembered that Cassandra had brought back a plate from school when she was about twelve. Everyone in her class had had to decorate a plain white plate with a picture of their favourite animal and she had chosen an elephant. I'd loved it immediately. The animal looked as though he were drunk. He was dancing a wild tango with a bunch of bananas in his trunk. Both elephant and the background were decorated in mad squiggles and asterisks of colour. I had put it in pride of place on the top shelf of the kitchen dresser where it wouldn't get knocked by mistake. If Pandora hadn't been off school with a bad cold, I would have had two decorated plates to enjoy looking at.

When I got home, the others stared at me in amazement as I flew into the kitchen, dragged a chair over to the dresser, climbed up and started scrabbling behind the plate.

"What *are* you doing, Mum?" asked Cassandra in a stunned voice.

She was probably thinking that she'd been right all along to suspect that her mother, like Humpty Dumpty, wasn't completely together again.

"Elephants never forget." I murmured, still rummaging.

"Right!" said my daughter. I could imagine the nervous look she gave Keith behind my back.

"Got it!" I announced, turning around to show them the small parcel clutched in my hand.

"What have you got there?" asked Joan in her matter-of-fact way. As if she were quite used to being around women who suddenly start behaving like lunatics.

"It's a present from Sam."

"Why did he leave it up there? Why didn't he just give it to you," asked Cassandra.

"It's a surprise – for a rainy day," I informed her happily as I climbed down from the chair.

They all watched as I carried the small parcel over to the table and peeled off the paper. Inside was a box. Inside the box was a necklace – a simple curve of silver. It was like a modern version of a torque. And it was beautiful.

"That man of yours certainly has good taste," commented Joan in an approving tone.

We were all agreed on that point!

Cassandra ran her fingers over the satiny surface. "Can I put it on for you?" Without waiting for an answer, she took it from me and placed it around my neck. It was surprisingly light and the silver felt cool against my skin. "It really suits you. You look great, Mum," said my daughter, standing back to get a better view.

I've put it on the bedside table. I keep looking at it, admiring its smooth, shiny surface and feeling touched that Sam wanted to give me something so lovely.

He hadn't got back when I rang to thank him so I left a message on his phone.

"I think it's the most lovely present anyone has ever given me. Thank you so much. And thank you too for being here for us today. Goodnight, Sam. I'll talk to you tomorrow."

The house is quiet now. Joan has gone home. The fridge is stuffed with left-over sausage rolls and other goodies.

As Cassandra said, "Great, Mum. Now you won't have to bother about what to eat for a few days."

Keith is staying the night – supposedly in the spare bedroom. I've told them both that they are to get on with their lives and, from tomorrow, Cassandra is to go back to her rooms in college and, under pain of death, is not to miss any more tutorials. I think that, finally, she's starting to believe me when I say I am managing and I just need some time and space to go on with the reconstruction of Hebe Sayer.

I'm going to think of Mum before I go to sleep. I want to think of all the nicest things about her. It's too late now to change anything about our more off-than-on relationship but I don't ever want to remember her with bitterness or in a disappointed sort of way.

I'm thankful that today is over and grateful that it went as well as it did. But I know it was the ending of a chapter. I know too that I'm probably well over halfway through my own life and I want this last chunk to be good. I want to try and heal the rift between Cassandra and Owen and I want the luxury of getting to know Sam and of loving him. While I'm mentioning all my wants, I want a long and happy life for Busby, by the way.

I think that, most of all, I want to be able to talk about Pandora to Cassandra without her turning on me or turning away from me. And I want to be able to lay the memory of what happened to rest.

Chapter Fifteen

Friday night. No Busby. He must still be out on the razzle.

The most marvellous thing happened today. Suzie is back! I got a call after lunch.

"Hello, Hebe! How are you, girl?" There was a slight hint of Australian in the voice.

"Suzie?" I couldn't believe my ears.

"The one and only! Listen, are you at home this afternoon?"

"Yes. Can you come round? I can't offer you a tinnie by the barbie, I'm afraid!"

"Ha-bloody-ha! I'll be with you in about half an hour."

I could hardly wait to see her. More or less the last glimpse I had of her was at a mutual friend's party before she went on her travels, just before Pandora died. I sent her an e-mail after the funeral but whole months went by after that when I couldn't bring myself to write any letters or even short e-mails. Suzie isn't a great correspondent herself but she rang every now and then and I still have the collection of mad, brightly coloured cards she sent when she found out that I was in the clinic.

I don't think she understood quite how unravelled I was around that time. Suzie isn't the sort of person who suffers from self-doubt, nerves or an over-vivid imagination. She's strong in mind and body and far too busy living her life to get emotional about things. No, that's not strictly true. She used to get extremely overheated on the topic of her ex-husband, Donal, commonly referred to by her as 'It'. They split up at about the same time as Owen and I but hers was a far more tempestuous parting of the ways. Horrible though our separating was, at least we didn't get around to slamming doors or chucking personal possessions out of windows. I think I remember her mentioning that she had hidden several crates of It's favourite port, which must have made him extremely angry.

When I opened the door to her a little later, I was nearly knocked off my feet by her bear hug. When we eventually disentangled ourselves, I saw that she was looking positively Amazonian – all five feet eleven of her – toned and dark brown, her eyes and skin glowing with good health.

"Blimey! You look marvellous!" I gasped. "Like an ad for Laura Croft, or whatever the name is of that one in the telly ad who spends her time leaping off precipices with a bottle of pop in her fist."

"Tennis! I played nearly every day. That and swimming and," she gave a dirty giggle, "marvellous sex nearly every other day. I tell you, it's the best recipe I know for keeping your circulation up to scratch." She stared at me with her large brown eyes. "You look as though you could do with a year in Oz yourself. You're terribly thin, Hebe. Beautiful but too thin. Was this because of what happened to Pandora or is there something else you haven't told me about?"

We took mugs of coffee out into the garden, which was looking decidedly autumnal with leaves all over the place, but the sun was shining and we sat in a sheltered corner, surrounded by late flowering roses and wind-bashed lilies.

She settled herself, stretching out her long, tanned legs in front of her (I've always coveted Suzie's legs. They are exactly what legs should be: smooth, shapely, slim-ankled and yards long – with not a bristle or blemish in sight – damn her!).

Gazing around the garden, she said, "This is looking a lot more cared-for than when I was last here. I seem to remember that you were going in for the natural look in those days – more designer jungle than cropped and tweaked! Where's Busby by the way? Don't tell me something's happened to him. I couldn't bear it."

"No, he's around somewhere. I think he's in love. I've seen him keeping rather dubious company with the flirty white cat from three houses down and he's not been coming home till late each night."

"But he's got no balls!"

"Doesn't seem to stop him from roaming. Perhaps it's a platonic relationship."

Suzie snorted. "There's no such thing!" She took a sip from her mug. "Come on, tell me what's been going on. You obviously haven't kept me up to speed," she observed, leaning back in her chair and pushing her thick chestnut hair from her face with long brown fingers.

So, I told her about how I hadn't been able to cope with

Pandora's death, that it had affected me so badly that I started to lose control of my life. I told her about what I remembered of my time in the clinic, of Dr Scheller and how difficult things had been between Owen, Cassandra and myself. I recounted my unfortunate remark to Lucy at the dreadful dinner and Dervla and Cassandra's reaction to what I'd said. And I told her about my mother's deterioration and death.

She listened, more or less open-mouthed, eyes fixed on my face. When I'd finished, she put her mug down on the ground and took both my hands in hers. "You poor darling! No wonder you're still looking a bit the worse for wear."

"Thanks," I said, smiling. "I thought I was looking a lot better. You should have seen me six months ago. I would have given Dracula's mother a run for her money in the gaunt and hollow-eyed stick-insect stakes. It wasn't a pretty sight!"

"Oh, Hebe, I feel really guilty. I had no idea things had been so awful for you. And all the time you were going through this, I was living the high-life in Melbourne."

"Don't feel guilty. I honestly believe that there was nothing you could have done to make things any different. I had to work my way through it all. No one else could do it for me."

"And *have* you? Have you worked your way through it?" she asked, her face serious.

"I've still a little way to go and a few more things to sort out but I'm getting there. Somehow, Mum dying, although I'm sad that she wasn't given a longer, healthier life to live, has freed me in a strange way. I hadn't realised that, for years, she was almost always present in my mind. I was carting around a whole load of baggage: I wondered if I was doing enough for her and whether I should have done things differently in the past. That and wondering why we never hit it off together. Was it my fault or hers? It crossed my mind that perhaps she wasn't getting the right treatment, that she was more miserable than I realised – all that sort of thing. Now, the anxiety has gone and it means I can concentrate on the other stuff in my life that has to be sorted."

"It doesn't sound as though Owen has been much of a support," she commented, pulling her mouth down at the corners and raising her eyebrows.

"He's done his best. But I'll never understand him. You'd think it would help to talk about what's happened but it's as though he's frightened to. I don't understand what he's frightened *of* – unless it's his daughter's temper. Perhaps he's frightened that if he shows me he's not as tough as he makes out, I'll take advantage of him. Or perhaps he feels that, if he really says what he thinks, I won't be able to take it and I'll go gaga again. I don't know! I really was one sandwich short of a picnic for some time. He and Cassandra had their hands full keeping tabs on me. And I know he blames me for what happened."

"Bloody hell!" exclaimed Suzie, sitting bolt upright. "How does he work that one out?"

"He says that if I had kept better control of the girls, they wouldn't have gone to the club that night. What he *hasn't* said in so many words, but I know he thinks, is that my row with them the night Pandora died was the catalyst for her behaving in a way that was completely out of character. If I had reasoned with her, explained why I felt the way I did about 'Spike's', she might have given in and backed down – in spite of any pressure from her sister."

"He's a fine one to talk! If I remember correctly, it was Owen who lost his temper and was always banning them from doing things or stopping their allowance. *You* were the one they turned to when he was being downright unreasonable."

Suddenly, the horror of that night a year ago flooded into my mind and I was back in the A and E department, looking down at my dead daughter. She was surrounded by resuscitation equipment, her face unbelievably pale and there was a large bruise on one cheek where she'd fallen when she'd collapsed. I can still hear the unemotional voice of the tired doctor telling me that it appeared that she had taken Ecstasy. Alcohol and one little white tablet of Ecstasy was all it had taken to kill her.

"It's all right, Hebe." Suzie's voice was gentle. "Don't go over it all now. Leave it. We'll talk about other things."

For a moment I couldn't look at her, just sat there with my head bowed, fighting the fear that I would become ill again, that I wasn't really cured at all.

Eventually I said, "It's just that, sometimes, I get panicked by the idea that I only imagine I'm coping, that really, underneath, I'm starting to crumble again."

"No, not you," she said in a firm voice. "You've so much sense and strength, Hebe, you'll win through. I know you will." She gave my arm a gentle shove. "And I'm back on the scene now. So things can only improve, right?"

She looked so confident, I couldn't help smiling.

"I can't tell you how good it is to see you. I've missed you so much," I said, rubbing a drip off the end of my nose with the back of my hand. "Now, you tell me what you've been up to and who is this lucky man with whom you've been having so much fun?"

It must have taken nearly an hour for me to hear about Lee (yes, even she was a little embarrassed at falling for an Aussie called Lee), about his surfing skills, his fine tennis-playing, his charm, his good humour and, of course, his ability in the bedroom department.

"What he lacked in finesse, he certainly made up for with energy and enthusiasm – and not a little imagination," she informed me with a wicked glint in her eye.

"And is he going to follow you back to Ireland? Or is he here already?" I asked.

"Good God, no! He wouldn't fit in to my life here. He knows it and I know it. Can you imagine? Not a roller in sight and only three days of hot sun a year – if we're lucky. No tinnies around the barbie with hordes of semi-clad Sheilas! He'd go into a decline." She gave me a sudden probing look. "And when did Hebe last have a good roll in the hay, may I ask?"

I laughed. "I haven't had one of those for longer than I can remember."

"Well, all I can say is, it looks as though I'll have to get myself organised pretty smartish and throw a few parties with every single attractive, unattached male I can think of inviting. We'll have to do something about the situation. You can't expect to get completely better without a good bonk every now and then. It's not natural to live like that."

"No need," I said.

"What do you mean, no need? You're not thinking of running away and joining a nunnery, I hope?" I shook my head and she continued, "You just said that you can't remember your last bonk. It sounds to me as though it's imperative we do something about that. It will be top of my agenda. I'll call it the Help Hebe Regain Health Holistically campaign!"

"No, you won't," I said. "I've met someone."

"Yes?" She suddenly looked anxious. "Not someone from the nut – clinic, I hope?"

"No, not someone from the nuthouse, Suzie! He's a writer."

She digested this piece of information for a moment. "Well, why haven't you gone to bed together. Or is he gay and this is just a meeting of lovely literary minds?"

"It's a meeting of minds all right. But he's not in the least bit gay and it's too early in our relationship to rush into bed."

"Oh, yeah?" The scepticism in her voice was palpable. "Of a nervous disposition, is he? Frightened of rejection?"

I remembered the smouldering look in Sam's eyes after we'd kissed. The idea of his being too timid to ask me to go to bed with him seemed so absurd, I laughed out loud. "You like reading novels. You may have even have heard of him, Suzie."

"And? You're doing this on purpose. For goodness' sake, who is he?"

"Sam Ellis."

She looked at me in amazement – just like Cassandra when I'd first told her. "You're not serious?"

"Completely."

"Oh, my God! He's even big down-under – if you get my meaning."

She continued to stare at me, so stunned by the news that it rendered her temporarily speechless. Temporarily. It takes a lot to silence Suzie – a stun gun might do the job.

I bent down and collected up the mugs. "I'm beginning to feel cold. How about going inside? I think we should celebrate your arrival with a proper drink."

She got up and followed me into the house. "And when you've made two large and very strong G and T's, I want to hear, in minute detail, about this Sam Ellis, where you met, what he said, what you said, what you did, what he did, etc etc."

She made it sound like a game of Consequences! Anyway, I told her everything I could think of and when she eventually left to go home it was late but she looked as though she was satisfied I had left nothing out!

I realised after she'd gone that I'd forgotten to ask about the recalcitrant boyfriend, left behind in Ireland while she went on her travels. Had she seen him yet? We'd been so busy catching up on our respective lives, I'd even forgotten to ask her about her son, Luke, and whether It knew she was back yet. I can just imagine her forgetting to tell him so that the poor man will suddenly bump into her when he's out shopping with his latest girl friend, who is years younger than Suzie.

It seems to be the norm, this adoption of pretty young things by our men-folk. Why can't they enjoy our more mature minds and experienced ways? Silly question. What man wants flabby roly-poly that wobbles when it runs rather than firm and fresh that doesn't? Oh, bugger them anyway! I hope to God that Sam won't find me tired and past it when we get around to being more intimate. I think I would curl up and cry if that happened.

* * *

Saturday night. Flaked-out cat at end of bed with torn ear and feeling rather sorry for himself. He's either been in a fight or his lady companion is fiercely passionate.

Sam rang this morning.

"I have some rather startling news," he said without any preamble.

"What?" I said, groggily, as he'd woken me up. (He has a habit of doing that but I really don't mind.)

"There's been a transformation in the office."

"You had the decorators in?"

"No, not that sort of transformation! What's been transformed is Sylvia." I waited for the dramatic pause to end and for him to carry on. "Guess who she's seeing?"

"How on earth would I know? For a start, I've never met the woman and I'm not exactly acquainted with either her or your friends. You'd better tell me."

"Maggie!"

"*Our* Maggie?"

"Precisely! I thought that 'our' Maggie had a certain spring in her step last time I saw her. At the time, it didn't strike me as all that odd that she'd called into the office rather than ringing. It wasn't until I saw her picking up Sylvia after work yesterday that the penny finally dropped."

"They might have been going to a business thing – a book launch or something. Don't you lot spend half your lives trying to get out of them?"

"No! I'm sure it wasn't a business thing. Sylvia was hyper all day yesterday. I caught her twice quickly putting down the phone when I came into the room and looking a bit flushed. They were both dressed up to the nines and quiet, understated Sylvia was actually wearing make-up.

She *never* wears make-up. She looked really very pretty too."

"Wow!" I said. "So, the days of lonely supper trays are over and she's going to start living a little."

"I sincerely hope so. I always knew that Maggie wasn't too pushed when it came to the male of the species but I've never actually seen her with another woman – not in a social context anyway. It's good, isn't it?"

"Yes, it is. I hope it works out for them. *I've* got good news too. My friend Suzie's back from Australia."

"Suzie with the ex-It."

"That's the one! She was full of plans to find me a man. She seemed to think I was lacking in that department."

"She doesn't waste any time, does she? I hope you put her straight."

"I most certainly did." I paused. "She was a little nonplussed when I said we hadn't made love yet but immensely impressed when she found out who you were. That is, once I'd assured her that you weren't either gay or scared stiff of intimacy!"

"Good Lord! Is nothing sacred to the Sisterhood? Is there *any* intimate topic that is out of bounds to you lot?"

"Don't worry! I told her that it would probably happen at some point."

"You did?"

"I did!" I paused before adding, "You don't mind, do you?"

"Of course, I don't mind but, from what you've told me, I expect she'll want to know all the gory details."

"Probably," I laughed. "So, perhaps we shouldn't be within phoning distance when it does happen."

"Might be another good reason to come away with me in a couple of weeks' time," he said, slyly. But he was very nice when I told him I was still thinking about that one. Not a hint of irritation or impatience. "All right," he said. Then he added, "Just don't take too long to make up your mind. I've been offered a particularly good deal for the Seychelles if I get back to them reasonably quickly. It sounds a really lovely place, Hebe – white beaches, turquoise sea, feathery palms, cloud-free skies, cool cocktails, absolute peace and privacy . . . you know the sort of thing."

If that isn't pressure, I don't know what is!

* * *

A little later because I can't sleep. Had to remove Busby from the end of the bed. He kept twitching and snoring and flailing his tail in his sleep.

It's nearly two a.m. and I'm wide-awake. So I thought if I grabbed my pen and notebook, writing something might act as a soporific. The same things keep chasing around my brain. I think one of the reasons I'm finding it difficult to relax completely at the moment is that I keep thinking I should be visiting Mum. For a moment, I forget she's no longer there and I have a sudden pang of guilt because I haven't worked out when I'm next going in to see her. I suppose if she'd been living with us when she died, I would keep thinking I caught a glimpse of her out of the corner of my eye – like I did for so long with Pandora.

I still haven't done anything with Mum's ashes either. She didn't leave any instructions about that. I'm tempted to bury them in the garden and plant something nice to mark the spot – but that's not very classy when you think of other options, like scattering her over the sea or from a mountaintop. And anyway, the garden scenario thing was what we did with Cassandra's hamster. I think Mum might be a little put out to be that brain-dead creature's neighbour in death!

Something else that's been bothering me is Pandora's room. I can't leave it like it is. I don't want it to turn into a sort of museum. It's a perfectly good room that would make a nice spare bedroom. Then I could turn what is now the spare room into a study for me. That would mean I could stop using the dining-room table for the computer and we might even have the occasional meal in style instead of on the kitchen table or on our laps in front of the sitting-room fire.

I don't know what Cassandra will feel about it though. Things have been so much better between us these last few days – just as long as I steer clear of two topics: her father and Pandora. I suppose I've put off doing anything about the room because I don't want to jeopardise my relationship with her. And I know that's me being futile. I have to keep repeating all the promises I've made to myself – to be strong and sensible and level-headed.

Another thing that is keeping me awake is this holiday with Sam. I don't know what's happened to me. I never used to get so wound up. A couple of years ago, I would have jumped at the opportunity and thought about any problems as and if they cropped up afterwards. It's as though this illness has made me into a different kind of person and I'm not sure I like her. I'm perfectly aware of the fact that it's not a good idea to lie awake, worrying about things. What was it Dr Scheller said? Something along the lines of – if all the negative energy expended by people worrying was fed into the national grid, the price of electricity would plummet. And I'm sure he was right!

Any more moans while I'm at it? Oh, yes! The screenplay. What the hell do I do about *that*?

And Owen. I can't just dismiss him like Suzie does with It. I know he's far from perfect as a dad and even less so as a husband but he deserves to be treated better by Cassandra. The trouble is, old Witchy Poo is whispering into his ear all the time and that makes it difficult for him to be objective – especially when it comes to me and my perceived shortcomings. And then his dissatisfaction rebounds onto his daughter.

I bumped into Lucy this afternoon when I was doing some shopping in the local supermarket. She didn't say much but I thought she looked very down. I got the strong impression that things weren't all that rosy in the Sayers' ancestral home.

Another thing I've got to get on with is sorting out Mum's things. Not that there are many of them. I came back from the nursing home the morning she died with a horrible black bin-liner containing all that remained of her personal possessions. When I tipped them out onto the kitchen table, it made me want to cry. It seemed so little to have left at the end of a life – some dirty nightdresses, a bed jacket, slippers and dressing-gown, two sets of day clothes and her reading glasses, which she hadn't used for goodness' knows how long. And then, her handbag, into which they'd put her wedding ring, pearl earrings and bracelet watch and a photo of the girls and myself and one of her and Dad on their wedding day.

Of course, I've washed her clothes and put them in a box ready to take down to the local *War on Want* shop. The rest is in a drawer in my bedroom. I know I won't ever wear them. Mum gave away any good jewellery to the girls and myself a long time ago. But I've so little to remember her by and, anyway, I couldn't bear the thought of a complete stranger pawing over her things in some antique shop.

Right! There are quite a few moans in there. I think I'll try and start my next entry off with some positives! Something along the lines of I'm still alive and breathing and I'm not living in a cardboard box. And Suzie's back!

Chapter Sixteen

Monday night. In bed with Busby and the electric blanket. It's blowing a gale outside and pissing rain. The temperature must have fallen by at least ten degrees.

Cassandra and Keith called in yesterday afternoon and we had an interesting and revealing discussion about Pandora's room. I'd got my courage up and made the decision that I would have to mention it when I next saw Cassandra.

"How do you feel about helping me clear out Pandora's room?" I asked her, a little nervously.

She didn't answer me straight away. Keith and I watched her, both of us wondering what her reaction would be.

"Why does it have to be done now?" she asked eventually, her face expressionless.

I knew that was a bad sign – when she has that particular look about her I know it's the calm before all hell breaks loose. But I also knew that, for both our sakes, it was something that needed dealing with and so I battled bravely on.

"I think it *does* have to be done now – not at this very minute, obviously, but in the next few days."

"I don't see why." Her voice was louder and she was looking at me as though I'd made an obscene suggestion. "It's been the same way for a year. Why can't we just leave it until some time later? What's the rush all of a sudden?"

"Because, it should be done. We can't leave it as a sad, no-go area. We have to move on, Cassandra, and I think that clearing out Pandora's room will help us both to do that. I'm not trying to erase the memory of her or anything like that."

She stared angrily at me. "You sound just like Dad. He's always telling me to pull myself together and get on with my life. Just because you're feeling better doesn't mean that you have to dismantle her room. *You* may be getting over her death but I can't forget. I don't want her room cleared as though she was never there. You can't do it! It wouldn't be right." She banged the table with her fist and glared, first at me and then at poor Keith, who, up until that moment, hadn't said a thing.

I was in the middle of trying to sort out how best I could calm her when he suddenly said in a low voice, "Sometimes, Cass, I think you believe you are the only one who really suffered because of Pandora's death."

She looked at him in amazement. "What do you mean?"

"I've heard you blame your mother and your father for Pandora's death and you once even had the gall to tell me that I should have been around the night it happened. You know in your heart of hearts that you fought your mother for the right to go out that night. You didn't listen to her.

You *wouldn't* listen to her. And all this year, you've refused to accept that you had any part in what happened. It's unfair and it's wrong, Cass, dreadfully wrong." He never raised his voice and somehow the effect of what he'd just said was doubled by his quiet delivery.

I stood, looking at him, speechless. Was this the same young man I had known for a couple of years – always so quietly good-humoured, taking more or less any guff from Cassandra that she thought she had the right to dish up? I knew that I'd never heard him criticise her like that before.

Neither had Cassandra, who was looking stunned. "Well, I was upset. I didn't think what I was saying," she muttered.

"Well, I was upset as well. And so was Hebe. Has it ever crossed your mind that I loved Pandora too? Have you ever thought that no one was in a better position or closer to her than you were? You could have talked her out of going to 'Spike's' but you didn't. You encouraged her to make a stand against your parents when you knew perfectly well that your mum had pleaded with you not to go. For Christ's sake, Cass, stop feeling so bloody sorry for yourself and start thinking about the rest of us for a change."

Slowly, he sat down in the nearest chair, not taking his eyes off her.

All I could think was, goodness, that was brave! I looked at Cassandra.

She'd gone very pale. She stared at him for a moment and then went towards the door. "You don't have to keep repeating yourself. I heard you the first time."

He shook his head, "But you don't always listen the first time someone says something you don't want to hear, do you, dearest Cass?"

She didn't reply, just walked quickly through the door and slammed it – hard – behind her.

He and I were left staring at each other. He took his glasses off, looking despondent, and ran his fingers through his hair. "Perhaps I shouldn't have said all that, Hebe. I'm sorry. I had no right to interfere."

I smiled at his worried face. "It's all right. I'm glad you did. I've thought of you as one of the family for ages. Some one had to say it and I think it will have more effect not coming from me." I looked at him curiously. "Was that true about you loving Pandora?"

He nodded slowly. "Yes, it was – although I hadn't meant to say that. Cass will probably never forgive me. Although she loved her sister, she was always comparing herself to her, always competing, trying to prove that she was just as worthwhile." He smiled slightly. "But you know, since Pandora died, I've seen another side to Cass. I hadn't realised before how vulnerable she is. And I *do* care for her, Hebe. I really do."

"You don't have to tell me that. It's obvious that you care for her," I said. "Did Pandora know that you loved her?"

"No," he stared down at the glasses in his hand and started to absent-mindedly polish them on the end of his sleeve. "I'd been going out with Cass for over a year before I realised that . . ." He gave an embarrassed shrug. "I'm sorry, this can't be easy for you to hear but I do love Cass. It was just that I fell in love with Pandora without realising it. There was a sweetness about her that got to me and when I realised what had happened, I couldn't have said anything. Cass would have taken it badly and it would have caused problems between them."

"And she never knew until today?"

"I don't think so. I never said anything. But I think there were times when she suspected that I was more attached to her sister than I let on. It would have been cruel to say anything, especially as she seemed to be convinced that her dad preferred Pandora." He put his glasses back on and looked at me, frowning. "And now I've let the cat out of the bag and made it all worse for her. That was the last thing I meant to do. But it just seemed so unfair, her wallowing in all that self-pity while you were picking yourself up off the ground and getting on with things."

"Oh, Keith! You know Cassandra," I said. "One minute blowing hot, the next cold. The fact that she banged out of here and thumped upstairs is just her way of letting off steam. She'll hide away for a bit, lick her wounds and have a good think about what you said. Her pride wouldn't let her admit that you were right when she was standing there in front of us. You'll see, things will work out," I reassured him, at the same time hoping that I wasn't spouting a whole load of guff and that in fact the opposite was true.

I had visions of my daughter upstairs, ripping wallpaper off the bedroom walls and planning to run away or refuse to have anything to do with any of us ever again.

By the time he left, I think I had managed to persuade him that his relationship with Cassandra could be salvaged. He agreed not to try and contact her until the next day. Wise move, I think.

I was just sitting down with a large mug of extra strong coffee when there was a ring at the doorbell. My first thought was that he must have left something behind and had come back for it.

But when I opened the door, I was astonished to find a very damp (it was pouring then too) and a very tearful Lucy standing on the step. I hadn't seen anyone look so miserable for a long time.

"I'm sorry, Hebe!"

Wondering what on earth she was sorry about, I let her in, at the same time hoping to God that Cassandra wouldn't decide to come downstairs again just then.

"If anyone should be apologising, it should be me after the other night. Come into the kitchen." I said, trying to sound cheerful, as I led the way. "It's nice and warm in there."

Following me obediently and without taking off her soaking raincoat, she sank onto one of the kitchen chairs, water dripping off her and onto the wooden floor. She looked completely done in.

"I'm sorry to disturb you, Hebe. I didn't know where else to go."

She looked so distraught that I was beginning to feel really uneasy.

"What's the matter, Lucy? Why are you so upset? Is Owen all right?"

"No!" she said, her eyes flooding with tears.

"What's happened?" I asked, handing her a piece of paper towel.

"I had a fight with Dervla," she said, giving a loud sniff.

"You did?"

"Yes, I'd taken a day of work because I wasn't feeling too good and so she didn't expect me to be at the house. She came round to bully Joan about something. I said I thought she should leave both of us alone, that I was going to run the house the way I thought was best and I didn't want her to keep coming around and changing things."

"Good for you!" I exclaimed, full of admiration. I honestly hadn't thought she had it in her to stand up to the woman.

She gave me a watery smile. "Well, I felt terrific after she'd stormed out of the place and Joan looked pleased – although she didn't say anything much – just went on polishing the silver as though everything was OK. But then Dervla must have rung Owen and told him what happened. He came back from the office after speaking to her and told me, in front of Joan, that I had no right to talk to his mother like that. When I tried to explain how she made me feel useless and that I didn't want her telling me all the time how I should be doing everything, he said I was lucky to have someone like her to put me straight on how a house should be run. He made it sound as though we would be living in a pigsty if it weren't for his mother."

She looked as if her life had just fallen apart irreparably. And I suppose, from her perspective, it probably seemed as though it had.

"Oh, *Lucy!*" I gave her a hug. The smart, on-top-of-things-looking secretary had dissolved into a little girl with smudged mascara on her cheeks and soaking wet hair. I got up and handed her a towel. "Give me your coat. Dry your hair and have a cup of hot coffee."

While I made the coffee, I wondered why she'd chosen to come round to me. Wasn't it just a little bizarre, to choose to take shelter with her lover's ex-wife? Surely she had friends, family that she could turn to?

As if guessing my thoughts, she said, "I hope you don't

mind me coming here. I know Cassandra doesn't like me."

"Don't worry about Cassandra. She has a habit of not liking people when the wind's blowing in the wrong direction but then she forgets herself and starts to be nice again," I said, cheerfully.

"It's just that my parents were so angry when I moved in with Owen, they said that they didn't want to have anything more to do with me. Really, they're worried the parish priest will hear about what a sinful life their daughter's living. I've only got one sister and she's living in Los Angeles. She's got three small boys and a job in the university and she wouldn't want to be bothered – and, anyway, she wouldn't understand. She thinks I'm a bit stupid and that I'm being selfish, upsetting our parents." At this point, she ran out of breath and subsided into the kitchen towel.

"What about your friends?" I asked her.

She raised her head and gave me a funny look and then said, "It's difficult in the office. The others know I'm living with the boss and, well, my own friends are all kind of young. You know, my age. They don't understand how miserable Dervla can make things." She hesitated for a moment, twisting the towel in her fingers. "But you know more about life than I do and you know Owen and Dervla. I just felt that you would be able to give me better advice than anyone else."

I looked at her blankly. "But, as Owen will tell you, I spent most of the summer in a psychiatric clinic. I don't think I'm really the right woman to turn to, Lucy."

Then she said the nicest thing. "Oh, I think you are. You're a good person. I think you're kind. You didn't turn against me when you found out I was living with Owen."

She looked at me, shyly. "I think I understand why someone like you couldn't live with him. You're . . . very different."

I really didn't want to get into why I had chosen to leave Owen. "Listen, Lucy. Drink your coffee while it's hot and we'll try and sort out what we can do about all of this."

She nodded and obediently drank the rest of her coffee.

Lucy stayed for a long time. I was beginning to feel tired but felt the best thing was to let her talk until she'd got it all out of her system. Owen had obviously behaved like a pig, first of all shouting at her and then giving her the silent treatment. What is wrong with that man? I do know one thing that's wrong – he can't see that, if he wants his relationship with Lucy to work, she should take precedence over his bloody mother – at least some of the time. How thick can you be not to see something so glaringly obvious? Mind you, he didn't cop on when we were married, so I suppose I shouldn't be too surprised.

One of the things Lucy told me was that she was sure Owen had been having an affair with someone he'd met at some business function or other. I was surprised because, although I knew he'd been unfaithful to me after a few years of marriage, their relationship was still in its early stages.

"What makes you think that?" I asked her.

"I've seen them together and the thing is, she's even younger than me," she said, tearfully.

"Younger? How *could* she be any younger?"

"She's only just eighteen. She won some important prize at the young Scientist of the Year competition and got hundreds of points for her Leaving. A real brainbox as well as looking terrific." Lucy gave her hair a savage rub with the towel.

I remembered what Cassandra had shouted at her father after the dinner party – something about Lucy being careful, about Owen and girls in school uniforms. From what Lucy was saying, it seems as though she might have been right.

"How do you know all this?" I asked, hoping that she had got the wrong end of the stick.

"I saw them together in the pub when they thought I was working late. I'd gone in with one of the other girls for a drink and she recognised her. She'd seen something in the paper. Her name's Georgina," she ended, her voice flat.

"They could have just been having a friendly drink together," I suggested. Even I knew that sounded lame.

Lucy looked at me with red-rimmed eyes. "They weren't behaving as though they were friends. They just weren't. Believe me."

In the end, I left Cassandra to sulk upstairs safely out of the way while I gave her supper, and tried my best to cheer her up. Although, I couldn't help agreeing with her that the situation looked pretty hopeless from her point of view.

We had just finished eating when the phone rang. It was Owen – ice-cold and very angry.

"Is Lucy there?"

I considered saying no but then thought better of it. "Yes, she is," I said, as calmly as possible.

"I might have guessed. I want to talk to her."

"One moment! What do you mean, *I might have guessed?*"

"Because you are a manipulative, bloody-minded woman, Hebe. That's why. First of all you turn my daughter against

269

me and then you encourage Lucy to go against my mother and me."

"Hang on a minute! She came round here of her own accord. I didn't even know she was coming. And can we just leave your damn mother out of this for once?" I found myself shouting into the phone. Calmness, you will notice, had disappeared in record time. "Why can't you see that you have to deal with people on a one-to-one basis, without involving her all the time? She's upset Lucy and so have you by taking your mother's part against her instead of trying to understand her side of things."

"Put Lucy on, will you please?" I could hear his uneven breathing at the other end. It sounded as though he were having trouble stopping from indulging in a little shouting himself.

It was on the tip of my tongue to mention the name Georgina – just to shut him up – but I managed not to. I looked over at Lucy and gestured toward the phone. She shook her head vehemently.

"I'm sorry, Owen but Lucy can't come to the phone at the moment," I said, attempting to make the excuse sound as though there really might be a plausible reason for her not being able to speak to him.

"Why, what is she doing?"

"She's – having a bath," I said, suddenly inspired. "She got soaked on her way here."

There was a silence while he considered that. Then he said, "Well get her to ring me when she's finished." And he rang off. Just like that!

I went and sat down beside Lucy. "You know you are going to have to sort this out with him, don't you?"

"Yes," she said, in a small voice.

I hadn't the heart to point out that, if she thought she was liberated and mature enough to go and live with a man like Owen, she must realise that she would have to deal with any problems that arose from their relationship, face to face, with him.

I feel really sorry for her. In a way, though, it might be a very good thing if she did finish with him. Perhaps then there might be a chance of her falling in love with someone her own age. But you can't say that sort of thing to a girl who's hurting so badly. It's obvious from talking to her that she's heartbroken that he appears to have so little respect for her. I did what I could before I rang for a taxi for her. I told her that I was there for her if she needed me to talk to – although I don't see that there's all that much I can do for her. I've just thought of another horror. What if she loses her job over all of this? The way Owen sounded, I think that's highly likely.

* * *

Wednesday, and it's still bloody raining. At least when I was in the clinic I didn't notice the weather.

I've just discovered that Suzie left son Luke behind in Australia. Apparently he wants to wander around the outback, finding himself. Sounds unnecessarily complicated.

"Perhaps going walkabout for a few months will help him decide what it is he wants to do in life. I hope he runs out of money and has to eat grubs and roots. Nothing like a bit of poverty to concentrate the mind," said Suzie in a cheery voice this afternoon.

Even though he drives her wild with his laziness, I

happen to know she'll miss him like mad. He's rather sweet and very good company.

I asked her about the boyfriend who lived in Foxrock. (The one she told to pull himself together and leave his wife if they were to have a future together.)

"Peter's decided that I'm too much of a risk to take on," she said with a grim smile.

"Did he actually *say* that?"

"No, what he actually said was that he has decided the honourable thing to do is to try and make a go of it with his wife. Poor man! He can't admit that I scare the shit out of him."

"But wouldn't that be a good thing?" I asked, somewhat tentatively.

"To scare the shit out of him? Probably!" she said, with a laugh.

"No, you lunatic! I meant wasn't it a good thing that he's having another go at making his marriage work."

"Perhaps, if it were true. But the truth of the matter is that Peter could lie for Ireland. I happen to have found out that he is having an affair with a much younger and more biddable woman and that he hasn't the slightest intention of going back to his wife."

"Oh, another one!"

"Another liar falling for a younger model, you mean?"

"More or less," I agreed.

"Well, as my old granny used to say, 'What goes round, comes round'."

"I'm sorry, Suzie. I know how fond you were of him."

"Oh, I'll get over it! I just hope that he'll get boils in awkward places and that his halitosis, first thing in the morning, gets her down. He was always a bit whiffy before he'd eaten his bowl of Crunchy Nut Cornflakes!"

Even though I hadn't liked him very much, I was sorry for her. And although she didn't want to admit it, I knew she'd been fond of him – bad breath and all. Plus the obvious thing that no one likes to be the one who is dumped and, in the past, it was Suzie who always did the dumping.

We moved onto the subject of ex-husbands. Apparently, she did run into Donal and the new girlfriend this morning. As I predicted, he was a little taken aback. So was Suzie, who hadn't known how very pretty she was. Girlfriend was also put out, having been told that ex-wife was safely tucked away in Australia for the time being.

"But why should I object?" said Suzie, taking a long swig of brandy and ginger ale. "After all, I can hardly pretend to have been behaving like a vestal virgin since the parting of the ways. Although I must say they looked a little ridiculous together. It is nearly completely bald now. They have one thing in common though – they're both bow-fronted. His pot-belly sticks out just about the same amount as her tits. She was wobbling along on three-inch heels with a pussy-pelmet that left nothing to the imagination." She waved her hands in the air. "I mean, when the sex is over what on earth do they *talk* about, for goodness' sake? From the look of her, I doubt she ever picks up a book."

I must say that Suzie doesn't let the grass grow under her feet. She's in the middle of making plans to start some sort of beauty clinic. She's a trained aromatherapist – a bit rusty, as she hasn't worked since before she got married but she says she'll do a refresher course to get herself back on track.

"I can see it now," she enthused. "I'll convert the basement and have it all dry-lined and painted a luscious pale pink and there will be under-floor heating. I don't know how I survived this climate before I went away. It's bloody Baltic outside and it's only the last week in October. Anyway, this place is going to be toasty warm. The clients won't ever want to leave." She gave me a dig with her finger. "And you, Missus, will be my first customer. I'll have you so pampered and spoiled you won't know yourself!"

"As long as you don't start messing around giving me two-inch nails and fussing about my broken veins and wrinkles," I cautioned, worried that, once she got the bit between her teeth, if I weren't careful, I'd end up having a face transplant.

"Don't tell me that you wouldn't like to get rid of a few wrinkles," she teased.

She looked a bit surprised when I said that, at the moment, I was more interested in getting rid of the wrinkles on the inside and wasn't too pushed about the exterior.

"But what about the DOH?"

"The DOH? What on earth is that?"

"Your *Desirable Other Half!* Wouldn't he like it if you suddenly looked ten years younger?"

"No, I suspect if that happened, he'd panic and do a runner," I replied. "And that's only one of the reasons I like him so much."

She still didn't believe me. And I could do without her using the term DOH. It makes her sound like some ersatz Homer Simpson!

That conversation reminded me that, from before Suzie

went away, Joan was convinced that she was for the birds. I caught her looking at her this afternoon with a slightly bemused look on her face as though Suzie had just landed from another planet. Mind you, Joan and I were drinking tea at four o'clock and Suzie was well away on her third brandy and mixer by then, waving her hands around like a windmill and talking at top speed.

Still, she's a good friend and she makes me laugh. She even takes the trouble to remember ridiculous jokes to pass on to me. I can *never* remember them five minutes after hearing them. I think if brain capacity could be measured in the number of cupboards you have there, packed with useful, intelligent, information, then I've lost the key to a considerable number of them.

* * *

Later, Wednesday night.

I had a call from Cassandra a few minutes ago. I was so relieved. She'd gone back to college on Sunday night, having hardly spoken since the set-to with Keith and myself.

As soon as I heard her voice, I asked her if she was all right. She sounded so subdued.

"Yes, Mum. I'm OK." There was an awkward pause before she said, "I'm sorry, Mum, for being such a cow."

"I would never describe you in those terms," I said, keeping it light.

"Keith was right. I realise that I have been sort of wallowing in how miserable I felt. And I never knew that he was so upset. I just sort of let him make a fuss of me and try to keep my mind off what had happened. I never

275

stopped to think about how he was feeling. And I knew you were ill and miserable but something kept stopping me for doing what was right. I knew I was behaving badly and I didn't seem able to be nice to you. I know that sounds pathetic. I'm really, really sorry, Mum." There was another pause and then she said in a husky voice, "Did you know that he loved Pandora, Mum?"

"No, I didn't. And neither did she."

"I know. He told me. He rang me yesterday and we talked a bit."

"Keith also told me that he loved you, Cassandra. Don't spoil your friendship with him, darling."

"I don't know, Mum. It's a difficult one. Finding out that he loved her just sort of made me feel I wasn't special to him any more – that I was second-best again."

She didn't say, 'like the way you and Dad used to make me feel'. But I knew that's what she was thinking and, remembering that she'd told Keith that her father loved Pandora more than he did her, she really must have a really serious hang-up over the whole thing. Either that or Owen *did* show her sister more affection. But if he did, it must have been when I wasn't around because I can honestly say that I never noticed it.

We talked for a long time and she agreed that she wouldn't make any hasty decisions about her and Keith. So, I'll just have to stand back and hope that she doesn't do anything she'll regret later. But, hell! Isn't that what being young is all about? Making all those idiotic mistakes and having to live with the consequences afterwards. And I know that she has to be left to make them by herself. I mustn't interfere. But I would be really sorry if Keith were to disappear off the scene. And I believe him when he says that he loves her. He'd have to – with all the nonsense she's given him over the past year and got away with!

At the end of the conversation, Cassandra said that it was all right with her if I wanted to sort out Pandora's room but she'd rather not be involved.

"I'm sorry, Mum. I know that sounds stupid but would you be able to manage it on your own?"

"Yes, of course, I can." I said. "Don't worry! I'll manage. And, Cassandra, I do understand."

"Thanks, Mum," she said in a quiet voice, before ringing off.

I just hope I can do it on my own.

* * *

Something important I forgot to mention: I had a letter from the clinic today with an appointment to see Dr Scheller next week. I can't believe that he's in any fit state to be back at work after seeing him at Mum's funeral. But, perhaps, burying himself in work will help him work his way through his grief. I feel rather nervous of seeing him again. I can't help feeling that it's not right that he should be shouldering the woes of other people when he must be feeling like death. What he needs is another Dr Scheller to care for him. I wonder if such a person exists.

Chapter Seventeen

Friday night. In bed with Busby. Much as I love this cat, I'm starting to wish it were a case of: In bed with Sam.

I've decided that tomorrow is the day I will tackle Pandora's room. Joan and Suzy have both offered to help but I fear it's just another of those things best done on my own.

Lucy rang this morning. Apparently, things have gone from bad to worse. Owen told her that if she couldn't cope with him having a drink with another female then their relationship wasn't going to work out. Apparently he was quite unpleasant about it.

"But I *know* he's not just having drinks with her! I just know!" she sobbed down the phone.

"What about the atmosphere at work?" I asked her.

"I *can't* go in to work."

"So, what have you been doing with yourself?"

"Hiding mostly. Oh, Hebe! It's desperate. He's so angry about everything and Dervla just makes things worse all the time. If it wasn't for Joan, I think I'd go mad."

"Have you tried sitting down calmly on your own with him and a stiff drink and explaining why you're upset?"

"Yes. And he won't listen. He says that I'm a fool; that I pay attention to the wrong people."

That, no doubt, was a reference to me. As far as Owen's concerned, he is all-wise and anything I say that contradicts his point of view, on pretty much anything, just confirms his idea of me as a fool.

"He doesn't love me. I was just kidding myself. I want to move out but I haven't anywhere to go. I rang my parents yesterday and, when he heard who it was, my father put the phone down," she said in a miserable voice.

I find that quite extraordinary. How could her parents turn their backs on her? It wasn't as though she'd committed a murder. But perhaps, in their eyes, living in sin with a man who's old enough to be her dad *is* a terrible sin. My own mother would have been shocked if I'd done that but, tricky though our relationship was, I really don't think she would have refused to have anything more to do with me.

So, opening mouth before engaging brain, I said, "Listen, Lucy, I'm going to be busy this weekend, but if you still feel the same way on Monday, you can come and stay here for a few days until you get yourself sorted out."

There was a relieved intake of breath from the other end of the phone.

"Are you sure?"

"Yes, but it's only for a few days."

"Hebe, thank you so, so much."

"Well, see if you can't get him to listen to you. Try again, just in case there is a misunderstanding."

She promised that she would and we left it like that.

Now, of course, I'm having kittens, wondering if my on-the-spur-of-the-moment offer was all that wise. What about Cassandra's sometimes rather violent antipathy towards Lucy? I know she's gone back to college but I don't want her to feel that she's not welcome to come and stay with me at weekends because of Lucy being here. She's so touchy if she thinks she's being in any way sidelined. I'm terribly aware of how careful I have to be not to make her feel that I'm putting her second after what she said about us having loved Pandora more than her. And, what if Lucy's got it wrong and Owen really isn't having an affair? But there's a part of me that can't dismiss the idea as totally impossible. I can't help remembering that he had a new woman installed in the house within a week of our separating. I had gone to drop the girls in to him to stay the night and this hard-faced creature suddenly materialised from behind the hedge and stood in front of the steps leading up to the front door, looking all proprietorial. I remember thinking that she almost looked as though she were daring me to go any closer. *That* had been a bit of an eye-opener! And not too good for the old morale either.

* * *

Sam says he needs an answer about the holiday by Sunday night. Of course, Cassandra thinks I'm completely loopy for not jumping at the offer.

"A fortnight in the Seychelles! Mum, you'd be off your trolley not to say yes," was how she put it.

She's probably right, but, Moan Number One: Being realistic about the situation, we've never spent longer than half a day in each other's company. Two: I don't really know him properly. How can I be sure that it's not just a case of my loins leading my head? Three: I haven't made love to anyone for so long I might not do it right any more. I'll probably be all dried up and useless. Four: How do I know he hasn't slept with someone in the last five years who's given him some ghastly disease that he doesn't yet know he's got? Five: Shouldn't I be settling down to some sort of steady routine and making a serious stab at writing – especially if I'm going to even consider working on a screenplay? Six: With Cassandra back at college, Busby would have to go and stay with Joan and, although he likes her, she's out at work all day and he won't have anyone to cuddle.

When I mentioned the proposed holiday to Suzie, she just said, "*And?* What is the problem?"

So I reeled off some of the above.

She looked at me as though I had two heads and said, "Didn't you tell me that you fancy him to bits?"

"Yes."

"Didn't you tell me that, not only is he incredibly dishy, he's funny, polite and intelligent?"

"Yes."

"And he's not married?"

"Not any more, no."

"And he's not involved with anyone else?"

"Not as far as I know."

She stared at me for a moment before adding. "Dearest Hebe, you've had a year that would be the end of a lot of people but you've soldiered on. I can't think of *anyone* who deserves a holiday with the delectable Sam Ellis more than you do. Don't be an idiot. Say yes, *please!* If you don't, I shall probably throttle you! And then I'll offer to go on

281

holiday with the man myself – that might make you come to your senses!"

"But, what if I'm not ready to take such a big step? What if I muck the whole thing up and he decides that he doesn't want to see me any more because it's too much like hard work? I'm sure he's never been involved with anyone before who's just emerged from a psychiatric clinic."

"You didn't hide the fact that you'd been ill. He knew early on about that, didn't he?"

"Yes. But I still haven't talked to him about Pandora. He knows that she died but nothing about the circumstances."

"Well, that's the sort of thing you will be able to tell him when you're together and relaxed and have all the time in the world, with no pressures on either of you. It's the perfect situation for finding out more about each other. Hebe, don't get cold feet and back out now. If you do, he might think that you don't want to commit to a proper, full relationship and then, maybe, the pair of you could easily start to drift apart. Go on! Be brave and stop *thinking* so much!"

She gave me a hug, before picking up her bag and coat from the chair. When she'd put on her coat, she turned and gave me a quizzical look.

"Are you going to be good?"

I smiled and nodded. "OK! I'll give it serious thought."

"And be positive about it!" she insisted.

"And I'll be positive," I promised, with a laugh, as I pushed her towards the door.

Perhaps, working on Pandora's room will help me sort myself out. Just the sheer physical effort of doing things is usually good therapy for an overheated brain!

* * *

Midday, Saturday 31st October.

I kept to my promise and made a start on clearing out Pandora's room after breakfast. At the last minute, I was tempted to put it off until another day and do something else instead. I stood with my hand on the door handle for a moment, undecided. Then I turned the handle and slowly pushed open the door. It was so horribly quiet in there. Everything looked, I don't know, sort of embalmed. I felt as if I were trespassing in a forbidden place.

I spent a long time just looking at everything on the shelves and desk and dressing-table. I picked up the necklace of blue beads that she'd discarded in favour of a different one on that last evening of her life and cradled it in the palm of my hand, remembering how I'd bought it for her on one of our holidays in Greece and how pretty it had looked on her slim, tanned neck.

When I saw one long strand of golden hair still entwined in the bristles of her hairbrush, I thought I wouldn't be able to go on, my vision blurred with instant tears. But after a few minutes of standing very still and steadying my breathing, I was able to pull myself together. I found myself running my fingers over her books and sheet music and the photos on her desk. Photos of herself and Cassandra, laughing, side by side on the garden seat, of Pandora half-smothered by a sleepily contented Busby, wound round her like a large, fake-fur collar, a photo of her and Cassandra with a smiling Keith, standing with an arm around each of them. They looked so easy together, so comfortable with one another – more like two sisters with a brother rather than a lover.

I sat on the end of her bed and studied the posters on her walls, of the *Greenpeace* sailing ship, the snowy owl with its savage, hooded golden eyes and a black and white study of Johnny Depp, whom she adored. As I sat there, I tried to fix it all in my mind so that I would be able to recall how her room had been before I'd dismantled it. I know I put off starting the job for as long as I could.

I began by stripping the bed. Joan had already washed the sheets and pillowcases and put them back on again but no one else in the house had ever used the pale blue cornflower-patterned bed linen. If I was going to change the room and repaint it, I wanted it to be completely different – even down to the sheets. I worked hard, once I got going, stacking things in boxes, some for Cassandra, some for me, the rest for the second-hand book shop around the corner or the *War on Want* shop and some for the attic – the things I couldn't bear to part with yet but that I didn't want to keep coming across.

I've decided to have a break before doing any more. I was beginning to feel really tired. Suzie warned me that this would be hard. She needn't have. I knew that already. Anyway, I'm sitting in the kitchen with a mug of strong coffee and some of Joan's crumbly brown bread – with a large hunk of cheese – and getting my breath back. It's tough going but I'm doing all right. I should have it more or less finished by this evening.

* * *

Later.

I'm shaking so much I can hardly write. But I know that I've got to write it down. If it's all there in black and white in front of me, perhaps I'll be able to make sense of what's happened. I've discovered why it is that Cassandra won't have anything to do with Owen and why he won't come into the house any more. It was all there in the diary Pandora had hidden in a carrier-bag at the back of her wardrobe. I nearly threw it away, thinking it was empty. I'd put it with a heap of other things to take out to the bin when the diary slipped out onto the carpet.

It was when I bent down to pick up the pile of stuff from the floor that the slim, black book slithered like a snake out of the carrier-bag at my feet. As I picked it up, I had a sense of foreboding. The skin on the back of my neck prickled and the whole house seemed to be unnaturally quiet – like the strange lull you experience before an earthquake. I almost didn't open it. I wouldn't have read her diary when she was alive and what right did I have, now that she was dead? But some instinct made it impossible for me to put it down. Instinctively, I turned to the last entry she'd made. The day that she died.

It was dated the 29th of August.

Cass says I should tell Mum about what Dad did yesterday but I can't. I've made her swear that she won't say anything. Mum wouldn't want to believe it and if she did, it would hurt her so much to think that he was capable of behaving in the way he did.

I wouldn't have told Cass it happened except that she saw him trying to kiss me, trying to push me back on to the bed. He thought the house was empty. He'd been out to dinner and I could smell drink on his breath. He didn't know that she was in her room. I will never forget that horrible pleading look on his face and the way he kept saying that it wasn't wrong, what he was doing, that he loved me. Loved me! He said that there was nothing wrong in him giving me a kiss. I tried to push him away but I couldn't. I don't know what would have happened if Cass hadn't burst into the room. She went wild and hit him again and again, screaming at him that he was a pervert, that he was wicked. He shouted at her, said that she was just jealous and stupid.

I don't know what made him go but he was suddenly not there any more and Cass was holding me and we were both crying.

I feel so ashamed. Did I do something to make him think that I wanted him to do that to me? I've started to wonder if all the times he seemed to go out of his way to be on his own with me were because he was testing me. I thought it was just that he liked being with me. I felt sort of special – and that it was nice that he wanted to spend time with me – although I realise now that it was usually when Mum was out. I knew our closeness annoyed Cass but she did make him angry when she wanted her own way all the time. I never guessed for one moment that he would do what he did.

Cass said she thought that might have been one of the reasons Mum left him in the first place, so that we would be safe – that she must have guessed what he was like. But wouldn't she have warned us if she had those doubts about him? I can't bear to believe that she wouldn't.

She always sticks up for him though when Cass says anything against him. Cass says that they gang up on us to stop us having any fun. She says that, now we are nineteen, they can't stop us from doing what we want. She says that I'm not strong enough, that I don't stand up for myself. She didn't say that, if I had been stronger, perhaps he wouldn't have tried anything on. Perhaps Cass is right. It was me he tried to kiss, not her.

I feel so rotten. I loved him but I don't think I'll ever be able to look him in the face again. I don't know how I can be normal around Mum after this. I have never felt so frightened or confused. It's as though the things that I thought were safe in my life have disappeared. Who can I trust if I can't trust my own father? What am I going to do?

You can understand why I'm shaking. That last entry of hers with that final *cri de cœur* breaks my heart. How *could* I have not known that he would do that to his own daughter? There must have been *something* that I should have picked up on – some clue, some hint. No wonder Cassandra was so distant, so unloving towards me afterwards. All the time, she thought I knew what he was like. For all these months she's been guarding this awful secret like a canker, harming her from deep inside. And all the time, I was a complete innocent – a complacent, gullible fool. But I *didn't* know that he would do something like that. That wasn't the reason for my leaving him. I left him for a dozen reasons – but not that. Not ever that.

All I can think of is how frightened and confused they both must have been. It must have felt as if their world had fallen to pieces around them. *Why* didn't Cassandra come to me? Surely she didn't think I wouldn't have believed her?

Now I understand why she lost her head at dinner last week. When she talked about pretending to be civilised but really being rotten, she was reminding him that she knew what he was really like and she wasn't going to forgive or forget.

My God! And after Pandora had suffered that, I played the heavy parent, refusing to accept that they were old enough to make their own minds up about what they did and where they went. And all the time, Cassandra was encouraging her to stand up to us – her wise, all-knowing parents, whose only thought was to protect them from harm. After what happened, the pair of them must have been filled with anger and disappointment and fear – and with their whole world toppling around them.

It's almost too much to contemplate what they must have felt on that last night together. No wonder they wanted to get out and away from the house, to be wild and to forget. It all makes dreadful sense now.

What am I going to do? Where do I go from here? Oh, God, I feel as though I'm drowning. Where am I going to find the strength to deal with all of this?

* * *

Later, same day.

I've spent the last, God knows how long, pacing backwards and forwards, trying to fight down the panic and to make myself think about what I have to do now. It's obvious that I have to confront Owen and tell him that I know. I've also decided that I have to try and persuade Cassandra that she doesn't have to hide anything from me any more and that I never, ever thought her father was capable of behaving in such a way. And I have to get Lucy away from him. She shouldn't be living with him. He'll only end up hurting her more than he has already.

If I do these things, perhaps I will be able to keep going and perhaps I will be able to live with what I now know. Whatever happens, I can't slide back down into the pit. I've got to be there for Cassandra. I've *got* to be strong.

* * *

Sunday, late.

Today has been a day I will never forget. The day
Pandora died was another such day. I didn't sleep at all last
night, just walked around the house with Busby in my
arms. He seemed to sense that something was wrong and
just wrapped himself round my neck and didn't even object
when I hugged him tight and buried my face in his fur and
wept. I can't seem to think of anything except what
Pandora and Cassandra must have gone through during
those last two terrible days of Pandora's life.

Sam rang early this morning and, for the first time in
our relationship, I didn't want to talk to him. I just wanted
to get off the phone as quickly as possible. I can't even
remember what I said to him. I know he asked me about
the holiday. As if the damn holiday mattered! I told him
that it was out of the question, that I had other things on
my mind, that I was sorry but now was not the right time
for me to go on holiday. I can't remember exactly what he
said. He sounded surprised and probably disappointed – I
don't know. I'm afraid that I didn't give him a chance. I
think I rang off very abruptly. Oh, I don't want to hurt him
but I can't, can't think about him and me just now. Not at
the moment.

I managed to pull myself together after a while and
went downstairs and gave Busby his breakfast. I couldn't
face eating anything and at nine o'clock I went straight
around to Owen's house. I knew that it was early and a
Sunday morning and that he would still be in bed but I
couldn't wait any longer to face him. I knew that by going
so early at least Dervla wouldn't be around.

When Lucy opened the door, she looked dreadful. She

looked as though she hadn't slept either. Her hair was all tousled and there were bags under her young eyes. I had hoped that it would be Owen who would come to the door and that she would be still asleep. I was frantic to talk to him but I could see that the poor girl was at the end of her tether.

"What's wrong, Lucy?" I asked.

She was biting her bottom lip in a brave attempt not to cry. "He didn't come back last night."

"Do you know where he is?"

"Probably with *her*." she replied, with tears in her eyes.

For a moment, I wondered if she meant he was with his mother but realised that she was probably referring to the girl called Georgina.

"We had another row and he stormed out after dinner, saying that he was fed up and that he wished he'd never bothered himself over me."

"Have you any idea when he might come back?" I asked, determined to stay calm.

"I know he's playing golf this morning at eleven and his clubs are still downstairs."

"Right!" I said. "Go and get your things and I'll drop you back at my house. I'll have to leave you there for a while on your own. I have to see Owen when he comes back here. You can give me the keys."

My manner must have convinced her that it would be a good idea to do what I said and not ask any questions.

Together and more or less silently, we packed a couple of cases. Her misery made her clumsy as she hurriedly wrenched open drawers and cupboards, items of clothing falling to the floor.

"Is that all?" I asked her, thinking she might have ornaments or books that wouldn't fit into the bags.

"Yes, that's everything."

"All right. Come on then."

The door to the sitting-room was open. She saw me glance at the painting over the fireplace as I hurried ahead of her on our way through the hall.

"I gave that to Owen as a present for his last birthday. He *said* he liked it." She sounded as if now she didn't care if he liked it or not.

I thrust the cases into the car boot. It seemed so little to be taking with her. I mean, she'd been living with him for nearly six months now but, apart from hair-curling tongs, the rest of her possessions seemed to consist of clothes and make-up and a few tapes.

When we got back here, I hastily showed her where the kettle was and the toaster and told her to make a cup of tea for herself and to have some breakfast.

"I may be some time but I'll be back as soon as I can."

She looked at me curiously but didn't ask why I had to see Owen so urgently.

As I was going out of the door, she asked, almost nervously, "Is Cassandra coming back today?"

"No," I reassured her. "You just make yourself at home. The fire's ready to light in the sitting-room. The spare room is upstairs and first on the left. There are clean towels on the shelf in the bathroom. Have a hot bath, stretch out and listen to some music. Do whatever you like. We'll talk later."

She looked so forlorn, I went back and gave her a quick hug. It was almost like having a second daughter again, seeing her, standing in the middle of the kitchen, her cases on the floor at her feet. But it wasn't the same at all.

Owen's car wasn't there when I got back to the other house. I let myself in and went into the sitting-room and waited. After a few minutes, I started to wonder if I'd missed him and that he had been back for his golf clubs. I ran downstairs. The golf bag was where I remembered he kept it, leaning against the wall of his study, behind the door.

Slowly, I went back upstairs and went over to the window. I stared out at the stormy-looking sea with its bucking grey waves and tried to get my thoughts in order. The waiting seemed to go on forever. When I finally saw his car draw up to the kerb, I backed away from the window, not wanting him to see me there and be forewarned. I heard his approaching footsteps and the sound of his key in the lock. He came into the hall and was passing the door when he saw me out of the corner of his eye. I'd startled him quite badly. For a moment, he looked as though he'd seen a ghost. Almost immediately he recovered himself. Frowning, he dropped his car keys onto the hall table and came into the room.

"What are you doing here?" he asked in an unfriendly voice.

"I've come to see you, Owen."

"Where's Lucy?"

"She's not here. She's left you."

He stared at me for a moment. "I suppose I have you to thank for that."

"She's staying with me until she sorts herself out."

"How kind of you," he said, his voice icy. Suddenly his look changed to one of suspicion. "How did you get in?"

"Lucy gave me the key so I could let myself in."

Up until then, I had been standing with my back to the windows, my hands clasped tightly in front of me in an effort to stop them trembling.

He came closer and glared into my face. He smelled of his usual cologne but there was another, faint scent that clung to him as well. He looked as though, at any minute, he would lose his temper. I could feel a pulse, thumping in my head.

"What *is* this all about?"

"I've found out about what you did to our daughter." I was having difficulty in keeping my voice level and if I hadn't suddenly sat down, I think I might have fainted. Before he could deny anything, I continued. "Don't try and pretend it didn't happen. Pandora wrote down what you did in her diary and Cassandra saw you."

His face darkened. "That little bitch spends her life causing trouble."

"That little bitch, as you call her, is my daughter, whom I love – as was Pandora. And you," I pointed a shaking finger at him, "and you spoiled everything. You turned her from being a trusting, biddable, happy girl into a frightened creature, who was reduced to rebelling against us both in order to try and deal with what you'd done to her. How *could* you? And how could you pretend that everything that happened afterwards was because I was a useless parent – who hadn't looked after them properly? You're a smug, evil monster. I should go to the police."

He looked at me for a moment. The only sound I was aware of was the pounding of my heart, the only sensation one of nausea as I watched him standing there, so handsome, so smart in his *Louis Copeland* suit, so respectable-looking. He's like one of those well-upholstered politicians, I thought, pretending to be on your side and yet, all the time, only interested in their own survival and wellbeing.

"You can't! How do you think that sort of investigation would affect Cassandra?" With his head slightly to one side, he gave me a calculating look. "And you've only just come out of that clinic. Are you prepared for all the probing and unpleasantness your accusation would result in? Not that there's any real proof. Girls often fantasise over their fathers. I think you should consider your actions very carefully, Hebe."

"At this precise moment, I don't care a damn about what you think. I wonder what your beloved mother would say if she found out what you've done."

Suddenly, all his belligerence disappeared and he collapsed into one of the chairs, his face pale. It seemed as though all thought of refuting what I'd said, all instinct to fight me back, had gone. The early morning sun, slanting through the windows, lit the side of his face. All of a sudden I was struck by how much older he looked than his forty-eight years.

He buried his head in his hands and mumbled something.

For the first time during the conversation, I felt suddenly unnaturally calm. I'm ashamed to say that the only feeling I had was one of impatience. "I can't hear what you're saying." My voice sounded like a stranger's – cold and hard.

He lifted his head but avoided looking at me. "It was a mistake. I don't know what happened to me. I know I had too much to drink. Christ! I only tried to kiss her. I regretted it immediately. I would never have done it again."

He forced himself to meet my eye. "For God's sake, Hebe, don't bring my mother into this, please. For all our sakes."

All of a sudden, I found him repellent. I couldn't spend another moment in his company. I got to my feet and somehow walked past him and out into the hall, with him following me, his face agitated.

"Hebe! Please!"

"I don't know what I'm going to do but I know that I don't ever want you to come anywhere near my house and don't ring. Leave Lucy alone. I'll tell you what I'm going to do when I've made up my mind. Until then, just keep away from all of us."

Startled, he backed away. I think I must have frightened him. I frightened myself with how I felt.

I don't remember the drive home afterwards. I was completely numb. Lucy must have been having a sleep when I got back and I was relieved that I didn't have to face her. I made myself a drink and sat in front of the fire. When I finished it, I went into the kitchen and made myself another. The telephone rang. I don't know why but something told me that it was Sam. I picked up the receiver and then replaced it without finding out if I was right. Then I switched the answering machine on. I know! But I don't want to talk to anyone. I want to sit on my own, quietly and get my thoughts together and do everything in my power to keep myself from going to pieces.

Chapter Eighteen

I rang Suzie this morning. After another sleepless night, I felt I'd go mad if I didn't talk things through with her. I could hardly ask Joan to drop everything and come round. Owen would immediately guess where she was. I don't want her to lose her job, on top of everything else.

Suzie didn't ask me what the matter was when I told her that I needed to talk to her. She knew from my voice that something was very wrong.

"I'll be with you in half an hour, my love," was her instant reaction. "Put the kettle on."

I'd tried, I think fairly successfully, to put on a brave front with Lucy and kept her company while she had her breakfast. I watched as she nibbled at a piece of toast and drank half a cup of tea. She looked better than she had the day before but she was still rather pale and far from happy looking. It was as though all her self-confidence had drained away. Even her blonde hair looked straggly and dull.

She came over and kissed my cheek before she left to go to work.

"I can't tell you how grateful I am, Hebe. You've been brilliant about all of this."

I gave her a reassuring smile. "Well, just keep your head down at work and keep busy. Try and think of Owen as the boss, nothing more. That might help you get through the day."

I was tempted to add that it might be a good idea to have a look in the job vacancies during her lunch break but thought better of it. She had enough on her plate as it was.

When Suzie got here, she gave me a searching look before firmly pushing me back into the kitchen and into a chair.

"You look done in. I'll make us some coffee and then you can tell me what's going on."

She looked so attractive in her cream trousers and soft mohair sweater in a glorious pink. Even though she hadn't had the time to put on her make-up, she still looked stunning. She seemed to fill the room with her presence and I could smell the lovely perfume she always uses. I found myself watching her with pleasure as she fished mugs out of the dishwasher and got out the biscuit tin and more milk from the fridge. Even though she was worried, she looked so full of life and energy that I started to feel a little better.

"Right," she said, as she put the mugs down onto the table. Sliding one of them towards me, she sat down herself, folding one long leg over the other. "Now, tell me what's up. Why are you looking like yesterday's leftovers?"

"I think you'd better see this."

I gave her the diary, opened at the last entry. Suzie read it from start to finish without speaking. Then she looked up, her face grave, her eyes searching mine.

"That explains so much, Hebe – Cassandra's behaviour . . ." She shook her head in disbelief. "You know I've never liked Owen very much on the few occasions that we've met but I never, for one moment, thought he'd be the sort of person who'd be capable of doing that to his daughter." She moved her chair nearer mine, leaned over and gave me a hug. "You must be devastated, you poor darling."

Of course, her sympathy meant that the floodgates opened, in spite of my promising to myself before she arrived that I wouldn't get all weepy and hopeless. I ended up leaning my head against her shoulder and sobbing. She held me until the worst was over.

In the middle of it all, the phone rang – for the third time this morning.

"Do you want me to answer it?" she asked.

"No!" I said abruptly, then smiled apologetically at her. "Sorry! The answering machine is on. Just leave it."

She didn't say anything, just looked a little surprised. I think she guessed that it might be Sam ringing and couldn't see why I wouldn't want to speak to him.

Eventually, I straightened up and grabbed the kitchen roll. After I'd blown my nose and mopped up, I swallowed some coffee.

I knew she was watching me carefully, trying to work out the best way to deal with the situation. I was well aware of the fact that it's not easy to know what to say or do when, out of the blue, a person is confronted with something unpleasant and unexpected.

I found myself apologising again. "I'm sorry for the waterworks."

"Don't be daft! Of course, you feel like crying. Why wouldn't you?" She laid a hand on my arm. "The thing is, what are you going to do about Owen?"

"I've threatened him with going to the police but, of course, I know that, once he gets over the shock of being found out, he'll know as well as I do that it's out of the question. I mean, he didn't actually rape Pandora, did he? And they won't be interested in the fact that he 'merely' kissed her and frightened her out of her wits. They've got more serious crimes to think about than that. No, what scares him is the thought of his beloved mother finding out about what he did."

"Well, I haven't seen all that much of Cassandra since I got back. But, judging from what you've told me, that poor girl has had a rotten time over the last year and I don't think telling his mother will make things any easier. You don't know how she might react, Hebe. She sounds such a vindictive old witch, she would probably refuse to believe you and it might make her turn against Cassandra. I know Cassandra thinks she hates her dad at the moment but she doesn't hate you and, if you can convince her that you never guessed he'd behave the way he did, she'll come round. I'm sure she will. She loves you and she needs you."

"I just don't know if she'll ever come round to really trusting me again! She's so *angry*." I couldn't stop myself – I suddenly banged the table with my fist. "*I* feel so angry, Suzie! I loathe him for what he's done. It was he who was responsible for me losing Pandora, he who's turned Cassandra's life upside down and nearly made me go out of my mind. Why should he just walk away from it all? Why shouldn't he be made to suffer for what he's done?"

"It doesn't matter what I think, Hebe. I just know that if he'd been *my* ex-husband, I'd probably have battered him to death when I found out what he'd done." She gave me a small smile. "But you're *not* me and you're the only person who can make the decision about the best way to handle the situation – a way that will cause the least hurt to yourself and Cass. After all, you're the people who matter now. Damn Owen! He's got to live with the result of his actions for the rest of his life and however together he may seem, I can't believe that, deep down, the bastard isn't suffering." She paused for a moment and then asked, "Have you said anything to Cassandra about the diary yet?"

"No, I wanted to try and collect my thoughts before I told her. I don't even know if she knew that Pandora kept one." I suddenly reached for her hand. I felt like someone floundering around in deep water, holding on to the nearest solid object in an effort to stop myself going under. "I'm frightened, Suzie. I'm frightened I won't have the resources to get through all this – to make the right decisions."

Poor Suzie! I hadn't meant to go to pieces like that. When I'd asked her to come round, I thought we would talk and that I could tell her everything without losing control. It wasn't fair on her. But, true to form, she was splendid.

"Now, slow down a moment!" She gave my hand a squeeze. "You have all the reason in the world to feel alarmed and angry about what you've found out. For God's sake! You were married to the man for years. And when you got married, you thought he was someone you could love and trust. No wonder you feel the way you do. But you will be all right, Hebe. I *know* you will. You're a fantastic woman and you'll come through all this." She gave my arm a gentle shake. "What did you tell me that lovely doctor of yours said? Something about you emerging into the outside world and spreading your wings in the sunlight."

"I was starting to feel that *was* what I was doing – until yesterday," I said, miserably.

"Well, I think you've got to keep that picture in your mind." She let go of my hand and leant back in her chair. "May I make one, very obvious, suggestion?"

"Of course."

"You can't be expected to cope if you're worn out. Have you got anything to help you sleep?"

"Yes. But I stopped taking them weeks ago. I was worried I'd started to rely on them too much."

"Well, I think you should take a double dose and have a proper night's sleep before you talk to Cassandra. Then you have some chance of making some sensible decisions when you're not exhausted and frazzled. Will you do that?"

She looked so concerned. I did my best to smile and look as though I agreed with her – that a good night's sleep would solve all my problems.

* * *

Tuesday.

Actually, I did as Suzie suggested and took a double dose of the pills I had brought home from the clinic. I can't say I woke feeling refreshed this morning. I felt ghastly at first, drugged and hazy and Busby's cross with me because I accidentally trod on his tail when I got out of bed. After a shower, I managed to pull myself together and got down on my hands and knees to entice him out from under the bed. He's an old softie and it didn't take long to persuade him that I was still his friend.

Suzie stayed for ages yesterday, in fact until Lucy got in. Which was just as well, as it happened. I'd given her a front-door key so neither of us realised she'd come back until she walked into the room.

"Lucy!" I said. "I don't think you've met Suzie . . ." and then I saw that her eyes were red-rimmed. "What's happened?"

She gave me a miserable look. "As of today, I've no job as well as no home."

As I thought, Owen had given her the sack. I could just imagine why. It wouldn't do to have someone so disenchanted and dispirited around the place. Bad for morale.

"But surely he's supposed to give you a couple of weeks' notice. He can't just get rid of you without any warning," said Suzie, indignantly.

Lucy sat down slowly with a tired shake of her head. "Oh, he's given me a very generous cheque to make up for that."

"And does it?" I asked her, gently.

"Yes, I suppose it does. I couldn't have gone on working there, Hebe. The atmosphere was awful." She looked as though she were about to burst into tears again.

"You look as though you could do with something stronger than tea. Can I get her a proper drink, Hebe?" said Suzie, coming to the rescue.

So we all had large gin and tonics around the sitting-room fire.

It was evident that, by the time Suzie was ready to leave, she'd developed a soft spot for Lucy.

"I've had an idea," she said suddenly. "Listen, Lucy. If you'd like to give it a try, there's a small self-contained flat in the house that you could rent if you liked it and I'm looking for someone to be my receptionist when the aromatherapy clinic is up and running in a few weeks' time. Would you be interested, do you think?"

For the first time in days, Lucy's face brightened. "I'd love to. Thank you so much."

"Well, that's settled then," said Suzie, looking pleased. She turned to me. "I know I'm being a bossy female, but can Lucy come with me and see it now? She can stay the night and get the feel of the place." She hesitated and then added, "Or don't you want to be left on your own at the moment?"

I told her I would be perfectly fine on my own and that her being there for most of the day had done wonders. She stared at me for a moment before agreeing, obviously not wanting to say anything more in front of Lucy.

On the way out, she whispered, "Give that man of yours a ring. It'll do you good."

I didn't say anything, just nodded and smiled. I couldn't explain that, much as I had needed her to talk to, I couldn't face the thought of having to tell Sam about what had happened. Especially when I remembered that on Sunday, I'd told him in such an offhand manner that I wasn't going to the Seychelles with him. The most important thing I had to do next was get in touch with Cassandra.

After having tried several times, I finally got through to her this afternoon.

"Cassandra, can you come home? I need to talk."

"Are you OK, Mum?" She sounded worried.

"Sort of. I will be when we've had a talk. Can you come today?"

There was a pause and then she said, "Yes, of course. I've no more lectures until late tomorrow morning. I can stay the night."

Then Suzie rang and I told her that Cassandra was coming and asked her if Lucy could stay another night with her.

"I'm sorry, it's very short notice. I know I told her she could stay here but I have to have Cassandra on her own without anyone else around. Would you mind, Suzie?"

"Of course not! She's a sweet young thing. She's fallen in love with the flat and wants to move in as soon as she can. I've lent her a toothbrush and she can go round to you and collect her things tomorrow. Don't worry! Have you rung Sam yet?"

"I have to speak to Cassandra first," I said, doggedly.

"Yes, of course," said Suzie, quickly. "I understand." But she couldn't keep the surprise out of her voice when she said it.

She's great, is Suzie, but I don't think she really understands how I feel about Sam. She'd probably find it ridiculous – this fear of mine about telling him what's going on and possibly spoiling things between us even more than I seem to have already. I don't want him to see me as a damaged woman, desperately trying to keep her head above water. I want that to be a thing of the past.

While I was waiting for Cassandra to arrive, I realised that part of my reluctance to ring him stems from my not wanting to use him as a prop to get me through the next while. I feel it's important that I make decisions and do whatever has to be done without him feeling he has to cancel his holiday and come dashing over here. I've *got* to prove to myself that Hebe Sayer has grown up and is managing. I just wish I believed that.

* * *

Later that night.

When Cassandra came into the room this evening, the first thing she noticed was Pandora's diary on the table beside me.

"What's that?" she asked as she leaned over to kiss me.

"I found it in Pandora's room today. It's a diary."

I looked at her face, watching to see how she would react. She looked genuinely surprised.

"I didn't know she kept one." Then her expression suddenly stiffened. "What are you doing with it?" she asked, suspiciously. "Have you been reading it?" Her voice rose angrily. "A diary's supposed to be private, Mum. You're not supposed to look at someone's diary, even if they're . . ."

"Do you know what your sister wrote, the night before she died?"

She looked at me, eyes widened, startled. Realisation flooded her face.

Her voice trembled. "You know?"

"Yes, darling. I know."

There was a sharp intake of breath. For several moments she stared at me. It was as though she were frozen, unable to speak. I took both her hands in mine. She was shaking. "Why didn't you tell me, Cassandra? Why didn't you come to me and tell me what happened?"

"I couldn't." Her voice was almost inaudible.

"*Why?*"

"I promised Pandora I wouldn't tell anyone. And . . ." she hesitated.

"Didn't you think I would believe you?"

She stared at me for a moment before answering. "You were married to him. You must have known what he was like."

"What do you mean? You seriously think that I knew he would do something like that?" She didn't answer, just stared down at the floor. "Cassandra!" I implored her. "You have to believe me that not once in all the years that I was married to your father, did I ever, ever dream that he would do something like that. Do you think, that, for one moment, I would have stayed with him for as long as I did or left either of you alone with him if I'd had the slightest suspicion?"

She made a sound that was more like a croak than a laugh. "Oh, I was never in any danger. Pandora was the one he fancied."

"Oh, *Cassandra!*" For a moment I was lost for words, knowing that what I said next could make her clam up and withdraw – irretrievably perhaps. After a moment, I spoke again. "I can't make you believe me when I tell you that I didn't know." I looked down at her hands, cold and rigid with tension but still in mine, and I saw that her nails were bitten to the quick. I felt overcome by a wave of remorse. How much damage had been done to her? "I have never lied to you, or your sister, about anything. I know I haven't been a perfect mother and I've done things my own way and sometimes upset you because I wasn't like the mother

306

you thought I should be, but I have always tried to be honest with you and I have always loved you and your sister. And," I said, tightening my hold of her hands, "I never loved one of you more than the other. Yes, there have been times when you've disappointed or angered me and I haven't liked your behaviour but I have *always* loved you, deeply."

I didn't dare look at her face. I couldn't risk seeing that look of disbelief in her eyes. To be honest, I couldn't think of anything left to say. If she was determined not to believe me, there seemed to be very little I could do about it.

Her silence seemed endless. Just when I had despaired of getting a response, I heard a small sob. When I looked up, tears were coursing down her cheeks. Neither of us said anything as she crumpled against me with a small sound of anguish. She cried in a way that was unspeakably awful; as though the tears would never stop. It was uncontrollable and gut-wrenching in its intensity. My own tears were over long before she finally lay still, her head on my chest, empty of emotion, her face white and drained of all expression.

I waited until she felt she could speak. I listened to every word with every ounce of attention that I was capable of giving her. She told me, at first haltingly, of how seeing her father molesting Pandora had made her determined that no one would ever take advantage of her in any way, of her hatred of him, of her despair, thinking that I could not be trusted, that I was somehow complicit in his actions. She finally admitted her feelings of guilt over the part she played in persuading her sister to go out on that last night and how she had tried to concentrate on blaming the rest of us in a vain attempt to lessen the pain of that guilt. She tried to explain how my becoming so confused and then so ill had made her feel as if there was no one there for her, no adult relative she could trust. As I listened, I realised how true that had been. My mother was in no fit state to give her the support and love she needed so badly and Dervla had no notion of what loving a child means. The only person she could turn to was Keith. Then she found out that he'd loved Pandora when she'd thought that, at least, she was uniquely special to him – and that, for once, she didn't have to come second.

Again, I held her, burying my face in her tangled hair, stroking her shoulders, clasping her to me, not knowing how to assuage her grief but, at the same time, realising that this outpouring could only be a good thing.

She's sleeping now, having agreed to talk more tomorrow. I've taken the phone off the hook so that it won't disturb her and I'm going to bed myself. I don't think I will need any pills to make me sleep tonight. I don't think I have ever felt so exhausted in my life.

* * *

Wednesday evening by the fireside and Busby lying on the couch beside me, purring intermittently.

Cassandra left half an hour ago to catch the Dart back into Dublin. As we hugged each other on the front door step, I don't think that I'd ever felt so close to her.

She came into my room early this morning, carrying two mugs of tea and got into bed beside me, laughing at Busby, who snuggled down between us, looking as though all his Christmases had arrived at the same time.

She looked worn out but there was something different about her this morning – as though my knowing the truth and making it possible for her to start telling me what she was really feeling had been like a load off her shoulders. We continued to talk but it was not a tearful anguished occasion like yesterday but calm and thoughtful.

She was against telling Dervla about what had happened. When she told me that, I was surprised by my own relief.

"Are you sure?" I asked her.

She nodded, stroking the soft fur on Busby's square head. "Yes. It's got nothing to do with her. When I feel I'm able to, I want to go and see him on my own. I want him to know why I feel the way I do. I want him to admit that what he did was terrible. I want him to take the blame for what happened. And, Mum, I want him to say that he's sorry for what he did to her, to you. None of this would have happened except for him. She would have been here with us and you wouldn't have been ill." Then she took a deep breath to steady herself. "And when he says he's sorry, I want to know that he's telling the truth."

I found myself looking at her in amazement. She was such a different person to the troubled, awkward girl I had known for the past year. It was almost as if she'd grown up overnight. For the first time in our relationship, I felt we communicated as two adults. When I finally got up to have my shower, although tired, I felt strangely exhilarated.

At some point, she must have put the phone back on its hook and switched off the answering machine because, just as I was coming out of the shower, it rang.

I eventually picked it up. "Hello?" I said, cautiously.

"Hebe!" said Sam. "I'd almost given up on you. What's

been going on? Every time I've rung, that blasted machine has been on."

"Sam," I said quickly, "I can't talk now."

There was a pause at the other end of the phone before he asked quietly, "Are you giving me the brush-off, Hebe?"

"No, of course not! It's just that I found something out a couple of days ago and because of what I discovered, I haven't been able to think about anything else. I'm sorry, Sam. I know this must sound dreadfully offhand, but could you give me a few days and then I'll promise I'll ring?"

"And the holiday?"

"What?" I asked, flustered. I'd completely forgotten that would be the reason for his call, to ask if I were going with him or not. "Oh, but I've already said that I can't go! I *can't*, Sam. Not just now."

"OK," he said.

His voice sounded so flat, I was tempted to try and explain everything to him but I stopped myself. I wasn't clear in my own mind so how could I? "Why don't you go without me. It will be lovely, I'm sure it will," I said, trying to sound enthusiastic. "And then we'll get in touch when you get back."

All he said was: "I think I'd better go now. Goodbye, Hebe."

* * *

Thursday 12th November. It's been over a week since I wrote anything down. Each time I remembered, I put it off until I felt more able to tackle it.

Well, I can't put it off any longer. It's silly. I know perfectly well why I didn't want to write down what is going on because I know that I've been too unsure of how I feel – mostly about Sam.

He hasn't rung again and I haven't rung him. I suppose he's off in the Seychelles by now. Most of the time, I've been too occupied with reassuring myself that Cassandra really is as together as she says she is. I've spoken to Keith, who seems staggered by the change in her. Apparently, she told him everything and that's given him a much-needed insight into why she's been the way she has since Pandora's death.

"I don't know what you said to each other but it's made the world of difference to her," he said, with a smile, when he dropped in yesterday for a cup of coffee on his way back from visiting a friend living nearby. "It's as though she's wiped the slate clean and wants to start again. It's amazing!"

"Did she tell you that she went to see her father yesterday?" I asked him.

"Yes, she did."

"Did she say anything to you afterwards?"

"No. She said she didn't want to talk about it any more – about what happened. I know it must have been a horribly difficult meeting and she was rather quiet afterwards – but not too upset. And that's good, isn't it?"

Yes, it is," I agreed.

At the same time, I was wondering if it would ever be possible for her and Owen to have any sort of relationship. For my part, I don't see a way of coming to terms with what he did. Perhaps it might have been possible, if the repercussions hadn't been so terrible. I've discovered that my feelings of anger and disgust have faded. I feel nothing for that man now. Absolutely nothing. All I want to do is distance myself as far as I can from him – and his hell of a mother. Whether or not Cassandra decides to do the same, well, that's her decision to make. I don't want to influence her one way or the other and I get the feeling that, now, she's in a much better position to make the right choice.

Chapter Nineteen

Late, Saturday night, some ten days later.

Just when I was starting to get really worried because he'd been missing for two days, Busby arrived back this afternoon, accompanied by the disreputable white cat from down the road, with three kittens in tow. He sat in the middle of the kitchen, meowing at the top of his voice, while the others lurked on the threshold. White cat looked very much the worse for wear. She came in when I offered her a saucer of milk and some cat food. The kittens are sweet and sort of piebald-coloured. They're rather like small rubber balls, the way they tumble and pounce on each other. I keep looking at Busby and wondering quite how he figures in all of this. As Suzie succinctly pointed out some time ago, he has no balls so he can hardly be the father. And yet, there he sits, all smug and paternal-looking, surrounded by frolicking youngsters. Very strange! Joan said that she thought the owners had gone on holiday, leaving white cat to fend for itself. Sometimes I think I can't bear to hear about the cruelty inflicted by people on animals. The mess humans make for each other is appalling enough.

I haven't seen Cassandra since last weekend as she's deep into some project or other to do with her coursework. But we've spoken on the phone several times. Each time I put down the receiver, I find myself marvelling at our newfound ability to hold a conversation without any awkwardness. She told me that she and Keith were going down to Cork this weekend to stay with some friends. She sounded happy about the way things were between them. I've been careful not to ask too many questions. I think we are both trying hard to respect each other's private space.

She did, however, mention that she'd met her father a second time, though not in any great detail.

"Mum, I don't really want to discuss it, if you don't mind. What we said was between him and me."

"I understand completely but tell me one thing: were all your questions answered?"

"Yes, pretty much." Then there was flash of the old Cassandra. "He's still scared that we'll tell Dervla what happened. I let him think that was still a possibility. I told him that I would try and be polite if we ever bumped into each other but that I didn't ever want to talk about what happened ever again. *And* I told him that I wasn't going to let him bugger up my life any more than he has already."

When I suggested to her the possibility of her going to see Dr Scheller, she didn't bite my head off like last time.

"I'm not sure, Mum. But I promise that if I find I'm not getting on with my life properly, I will think about going."

"Promise?"

"Promise!"

And we left it like that, for the time being. I hope it won't be necessary but it's comforting to think that there *is* a safety net there if we need it.

I wonder how Dr Scheller is? I hope he can benefit from all that wisdom and compassion that he makes so generously available to his patients. I still miss our conversations and, although I was sorely tempted to go back to him after finding Pandora's diary, in a way I'm glad I managed not to. I really do feel that I'm getting mentally and physically stronger all the time – even without that dear man's help. And I have to say it, even without Sam's comforting presence.

* * *

Suzie dropped in this afternoon. As is her habit lately, she scrutinised me carefully before asking how I was.

"I'm doing all right," I assured her.

That is only half true. I'm missing Sam. And I know I'm still dealing with the Owen thing and I still, quite often, wake up in the night with a jump and I realise that I've been dreaming about Pandora. But I am getting over the past couple of weeks. I'm just feeling appallingly guilty that I seem to have managed to alienate the nicest man I've ever met. I pushed him away and now I don't know what to do about the situation.

"Well, at least you're beginning to look semi-human again."

"Thank you so much!"

"I've been very good and I've not mentioned his name for nearly a week. But I can't hold out any longer. What about Sam, Hebe? What's happening about you and him?"

"I don't think there *is* a me and him any more."

315

"I don't see why," she said with a look of frustration. "Mind you, if there isn't, it's not exactly his fault, is it?"

I suddenly felt resentful. Why would she say something like that? She knew damn well just what a shock it had been for me finding out about Owen's betrayal of his daughter. But then, as quickly as it came, the feeling subsided. She only has my best interests at heart. I know that.

Hoping to change the subject, I tried to shrug it off. "Oh, I'll get over it."

But she was having none of it. "Don't lie to me, Hebe! I've never seen the two of you together but I *have* seen the way you lit up when you first told me about him. A blind person could see that you're madly in love with him. You can't just drop him because of what's happened. You insisted he left you alone while you dealt with everything. Which he's done. Now, you're getting back on your feet, you should be doing something about getting in touch again. Good God! You pushed him away and so it's up to you to do the spade work to save what you had."

"I really don't want to talk about it."

"You sound just like Cassandra being difficult," she retorted.

She could have a point.

My attention was diverted from puzzling over what to do about Sam when I had a call from Maggie, asking if I felt up to going over to London to meet people from the film company about the proposed screenplay.

"I know it's short notice but a couple of the chaps are coming over for a flying visit and they have to go back the day after tomorrow. I know a lot can be done over the phone but they're rather keen to meet you. What do you think? Could you pop over for the day?"

"Tomorrow?"

"Tomorrow." There was a silence while she waited for my reaction.

I found myself hurriedly thinking, why not? Cassandra's busily getting on with her life and my diary is horribly blank for the remainder of the year – and probably the year after.

"I'll come over but what about getting a ticket?"

"Don't worry about that! I'll organise it from this end and ring you back when I have the details. You can collect the ticket before you check in tomorrow."

She didn't mention Sam. Not then, nor when she rang back half an hour later to tell me the flight time. She was as friendly and efficient as ever but, given her teasing of me after Sam had stayed on in Dublin, it looked to me as though she was avoiding the subject. When I think about it, she's known him far longer than she's known me and I know how fond she is of him. I'm sure she wouldn't want to see him getting hurt. Has he said anything? What does she know that I don't? There are so many questions I wanted to ask her. How is he? Did he go to the Seychelles? Was he alone or did he find someone to travel with at the last minute? I really don't want to think about that last possibility.

I've rung Joan and asked her to come in and check up on Busby and his entourage tomorrow. The white cat and kittens have the run of the kitchen and they bop happily in and out through the cat-flap. Because they are a mixture of chocolate, cream and a sandy biscuit colour, Cassandra has given them appropriate names. They are now called Choc, Chip and Cookie! They all sleep, intertwined, so that it's difficult to tell which tail belongs to which body, in a large cardboard box in the corner. Although I've noticed in the past couple of days that the bold Busby is looking a little dazed. He seems to be finding the domestic scene rather too hectic for his liking and, several times lately, has demanded to come through to the sitting-room with me on his own for some peace and quiet.

* * *

Monday 23rd November. Back home again, thank God, and in bed with Busby, who's looking as though he's had a hard day at the office. His whiskers look a bit bent. Perhaps the kittens have been having a good chew.

I got back this evening to find a chicken casserole in the oven. I'll ring Joan in the morning and thank her from stopping me going to bed on an empty stomach because I was too weary to do any cooking myself.

When I arrived at her office this morning, Maggie couldn't have been nicer, greeting me with a kiss on the cheek and thanking me for going over at such short notice. She took me out to lunch at a small, and very good, Italian restaurant just around the corner, where I was introduced to Chuck Weinsteen and Harvey Delmonte. I had to fight back a strong impulse to burst into laughter at their names but, when we sat down afterwards, I couldn't help thinking that they suited them perfectly. The pair of them were so very *Hollywood* with their oh-so-casual but horribly expensive-looking designer clothes and haircuts. Chuck went in for a light peppering of designer stubble and highlights and Harvey for beautifully manicured hands and goatee beard. I found myself trying to camouflage my own hands under my napkin in case he noticed the state they were in. I had spent some time choosing clothes that I thought would be suitable for the occasion. I ended up wearing a dark green woollen dress under my camel coat. I even managed to track down a good leather handbag, at the back of a cupboard, to match my tan leather shoes. I hadn't had time to get my hair done but at least it was clean and relatively tidy. Anyway, I reckoned they wanted to talk to me about my writing not check up on my wardrobe.

Lunch lasted a good two hours with Maggie mostly watching and listening and occasionally joining in. I noticed that when she did make a point about something, they both listened to her very carefully. They may have looked like amusing stereotypes but they were no fools. They asked searching questions about what changes I would be happy to make, alternative titles, about the introduction of characters that, as far as I can remember, don't even exist in the book I wrote and countless other questions and suggestions about plots and subplots, locations and timeframes and goodness knows what. I felt dizzy at the end of it and was beginning to wonder, if the thing were ever made into a film, what similarity it would have to the original story. Possibly none at all. But, although it was exhausting trying to keep up with them, it was also interesting and stimulating. I realised that I hadn't used my brain in that way for a long, long time. Perhaps never!

After we parted, with much kissing and handshaking and honeys and promises of getting back in touch in the near future (they'd just *loved* my Irish accent, by the way – that came up two or three times!), I stood on the kerb beside Maggie, waving them off in their taxi and feeling a little weak at the knees.

She turned to me, smiling. "Well, that went pretty well."

"Did it? I've no idea of how it went, not having any similar occasions to act as a yardstick. We certainly did a lot of talking! Do you think they really are interested?"

"There's no guarantee but I think there's a good chance. One doesn't usually go into such detail without there being serious interest. And those two haven't got any spare time to waste." She beamed at me, her fuzz of blonde hair bright in the winter sunlight. Pulling her coat more tightly around her, she said, "Hebe, I'm sorry but I have an appointment in half an hour that I really mustn't miss. Will you be all right? You're not too drained after all that?"

"No, I'm fine. I'll do some Christmas shopping and it only takes a little while to get to City Airport. Don't you worry!"

She gave me a kiss. "Well, it was lovely to see you again, Hebe. I'll be in touch as soon as I hear what's happening. Take care! We'll talk again soon."

With a wave of a hand, she was off, weaving her way at high speed through the crowded pavement like a small missile, disappearing out of sight in a couple of seconds.

She still hadn't mentioned Sam and she hadn't given me the opportunity to bring up his name.

It occurred to me just then that I had his address with me. Well, that's not strictly true: it didn't just occur at that moment. I had taken the trouble to bring it with me. Just in case I needed it. He'd told me that the office where his secretary, Sylvia, worked was in the basement of his house in Knightsbridge. Even if Sam wasn't around, I could always go incognito and perhaps find out from her if he was still away. And if *she* wasn't around, I could always go to the Versace exhibition at the V and A.

So I took a taxi to Brompton Square and stood outside

the tall cream building with its elegant window-boxes, balconies and railings and shivered. I shivered, partly because of the cold and partly from nerves. I wasn't really sure what I was doing there and that if I did see him, I hadn't the slightest idea of how he would react to my presence.

After getting some odd looks from a chauffeur in a shiny Daimler, sitting outside the neighbouring house – I think he thought I was loitering and up to no good – I eventually plucked up the courage to climb the four steps to the front-door bell. When I'd rung it, I waited, my heart pounding, staring fixedly at the decorative grill to the right of the glossy white door. After a few minutes, I rang again but there was no answering click and crackle of an intercom. No sound of Sam's voice. Slowly, I turned round and went down the steps to the door in the basement. The blinds were closed and the door locked. When I rang the bell, nothing happened. I looked at my watch and saw that it was 3.30. Hardly lunch-time any more!

I did wander around Harrods briefly, meaning to go to the museum afterwards. I somehow managed to get lost in the enormous shop. It was full of extraordinary things I didn't want to buy and rather ordinary shoppers. I had expected it to be bursting with mink-coated celebrities, all spending thousands on diamond G-strings and leopard-skin cat suits with chinchilla collars. My disappointment at not seeing Sam made me feel even more exhausted than ever so I ended up by going to a small café nearby and consoling myself with tea and scones.

All the way home in the plane I was kicking myself for not having the sense to, at least, ask Maggie where he was. And, of course, if she was in a relationship with Sylvia, she'd also know why she hadn't been manning the fort while he was away. I'm stupid, stupid, stupid.

If I can't say it to Sam's face, I can at least write it down here. I love him. I know I've only known him for a short while but I love what I know of him. I love his thoughtfulness, his intelligence, his humanity, his humour, his voice, the way he looks and how he reacts to other people. When I think of perhaps never being with him again, my heart aches and my stomach sinks to my boots. I want to see him and tell him how I feel, even if he doesn't feel the same way any more. I just want to let him know that I love him.

* * *

Wednesday. It's only the 24th. of November but it's bloody well snowing!

Choc, Chip and Cookie can't make it out at all! They keep making sorties outside and patting the snow-covered ground with their paws and then looking surprised and hastily retreating. Joan arrived this morning with a dusting of snowflakes decorating her hair and eyelashes. When we sat down together to have our usual chat and cup of coffee, she asked me when Sam was next coming over. I now have a trio of people asking me about him because Cassandra's joined in the act as well as Suzie. When I told her I didn't know, she looked at me sideways and then said she just hoped it would be soon.

After she'd gone, I sat down at my computer and wrote for a couple of hours. I started writing yesterday, staring at the screen and making countless abortive attempts to get something, anything, down. I kept returning to the idea I'd had several weeks ago about writing a series of letters to

Pandora. But somehow, I couldn't get started on it. Partly because I couldn't help wondering if it wasn't rather morbid, writing letters to my daughter who would never read them. But I kept going back to it. Then I began making notes, remembering all the happy times, the birthdays and celebrations and holidays and the countless funny, silly, inconsequential things that happen in any family. I don't know what form this is eventually going to take but, for the first time since Pandora died, I'm feeling excited about writing. I haven't told anyone yet what I'm doing. It's too early for that and I feel it's something that I have to coax out of myself and nurture carefully and privately.

Suzie rang at lunchtime.

"I hope you've got something spectacular to wear," she said, without any preamble.

"Why?"

"Because I'm giving one hell of a party on Saturday."

"*This* Saturday?"

"Yep! Eight o'clock. Dress formal. Anyone beautiful – and that applies to the males as well as the females, by the way – anyone interesting or the slightest bit sexy is going to be there."

"Then why are you asking me?" I said. I couldn't help laughing. I'm used to her suddenly deciding to throw a party at the drop of a hat – have a barbeque in the rain or a picnic halfway up a mountain to watch the dawn or hire a launch, complete with band, for a crowd of people, to wine and dine as they chug along the Liffey for a couple of hours.

"I'm asking you because you were the first on my list. In fact, you are my star guest."

"Hang on a minute, Suzie!" I remonstrated. "You know

perfectly well that I would *hate* to be the star guest, quite apart from the fact that I don't qualify in any way for the part."

"That's just where you are wrong, darling Hebe!" She continued blithely, "Don't worry, I'm not going to *tell* anyone that you are the most important person there and the reason that I'm giving the party in the first place. That's just for you and me to know. But who else has done what you have in the last year? I can't think of any other of my friends who have battled so bravely against all the odds and won through as splendidly as you have." She suddenly sounded more serious. "I just wanted to show you how very fond I am of you, how much I admire you and I wanted the chance to make a bit of a fuss of you and give you the opportunity to let your hair down and really enjoy yourself for a change. Plus the fact that I adore giving parties! Got the picture?"

"Yes, I think so." I said, overwhelmed. It was a typically generous gesture on her part but I wasn't quite sure if I really deserved such spoiling.

"So, make sure you look utterly desirable and glamorous and I'll see you on Saturday. Lucy's helping out and Joan said she would pop in to lend a hand. Cass is coming with Keith, so you'll have all your favourite, familiar faces around you and I'm sure there will be lots of people there who you'll like enormously. It's going to be a fun evening. You wait and see if it isn't!"

As soon as she'd rung off, I found myself thinking that I might be happier, curled up in bed on Saturday night with a purring Busby rather than trogging out into the snow to be all chirpy and the life and soul of the party. But I could have hardly turned down the invitation, could I?

* * *

324

Sunday.

It turned out that Suzie's party was definitely the best I've ever been to!

I'd decided that, if it was going to be a glitzy affair, then I might as well wear the dress I bought for the press conference at the Shelbourne, substituting for *Prada* shoes something a little more practical, given the weather situation, and topped off with the rather beautiful second-hand fur coat I'd bought a couple of years ago for only a hundred euro. I decided to give my favourite dangly gold earrings another airing and set off in the taxi, smelling good and feeling really quite elegant. I'd had my hair done that afternoon. I was surprised by how pleased to see me the girls at the hairdresser's were after such a long break and Sharon did her stuff when I told her I needed to look really good for a special occasion. When she showed me the finished result in the mirror, I didn't recognise the soignée-looking female in the reflection!

When the cab pulled up outside Suzie's pretty Georgian town house, the front door was wide open. The whole place was lit up like a Christmas tree and light spilled out into the snow-filled street from all the windows, making even the slush in the gutters look attractive. A lot of people seemed to have arrived before me and the decibel level had started to climb. Noise is never a problem with Suzie as all the neighbours within hearing distance are automatically invited to any entertaining she does involving more than twenty people.

As soon as I went into the hall, she swooped down on me. We exchanged affectionate hugs. She was looking pretty amazing in a shocking pink affair with a plunging neckline that showed off her tan to great effect. I caught sight of a remarkably happy-looking Lucy in the distance and waved. She waved back enthusiastically. I noticed that she was looking especially pretty and was surrounded by two or three handsome men, made even more handsome by evening dress. I was glad to see that they all looked a good twenty years younger than Owen.

As I removed my coat, Suzie took it, at the same time looking approvingly at my dress. "Terrific!" she exclaimed. "You look a real wow in that!"

She led me into the front sitting-room. I've always loved that room. It's perfectly proportioned, with its intricate plasterwork, deep cornices and fine marble fireplace, its Wedgwood-blue walls and its folding doors leading into an equally lovely room beside it. Fires were blazing in both rooms and everywhere there were trays of delicious-looking miniature quiches and pastries and other goodies. Even though the night was young, everyone looked as though they were enjoying themselves hugely, knocking back champagne and involved in animated conversation. She led me straight over to a tall blond man standing near the window and introduced us.

"Hebe, this is Blaise O'Gorman. He is a *very* clever man. He designs the most perfect houses. Blaise, this is Hebe. You remember, I told you about her. She writes extremely good novels." She beamed at me. "I'll just go and get you a glass of champers. Back in a minute!"

And she was gone, leaving me with a sinking feeling. My worst suspicions were confirmed. My very dear, but extremely devious, friend was apparently intent on indulging in some serious matchmaking. That was what the whole evening was about. She hadn't told me because she knew I wouldn't have gone if I'd known the truth.

Making a supreme effort to be polite, I smiled at Blaise O'Gorman. "So, you're an architect?"

His answering smile was attractively natural and lit up his face. "I am. And I have to say that not all my clients would agree with Suzie that the houses I design for them are perfect!"

"Why?" I asked. "Are you one those architects who designs buildings that are too adventurous for most people's taste? All glass and metal and acres of open space?"

I was distracted from his reply by a sudden flurry of activity outside the room. It sounded as if one of Suzie's better-known celebs had just arrived. I suddenly realised that the architect was looking at me, as though waiting for a response.

"I'm sorry! What did you say just then?"

"I'm an *aficionado* of Corbusier. Do you know his work?"

I vaguely remembered seeing curving sweeps of whitewashed walls against a Mediterranean sky in some coffee-table book, or perhaps it had been in one of the magazines at the dentist. I couldn't remember. "Not really."

For a moment, we both seemed to run out of things to say. He probably thought I was offhand and uninterested. I really didn't mean to be rude but I definitely wasn't interested. All I could think about was how much I would be enjoying myself if Sam were at my side.

I felt a hand touch my elbow.

"Suzie asked me to give you this."

I swear my heart missed several beats.

I turned and there was Sam, standing not six inches away from me with a lopsided grin on his face, his dark eyes taking in my reaction. Forgetting all decorum, the startled Blaise O'Gorman and the dangerously full glass of champagne in

Sam's hand, I stepped up to him, put my arms around his neck and kissed him on the mouth. He kissed me back and held me tightly against him with his free hand.

"Oh, Sam!" I said, after we'd disentangled ourselves. "I didn't think I was ever going to see you again."

"Nor I you," he replied, smiling again.

At that moment, we were joined by Suzie with Keith and Cassandra. Both of the women were looking incredibly pleased with themselves.

Sam gestured towards them. "If it hadn't been for your daughter and your Machiavellian friend here, I might never have known that you didn't hate my guts and that there was a faint possibility that you might quite like to see me again."

Still feeling stunned, I turned to Cassandra. "How did you manage to engineer all this?"

"Quite simple really. Suzie and I were cheesed off by you being as miserable as sin without him but, at the same time, paranoid about picking up the phone and telling him how you felt. So I rang Sylvia and explained the situation – I got the number from your bag – sorry, Mum! – and then we worked out a date when Sam was free and Suzie arranged the party. And the rest is history!" She looked from Sam to me with a broad grin. "Seems we did the right thing, eh, Suze!"

"But, you weren't in your office. Neither was Sylvia," I said to Sam.

He looked puzzled. "How did you know that?"

"I went over to London last week. I had an appointment with Maggie and I thought I'd drop in to see you at the same time. But the place was all locked up," I said, a little embarrassed by the surprised stares from Suzie and Cassandra.

"Oh, I didn't know you had plans to come and see me,"

he said, looking amused at the sight of my burning cheeks. "If I'd known, I would have immediately cancelled the rest of the book tour and gone back to London."

"You were doing a book tour?"

"I was. Sylvia took the opportunity to take some time off while I was away. As book tours go, it was a pretty hellish one, spent dashing around the good old US of A. I must have covered at least twelve states and I can't remember how many different cities and television stations. I'm not exaggerating when I say that you see before you a seriously depleted being with battery levels dangerously low."

He didn't look depleted to me. He looked perfect.

So, as you can imagine, the rest of the evening went by like a dream, with me floating several inches off the ground and feeling indescribably happy.

I can't remember it all in detail, only that I was enjoying myself immensely and that I even managed to be nice to Blaise O'Gorman to make up for my lack of good manners earlier. It was easy with Sam joining in the conversation. I was aware of a lot of people coming up to him and saying how much they enjoyed his books – and a lot of women watching him – with a lot of interest.

I did ask him if he'd gone to the Seychelles and he said that he had.

"Did you take anyone with you?" I asked, in spite of myself.

"No, dearest Hebe, I went because I thought you didn't want me and I thought it was as good a place as any to lick my wounds. The idea of taking anyone else didn't cross my mind, I assure you," he replied, giving my hand a gentle squeeze.

I also remember Joan handing me a plate of food and commenting, with a chuckle, "Thank God someone had the sense to get the two of you back together. You were made for each other. Or didn't you know that?"

When Sam and I got back here, I felt it was a true coming home. We went straight to bed and proved how wise Joan's words were. And now, I'm sitting up in bed with Sam sleeping at my side. Busby's stalked over to the chair by the window. He's feeling put out. I always know when he's sulking because he nests on the cushions with his back facing me. But he'll come round!

I promised Sam last night that, this morning, I would tell him everything. I've just been thinking how much Pandora would have liked him and I want to try and describe her to him so that she's as real as possible to him because I have the feeling that the beautiful man sleeping so peacefully at my side is going to be an important part of my life and my family from now on.

THE END